PRAISE FOR *BOY ON HOLD*

"JD Spero's *Boy on Hold* provides an especially poignant, compelling, and beautifully written update on the tale of the troubled child who witnesses a shocking event. Hen Trout and his off-kilter fascination with the world will steal your heart. Equally unforgettable are his stoic mother and all-too-teenaged brother, whose concern for Hen, even as they push through their own daily struggles, is equally moving. This family, under extreme duress, demonstrates how wisdom, kindness, and concern for one another can overcome even the greatest challenges. An utterly impressive novel that reveals incredible promise from this gifted writer."

~ David Corbett, award-winning author of *The Long-Lost Love Letters of Doc Holliday*

BOY ON HOLD

JD SPERO

Appropriate for Teens, Intriguing to Adults

Immortal Works LLC
1505 Glenrose Drive
Salt Lake City, Utah 84104
Tel: (385) 202-0116

Cover Art by Ashley Literski
http://strangedevotion.wixsite.com/strangedesigns

ISBN 978-1-7339085-3-5
ASIN (Kindle Edition) B07T3RZLT3

For my boys, especially Adam Henry
and for my dad

What are heavy? Sea-sand and sorrow:
What are brief? To-day and to-morrow:
What are frail? Spring blossoms and youth:
What are deep? The ocean and truth.

Christina Rossetti

Henry Trout snuck downstairs, skipping over the creaky bottom step. He brushed his bangs out of his eyes with a Tai Chi salute and slunk through the dark house. Past Mom's room. Through the kitchen. The youngest-ever nighttime ninja at seven years old, he slipped out the back door without a sound.

Dark quiet all around made his belly go goosy, even though his big brother, Tyler, taught him long ago not to be afraid. "Think of this, Hen," he'd said. "When it's dark, it's dark for everyone. You don't even need to hide. It hides you."

Hen pulled on his Spiderman hood. The cold night air stung. Hen's teeth chattered, making clicky sounds. But the Adirondack Mountains hugged him all around. Where they lived in Severance, near Paradox Lake, their street was like a patchwork quilt—the Hoggs on their left was a dark square, and Miss Sally on their right was a bright square. Their house sat in the middle, their square a blend of autumn colors.

Crickets chirped in the distance. How far away were they? Maybe hedgehogs were there too. Hedgehogs were the coolest nocturnal animals, with tough-guy spikes on the outside and soft fur on their bellies. Miss Sally would know. She knew lots of things. Like, that hedgehogs sleep all day during school and are ready to play in the afternoon. Hen already had a name picked out for the one he was going to catch—Louis. He always liked the name Louis. It was the best name for a pet.

Aha! Maybe Miss Sally would babysit Louis while Hen was in school, like she babysat Hen while Mom was at work.

Tonight, in the deep night, Miss Sally's bay window blinked different colors into the dark quiet. Like a disco ball. She must've fallen asleep in front of the TV again, slouched in her worn plaid chair. Hen smiled at the light. Wait 'til Miss Sally saw his new pet. Hen couldn't wait to see him, too. If only Louis would come out from wherever he was hiding so Hen could adopt him right and proper. Tyler said he needed a trap. But Hen thought if he was patient enough, Louis would come to him. Right in their backyard.

Hen ducked into his play tent and waited.

And waited. And waited.

Not Louis, but sleep kept coming for him. The tent floor was like a bed—the grass underneath soft and comfy. The moon made the green canvas glow like a nightlight. He yawned so big it made a whooshing sound. He lay down, but made a promise to stay awake.

Louis could be there any minute! A little ball of spikes wobbling into his tent, his tiny claws scratching, his nose twitching. Hen could see it now. He closed his eyes. It was easier to keep still that way.

Stay still.

Stay quiet.

But stay awake.

He could do it. Don't fall aslee...

A SCREAM. Shrill and high-pitched.

Hen shot up, knocking against the tent's piping. Dark quiet was everywhere. Was he still asleep? Inside a bad dream? His stomach flip-flopped.

Another ugly noise. From next door.

Miss Sally's house!

Hen scrambled out, rubbing sleep away.

Light from her window. Not a disco ball, just gray. Like fuzz on channel three. The sounds weren't from channel three, though. Not from a dream, either. They were real.

Everything got really slow. Like someone hit slow motion on the VCR.

A jagged shadow stretched across the window like a Scooby-Doo monster.

Someone was inside Miss Sally's house!

His heart moved into his brain, beating between his ears. He shook his head to clear it like a dog shook off water.

He looked again. Two shadows. The Monster. And another shadow—small, soft, hunched over. Miss Sally? They faced each other, like they were arguing. The voices were muffled, but angry.

Fear pierced his heart. He stared so hard his eyeballs went dry.

What was happening?

Something grew out of the Monster. A weirdly-shaped object. Heavy, by the slow way it swung around. Shadows splashed together. Then one huge, heaving blob, with sharp angles jutting out. Like a fight cloud in a comic strip.

Was that what he was watching? A fight? It changed so fast. Like the darkness was trapped in a net. Hen wished he had night vision.

He inched toward Miss Sally's house, gulping pockets of air like he was about to go underwater. He had to get closer. He had to see.

All of a sudden, it was really warm. Hot. His Spiderman sweatshirt was too much. As he crawled across the grass, wetness soaked through the knees of his sweats. It traveled up his legs and into his stomach and heart and brain. He was wet all over. Was it sweat? Or pee? Maybe both.

"Don't be scared." Tyler's words rang clear in Hen's mind. "When it's dark, it's dark for everyone. You don't need to hide—"

It wasn't working. The moon was a spotlight on him. He hid inside Miss Sally's willow tree and peeked from the curtain of its long, wispy branches.

"Put it down!" Miss Sally's clear voice. "Get out of my house this instant!" A voice folded over Miss Sally's. Then a thump. Like something heavy dropped. The shadow blob flung apart like an explosion, leaving only one shadow standing.

The Monster.

"Miss Sally?" Hen whispered, the night taking his words in a steam cloud.

Hot tears pricked. But Hen wouldn't blink.

Another voice. Distant, angry yelling. Hen felt a chill, recognizing it...

Marcella willed her eyes to focus on the textbook that lay open in front of her. She'd set up the coffee to start brewing at 4:45 am. Up and at the table by five. That gave her at least an hour to read her assigned chapter before the kids got up.

It really was ideal. A perfect environment to study. The house—heck, the whole world—was library quiet. The hum of her refrigerator the only sign of life. Her kitchen table was sturdy and clean. The overhead lamp was so bright it almost felt like daytime.

But her eyes were sticky from sleep. Yawn after yawn came in waves like she had a strange tic. It made the words blend together on the page. Coffee stung like acid in her empty stomach.

She had enrolled in the Coastal Community College telecourse a month ago, the same day the yellow flier was delivered to her mailbox advertising new offerings for the very first "virtual college" in the country.

Work toward your degree in the comfort of your own home! Affordable! Accessible! With Coastal, college comes to you!

Surely, it was a sign. A sign that even she—a single mom living on a pittance in the remote Adirondacks—could obtain a proper education. Make something of herself. Turn things around for her children. Tyler might soon be eighteen and out on his own, but Hen was still little. He needed her. He'd need her for many years to come.

She bit the inside of her cheek, a wide expanse of time yawning in her face. She could do both. She could be a good mom and get her degree. There was time to become the kind of woman her children would be proud of.

She now wondered if the hundred-fifty-dollar registration fee—such a splurge, it was downright dangerous—was a smart investment or a desperate grasp at an impossible dream.

A business degree was the obvious choice in order to get a good job, she reasoned. Her first class was Marketing 101. Perfect. No in-the-clouds philosophical mumbo jumbo. Nothing too mathy. Marketing was something she could see. Advertisements were everywhere. This was a good first step.

But these books didn't talk about commercials or billboard ads. They talked about market strategy and product development. They talked about focus groups and customer acquisition. The chapter she started this morning was on pricing and distribution.

On and on and on. Case studies about these things called "widgets" and economies of scale and profit margins and...

Words, words, words.

Mumbo jumbo, mumbo jumbo.

By the time the alarm went off on the microwave clock, she'd only read one paragraph. And she didn't comprehend a single word. Not a one.

She cut off her next yawn, spite cutting through her. How did that hour go by so fast?

The uneven song of larks ushered in the sunrise. A rosy hint peeked through the trees out the window. These classic signs of promise felt like a slap in the face.

She thumped the thick textbook closed with a mixture of relief and grief. She pressed on the glossy cover with both hands, covering that ridiculous image of a lightning bolt striking an accounting spreadsheet.

She was wide awake now. Sigh.

Tomorrow, she'd set the coffee for 4:30 and get started by 4:45. That would give her a good fifteen minutes to let her eyes adjust and her yawns to subside before she really had to concentrate. Tomorrow would be better.

But who knew? Sometimes your brain absorbed what you think you didn't understand. Didn't she read that while waiting in line at Stewart's yesterday? The magazine showed a cartooned brain with a porous, spongy texture. "Subconscious Learning" in bold letters leading to page fourteen where a SUNY-based scientist discussed his study. It claimed lots of what people learned was by osmosis, kind of. They didn't even realize they were learning it. That was the basic gist. No matter she didn't get through the whole article before the clerk rang her up.

Deep breath. Let osmosis do its thing.

Time to Mom up. She cinched her robe tighter.

She padded through the house, the worn wood floors gently creaking under her slippers. Upstairs to wake up Hen. Sweet boy would be hungry soon. Before she knew it, he'd be off to school.

"Good morning." She tiptoed in.

Across the room, Tyler's snoring shook the walls. She bristled at the sound.

Hen's pillow had slid off his bed. His covers were crumpled like he'd—

"Hen?" She flinched, confusion smacking her consciousness. He wasn't in bed. She checked the bathroom. No sign of Hen.

"Where in the world?"

She hurried back downstairs, dread closing in. He couldn't have crawled into her bed without her realizing, right? Could he have slept there through her dual alarms and coffee percolating and yawning and grumbling over her studies?

No. He wasn't in her bed. Not in the downstairs bathroom, either.

That sinking feeling hit, like when she'd lost him in Ames for a full five minutes.

Not on the couch. Not hiding in the closet.

Oh, no.

Blood roared in her ears. Panic rose up in her chest. She glared at her textbook, blaming it. What was she doing, reading that crap while her son was missing?

She stood in the middle of her living room, arms out, her balance precarious.

My boy. My boy. Where is he?

Where could he be? What was she not seeing?

A cast of sunshine splayed across the kitchen floor. It fell on her left slipper, warming it. She looked to the back door and gasped. Outside!

Could he be out there in the backyard? He always went in his play tent in the summer. It was the tree house he'd never have. But he couldn't be in there now, could he? That would mean—

Her slippers skated across the kitchen linoleum, and she flung open the door.

"Hen!" she called, frantic.

There he was—a dark splotch inside his play tent.

The earth righted on its axis. The air had oxygen again. Whew.

But why was he hiding there?

No matter. Her relief was so great she didn't care. She palmed her chest to settle her pounding heart. Hen scrambled out, his face scrunched against the morning sun.

"Mom?" His voice was scratchy.

She rushed to him. "Hen, what on earth are you doing out here?"

He rubbed his eyes and looked to Sally Hubbard's place where he spent every day after school while she worked. Marcella fought a flutter of something—was it jealousy?—and led him inside. To his own house, where he belonged.

"I went to wake you up and you weren't in your bed. Do you know how much that scared me?" She hugged him hard and noticed he was shaking. A ripple of worry went through her. "Oh sweetie, you have a chill from being out. How long were you outside?" She brushed his too-long bangs out of his eyes. "There are pine needles in your hair." Some loosened, and the sappy end bits stuck to his Spiderman sweatshirt. His sweat pants were grass stained at the knees. "You're not in your pajamas. What were you doing in the backyard at the crack of dawn? Tell me the truth."

His huge hazel eyes beamed up at her as if they could talk. Oh! Those eyes. Her heart swooned. How she loved this boy. If she could, she would jump into those eyes and see the world as he saw it. It had to be better than her view.

But his standard silent gaze would not do right now. She refolded her arms. "I can't read your mind, Hen. Tell me."

"I was outside, and—" He cut himself off. His lips trembled. Tears were on the way.

Enough.

"I'm going to say this once and only once." She wagged her finger at the back door, as if it were in trouble. "You're not allowed to leave the house without permission. End of story."

She shuffled him into his seat at the table and promptly slid that awful textbook into her tote bag. Out of sight, out of mind.

She went about preparing his breakfast, enjoying the easy breath that marked the shift in a stressful morning. Marcella took comfort in these small nurturing acts. It reinforced her role as a mother. A good mother. For now, everything seemed normal and fine.

She hummed absently while she flitted about the kitchen, urging the day to remain positive. She forced a smile at Hen—eyes bright!— who seemed to need it more than she. The way he looked at her made her pause, like he needed help but didn't know how to ask for it.

Mom always made things better. "Maybe in the summer Tyler can take you camping. We might be able to borrow a tent. Maybe Miss Sally has one. Or Bernie."

The last flake of cereal fell into Hen's bowl. The now-empty box had been the last in the pantry. Ugh. She'd need to buy groceries. If not today, then tomorrow.

Hen's sullen eyes were altogether too much. She poured his milk and excused herself. "I've got to get into my uniform."

She avoided the mirror as she changed. A run in her stocking. Again? As she dabbed the end with clear nail polish, she heard Tyler stumble down the stairs.

The fridge door swung open.

"Why don't we ever have any OJ?" Tyler sounded like a chimneysweeper. His voice change was not from hormones. He must've smoked a thousand cigarettes—or worse—last night with Derek.

The fridge door slammed shut.

Marcella clucked her tongue. She emerged from her bedroom, tying her apron behind her hips. She started at the sight of her oldest son.

Tyler's hair was spiked and matted from sleep. He still wore last night's clothes. She almost laughed. "What's this? Is this what they call grunge?"

Tyler stared back at her, unseeing. She felt the smile fall from her face. The chill in the air had nothing to do with the drafty window over the sink.

Hen's slight voice barely reached them. "Tyler, where's your bracelet?"

"What bracelet?" Marcella looked from Hen to Tyler.

Tyler rubbed his wrist. "Oh. Nothing. Just something Hen made at school." His neck flushed crimson, Marcella noted with surprise. He was ashamed. "I dunno, buddy," he told Hen. "It'll turn up. Must've fallen off or something."

Marcella put herself between her two sons. "Your baby brother makes you a gift and you can't even keep track of it?" She studied Tyler. His bright blue eyes—eyes of his father—were bloodshot. "I didn't hear you come in last night, Tyler. I hope you weren't out too late."

Tyler shrugged. What kind of response was that? What—no one used words anymore?

"The night before Halloween." She filled the silence, her hand working the air. "I know that's when you teenagers do all those pranks. I hope you weren't egging people's cars or toilet papering trees. What do you call it—the night before Halloween?"

Tyler smirked. "Cabbage Night."

"Cabbage Night. As if you need a special night to act like fools." She shook a finger in his direction. "Tonight, you're taking Hen trick-or-treating. Don't forget it."

As Tyler trudged upstairs to get ready, Marcella swung her attention to Hen. Lightened her voice for him. "Sweetie, you're not eating. Are you feeling all right?" She swept a hand down his cheek and cradled his chin. "You're not sick, are you?" She held her lips to his forehead. His hair smelled like winter wind and burlap. If she could inhale him, she would.

"I think I'm sick." His meek voice was wavy, like he still struggled against tears.

Oh, no. That was not what she needed to hear. Why did boys do crazy things like go outside willy-nilly and get themselves sick? She wracked her brain. Sally might be able to keep him. But—"You don't feel hot."

The phone rang and interrupted her thoughts. She gave Hen a stiff smile as she answered.

"Oh, hi, Bernie."

Sally's only son, Bernie, was Marcella's handyman and the only reliable man she'd ever known. His unceasing good spirits were a constant comfort. Now on the phone, though, his voice was strange. "Ma won't be able to watch Hen after school today."

"Oh? Is everything all right? You sound—"

"I can't talk about it right now." His voice cracked. "I can come by later—"

"Tyler can come home early to watch Hen. Don't worry about that. Is there anything I can do?"

Bernie's silence was loaded.

"What is it, Bernie? What's wrong?"

A thundering down the stairs. Tyler now wore his favorite red and black Baja hoodie—the one that looked like a throw rug and smelled like body odor masked by incense.

"I'm out." He pulled on his hood.

"Oh—sorry, Bernie. I have to go. I'll call you in a little bit. Promise." Marcella hung up. "Tyler, wait. I'm leaving for work in ten—no, five—minutes. You need to take Hen to the bus stop."

His eyes were half closed in her direction. Or maybe he looked at the floor. "Derek's here," he grunted.

Sure enough, through their bay window, Derek's black Ford idled in front of the house. Exhaust fumed from the muffler. Derek sat behind the wheel in a fog of cigarette smoke. Ominous. The whole contraption looked like a simmering bomb.

All hope began to sag. Marcella felt it in her shoulders. "Okay, fine. But you need to come home early to watch Hen. Sally can't watch him today."

Another shrug.

Really? She could scream. She followed him out the door, her voice projecting with sarcasm. "Sure, Mom. No problem! I'll be here to babysit my little brother. Anything to help you out, Mom!"

Tyler slunk into the passenger seat. Smoke billowed toward her from the open truck door. Marcella shivered, feeling the frozen pavement through her slippers. Snow felt imminent. Typical autumn in the Adirondacks. She clutched the door, forcing it to stay open.

"Tyler, did you hear me? About today?"

She waited until he made eye contact. It took ages.

His father's ice-blue eyes still had an effect on her, even coming from Tyler's face. "Anything for Hen," he said, bitterness souring his words.

The truck door slammed between them, the window showing Marcella's pursed-lip reflection. She searched for Tyler beyond the glare, trying to find that scared little boy whose own imaginary friends turned against him, triggering endless night terrors. Day terrors, even. The little boy who'd run in from the backyard, shaking with such fright he was unable to speak of it. He'd find peace only in his mother's arms. Hours she'd spend, singing to him and rubbing his back. He'd give himself up to her. And she'd make it right. That sweet, sad little boy. Where did that boy go?

Hesitantly, she tapped a fingernail on the glass.

Look at me, Tyler.

Tyler's gaze remained steady, out the windshield. He didn't acknowledge her again before the truck roared away, stripping a layer of maternal instinct Marcella was not aware she possessed until she felt it leave her.

The night terrors weren't always the same, but they weren't anything new. Ty had thought he was used to them. Told himself they didn't affect him anymore. Five years ago, he would have stayed home had he woken up feeling like he did this morning. His head was full of hot tar. An inky serpent swirled in his gut. A vivid sense of shame—its origin a mystery—consumed him. His whole body seemed to be infected by it. Years ago, it would be an automatic pass from school.

Marcella would've known. She'd have kept him home. And even though she'd had to call in sick to the diner and even though she'd had a two-year-old toddling around, Marcella would stay with him for hours until it passed. Curled on the couch with a blanket over his head, his mother's cool hands rubbing his back and her soft voice singing a country song about heartbreak and whiskey.

"Breathe," she would tell him.

Impossibly, he would. And the shaking would stop. Eventually, the demons would leave his brain.

Part of him wished he could be twelve again. Part of him wanted

Marcella to mother him that way again. But he was seventeen now. Almost an adult. Nightmares were kids' stuff.

He had to fight the demons alone.

And there was no orange juice in the house.

Marcella had followed him out to the truck, yelling. On and on. He wanted to ignore her, but it was about Hen.

As he'd ambled into Derek's truck, his mother's nagging was sidelined by Hen's little voice echoing in his mind: *Where's your bracelet?*

...your bracelet?

...bracelet...

Derek's door wouldn't close. Something had been blocking it. His mother. "Tyler, did you hear me? About today?"

He'd inhaled Derek's second-hand smoke. It helped the nausea some. He'd been able to look up without puking, at least.

She'd been asking him to watch Hen after school.

Hen...

Where's your bracelet?

His little brother's face had crumpled as he said it. He'd made it especially for Ty—with plastic beads and pipe cleaner. Made a big show of giving it to him just before he went out last night.

I dunno, buddy. It'll turn up. Must've fallen off or something.

Ty swore he'd put it right on his wrist. How could he have lost it so soon? Heat traveled up from his chest, making his hair sweat. His stomach churned. Was he coming off a bad high? A knife of panic cut through him.

He had to make amends. For what, he wasn't sure. That bracelet had everything to do with it, though. Today. He'd make it right today.

"Anything for Hen," he'd said, valiantly meeting his mother's eyes so she'd know he meant it. It was true. He would literally do anything for that kid.

The door finally shut, closing him in to the glorious smoke that filled the truck's cab. Another breath in, another demon out.

Tap, tap on the window glass. His mother was still there? She tried to get his attention. He could kind of see her in his periphery, and his pulse raced from anxiety. Why wasn't Derek driving off?

He couldn't look at her. Not now. Not yet. There was too much sick inside him. It would infect her.

Finally, the truck started to move.

Motion was good. Another breath in. And the hot tar cooled. And the inky serpent slept.

Derek handed him a cigarette without a word. Even lit it for him. Those small acts of kindness from his best friend overwhelmed Ty. Rendered him speechless. Derek didn't need a thank you or anything. That was the best part.

Ty opened the window and smoked deeply, urgently. Gratitude filled him. This cigarette was saving his life.

With the demons gone, beauty moved in.

His thoughts automatically went to Roxanne Russo. Oh, what bliss it would be if he could ride all day in his friend's truck, daydreaming about Roxanne. Feel that magnetic pull toward her even when she wasn't around. Little things. The freckles near her ear when she wore her hair pulled back. The infinity ring on her right hand. Her beautiful hands, her skin the perfect shade and softness. How she laughed during study hall, flashing a crooked tooth on the bottom row.

Ty tried to fix his hair in Derek's rearview, tipping his head out to catch the wind. A futile effort.

"S'okay. It's Halloween anyway." Derek sniggered, and then studied his friend. "Hey, you aw'right?" Derek read Ty better than anyone.

Ty cracked his knuckles, ignoring the question. He was antsy and running hot. What was wrong? It wasn't school. Not his mother. Not Hen. Something bigger. The demons this morning were more persistent than ever. He'd been coming off a high. Was it a bad trip?

He ran through his memory of last night. With Derek at Leon's, the bonfire—where Roxanne Russo was decidedly absent—and then... So many impossible images came to him. He didn't know which, if any, were real. Sensory overload. He couldn't talk about it to anyone. Even Derek. He'd sound like a crazy person.

He was probably still coming off that high.

"You watchin' Hen after school?" Derek asked.

"What? Oh, yeah. Yeah, I have to. You heard my mom."

Derek chuckled. "I'll keep ya company."

"You don't have to." Ty had an idea. "I'm going to teach him how to ride his bike."

"Wow. Ambitious. I'll keep your couch warm."

They parked in the lot near school and that familiar queasy feeling hit Ty. School was not his favorite. It was like accepting hugs from a distant aunt who wore stinging, choke-worthy perfume. Teachers' lectures drifted like wind in his hair, and only bits stuck here and there. It all sucked. Except Roxanne Russo.

They shared a class first period: English. And her assigned seat was right next to his.

Ty wasn't sure if that was a good or bad thing.

Roxanne Russo, the most gorgeous girl he'd ever seen. But it didn't matter how she looked. It mattered how she made him feel. It was magic. He didn't know how it worked. It was some sort of cosmic energy or something. But she made him feel so good inside. Better than good. Light. Filled with light—a warm glow that could only be happiness. Nothing and no one had made him feel quite that way before. How could he not want to feel that again? How could he not want that all the time? Even after what happened. He could forgive her. Even after what Derek told him, he couldn't stop yearning for that feeling. Despite everything, he still loved her. He couldn't help it.

She wore a white sweater today. So white, it glowed. Her lips and fingernails painted a deep red, almost maroon. She popped gum. The scent of peppermint wafted toward him. He couldn't look her way, though he desperately wanted to.

Hi.

Why couldn't he say hi to her? One word. Not even a real word. Kind of just a sound. Still, he couldn't get it out.

He kept his gaze straight ahead where Marla Searles happened to sit. Some guys thought Marla was a catch. Her name was a tongue twister, though. Too many Rs in weird places. Not like Roxanne Russo, where the Rs were placed just right.

Imagining a future with her was pretty much off the table after what happened. Still, he could delve into the past. Revisit better times. Innocent times. Like, just last year on Halloween when serendipity pushed them together as he took Hen trick-or-treating. She'd been dressed as a baby doll. She looked adorable and ridiculous with big red circles painted on her supple cheeks. Huge eyelashes rimming her bright eyes. Her long hair in pigtails.

Another pop of her gum. Another whiff of peppermint.

Ty blinked at Mrs. Finley, who was talking about mythology. "Medusa is a woman whose hair is made of venomous snakes. One look from her and you'll be turned to stone."

Marla's long coppery hair caught his attention. Before his eyes, it became a tangle of snakes. Red and yellow, deadly fellow. Ty's pulse quickened, yet he felt he'd already been turned to stone.

Boom. A desk crashed into his. Snapped him out of it.

Roxanne Russo was there, real close. Her delicious, musky scent battled through the peppermint. His senses filled with it. Her desk was right up against his.

"Want to be partners?" she asked.

"Partners?"

"Okay, so at least one of us was listening. We're supposed to research mysteries of mythology and report on them. I already have an idea. Do you want to partner up or no?"

"Sure." If Derek were in this class, he couldn't help but think, would she have picked him instead?

She kept talking. Her bright white gum flashing, matching her sweater. Her teeth, too.

He blinked at her mouth as it moved, talking around the gum. Focus! Listen! She was talking.

She pointed to a page in Bullfinch's Mythology. Her fingernail was so glossy, like a glazed cranberry. Absently, he pressed it like a button.

She giggled. "You're funny."

"Me?"

"What do you think of my idea?" She fanned her fingers near her lips.

"How do you do that?"

"Do what?"

"How do you get your lips to match your nails like that?"

She blew a kiss into the air. "I dunno. I've always done them this way. I guess I see naked nails as, like, rural, you know?"

"And painted nails are...cosmopolitan?" He remembered the magazine.

She open-mouth laughed, showing her snaggletooth. How easy it would be to lean over and put his lips on hers.

"Yeah, I guess. Here we are up in the boondock mountains. Someday..."

Someday, he would kiss her.

"Someday, I'm going to live in the big city."

He felt a pang of loss, as if she'd already boarded the train. Shock, too. Who complained about living here? The Adirondacks was the most beautiful place on earth. "You mean, New York City?"

"Yeah. I'm going to be a famous actress."

He forced a smile. "And your nails will be ready."

"Always." She held up the open Bullfinch's. "So what do you think? It could be fun."

"Oh. What?"

"Shape-shifters."

"What are they?"

"Creatures that take on different forms at will. Look here." She pointed with her glossy nail. Ty's eyes wandered back to Marla's hair. That's what it was. Shape-shifter. One minute regular hair. The next, snakes. He wasn't crazy. There was an explanation. He nearly laughed out loud.

He interrupted Roxanne. "You see it too?"

"See what?"

He pointed to Marla's hair. "The snakes."

"What are you talking about?"

Ty deflated. "Nothing."

She tensed. "Do you want to do your own thing, then? As usual?"

"What's that supposed to mean?"

"I think you know. Derek told me."

Ty's chest tightened. "What did Derek tell you?"

"Nothing. Just that sometimes you're in your own head. Don't listen to nobody. Not even to be polite."

A stab of devastation. He said nothing. Derek was his best friend. Betrayal now smudged out the bitter jealousy that had been growing mold in his heart.

"Never mind. Really. It's fine." She skirted over to join—of all people—Marla Searles. She whispered into her copper snake hair. The girls snuck looks back at Ty, giggling into their hands.

Marla fluffed her hair. "Watch out, Ty. Snakes are coming for you. Turning you to stone."

Roxanne collapsed against Marla, all-out cracking up now.

No snakes for Roxanne's hair. Her luscious, dark waves. His mother probably had that kind of hair when she was younger. Before strands of gray showed up. Roxanne talked to Marla with her hands, her glossy nails popping like fireworks.

He exhaled. "So, are you guys going to do shape-shifters?"

"No. Hera and Zeus," Marla said.

"You can take shape-shifters." Roxanne kind of smiled and held his gaze.

What a royal screw up, losing Roxanne to Marla like that. She'd been so close. They'd been talking. She told him about her dreams of becoming an actress. They were getting somewhere. He wanted to pound his head on the desk.

Ty didn't care about the project. He stared at the Bullfinch's Mythology. Whatever. One more school thing to get through.

But then he read the paragraph about shape-shifters.

Arachne turned into a spider. Rhea into a dog. Terrifying illustrations. Weird, though, how they comforted him. Here it was in print, documented a long time ago. That had to make it legitimate. Other people must have seen it, too. Maybe he wasn't such a freak after all.

His heart picked up its pace as he made a list of all the things he'd seen transform. He couldn't remember ever feeling this way about a school thing. But this was—holy shit—relevant.

"Nice work, Tyler." It was Mrs. Finley. How long had she been standing there, hovering like a raptor? Did she read his list?

He slid his notebook beneath Bullfinch's. "Shape-shifters."

"A decent choice. Actually, I have a book you might like." She retrieved a paperback from her desk. "It's not mythology, but it's probably the most realistic depiction of shape-shifting."

Ty read the cover, "*The Metamorphosis*. Franz Kafka. What's it about?"

"About a man who changes into a bug."

Ty's hands went hot as he stared at the cover image: a giant insect climbing out of a man's head, which was hinged open like a Fabergé egg. His tongue swelled. It was the most frightening thing he'd ever seen. And familiar.

"You can borrow that copy, if you'd like." Mrs. Finley left before he could answer.

Ty couldn't shake the thought. A man who changed into a bug. He slipped the book into the kangaroo pocket of his drug rug, not wanting Roxanne or Marla to see it.

It would be mortifying if they saw a resemblance in him too.

1 01 *Facts About Nocturnal Animals* lay open on Hen's lap, the jerky rocking of the bus making it slide around. Miss Sally had let him borrow it and he liked it so much she told him he could keep it. He loved that book. He looked at it all the time. But not now. He wasn't in the mood. Hedgehogs weren't in his thoughts. Not today.

He closed the book and got a whiff of Miss Sally. Her Juicyfruit house, her plaid chair, her snickerdoodles. He opened the book, shut the book, and smelled the air that came from it. It was like dessert. Open, shut, breathe in. Maybe he should save it. He didn't want to use up the smell. He closed it up in his backpack.

The bus put him to sleep sometimes. The bouncy rocking, snuggled in his big puffy coat. Hen didn't try to fight it this afternoon. It had been a long day at school. He'd spent the whole time trying not to think about what he'd seen from his play tent last night. Through Miss Sally's big window.

And he needed lots of energy for trick-or-treating too. He let his eyes close and gave in, not thinking in a zillion years he would dream...

A scream. Shrill and high-pitched. From Miss Sally's house! Light from her window. Ants on channel three. Slow motion on the VCR. An ugly, jagged shadow like a monster from Scooby-Doo. Another shadow: Miss Sally. Muffled, angry voices. Shadows splashed together. Darkness trapped in a net. "Put it down!" Miss Sally's clear voice. "Get out of my house this instant!" *Thump.* Like something heavy dropped. The shadow blob flung apart like an explosion. Leaving only one shadow standing—the Monster...

"Hey!"

Hen felt an elbow poke his arm. It was his pal, Murphy.

"Hello? Hen? Earth to Hen? Are you really asleep?"

Hen shook away the dream. "No. Not sleeping."

Murphy laughed. "Yes, you were. I heard you snoring." He snorted. "You were crying for your momma! Must've been a nightmare."

"I wasn't sleeping." Hen's voice was sharp.

"Okay. You kept yawning at school today. Whatever. Your stop's coming up, is all."

Hen looked out the window. Almost home.

"Let's meet up for trick-or-treating later," said Murphy.

"Okay."

"Your brother's taking you, right?"

"Yeah."

Murphy hopped in his seat. "Did you end up giving him that bracelet?"

That made Hen stop. "What?"

"Yesterday we made those bracelets in class. With the beads? And you kept bragging about giving it to your brother. I'm keeping mine. But you kept saying, 'I'm gonna give it to my brother.' You said it, like, a hundred times. You were loony about it."

"Was not."

"Was to." Murphy's smile was jokey and friendly. "So, did you?"

"Did I what?"

Murphy threw his hands up. "Did you give your brother the dang bracelet?"

Hen didn't want to answer. He had been excited to give it to Tyler.

And Tyler had put it right on his wrist. He said thank you and gave him that proud smile he did sometimes. And then Tyler lost it after only a few hours. Just...lost it. Like it was a piece of trash.

If Tyler didn't care about the bracelet, neither did Hen.

"Did you keep yours?" he asked Murphy.

Murphy answered by showing it on his wrist. "It's my good luck charm."

"Cool." Hen checked out the window again. "My stop is next."

"Dude! Did you give it to him or not? 'Cause if you didn't we could match. Like, it could be our secret super power thing. We could be partners. It could be part of our costumes tonight."

The bus gurgled to a stop. Hen sidestepped to the aisle. "I didn't give it to Tyler. But I don't have it anymore, either."

"What do you mean?"

"I don't know. Lost it, I guess." Hen remembered what Tyler had told him this morning. Why lie to Murphy, though? He turned away from Murphy's sad face, telling himself he didn't care.

Off the bus, he saw Tyler in their front yard pumping air into his bicycle tires. When he spotted Hen, he waved with a big smile. Hen picked up his pace, smiling too, not caring about the stupid bracelet anymore.

It had turned into one of those cool autumn days warmed by a thick blanket of sunshine. Perfect conditions for what Ty had planned. He pumped air in the tires and wiped off cobwebs, fighting that pesky pang of shame that hadn't quit all day at school. Also guilt. Hen had his bike for over a year and hadn't yet learned to ride. Honestly, Ty was a crappy brother.

"What's that?" Hen asked, out of breath from running off the bus.

"What do you think it is? It's your bike."

"I know that. What are you doing with it?"

"Today, little dude, you're going to learn how to ride it."

"Aren't we going trick-or-treating?"

"That's not 'til later. Right now you're gonna ride."

Hen frowned at the bike. "There aren't training wheels."

"S'okay. I'm gonna be right there to catch you if you fall." Ty grinned so hard he felt it in his ears, but Hen didn't seem convinced. "Come on. Put down your backpack and hop on."

Hen did exactly what Ty asked, which gave him pause. Hen's unwavering trust in him was off-putting. He scarcely deserved it.

"Aw'right. Let's go."

One hand on the seat, one on the handlebar, Ty pushed and ran alongside.

Hen worked the pedals, his face wide with awe.

"Great job. You got this." Ty chanted, at a loss for how to actually instruct pedaling a bike. Hen's instincts were spot on, thank goodness. He'd get a few good strokes before tipping. Each time Ty was there to right the bike, he felt fortified. All that sourness dissipating.

"Good! Now, pedal faster and get some speed. That'll help your balance."

This. This was the best high. The best drug. Out in the open air with his little bro. So wholesome and honest—as American as apple pie. Hen squealed, giddy. Ty laughed into the wind.

From the tall oaks, stray leaves fell in the sunlight like golden snow. Leaf piles lined the street like molehills.

Hen's bike headed right toward one of them.

"No!"

Hen yanked on the handlebars. The bike slid into the leaf pile like it was third base.

"They're just leaves," Ty said. "They don't bite."

Hen hovered over the mound, fists clenched. "Tyler, hedgehogs hibernate in there. Miss Sally read it in a book. It said sometimes they get scooped up with the pile. Like, with the street cleaners."

Miss Sally.

A dark aura came over Ty. He stared at the leaves, trying to think. Impossible images swirled, like a nightmare he couldn't shake. He shifted from one foot to the other, uncomfortably hot.

Hen stared at the leaf pile too. "There could be a hedgehog in there."

"Nah." Ty tried keeping it light. And fun. "Nothin' there, but—"

Ty trembled. The fluffy mound spoke to him. Impossible images. His brain folded in on itself. Stirring around, trying to find something. And then—*zing!*—a sharp whistling sounded from the base of his neck, ringing through to his eye sockets. He pulled at his hair, trying to pinpoint the sound. "Wait—"

A gasp escaped him. Hen was right! There was a creature inside. It was screeching.

"Oh, my gah—you're right!" Ty wailed, kneeling at the mound. He knew what he had to do. His pulse quickened as he slapped the dry leaves off the top. "I can hear it. Holy shit. I can hear it screeching."

Under that top layer, leaves were moist. Smelled like mulch and soil. He scooped that layer away, his breath hard and fast. The screeching got louder. It was working. Wasn't it? He must be getting closer.

"Can you hear it?" It was deafening. Almost unbearable. Ty wanted to cover his ears but had to find the thing. Save it. It was hurt, maybe.

"Tyler?" Hen's voice was far away.

Bottom layer—wet leaves. Sodden. Ty peeled them from the pavement singly, his heart thudding. They kept falling apart. One piece after another—odd shapes that didn't look like leaves anymore. Tedious work. Eventually, his breathing normalized. The sharp whistling noise faded away, like a balloon deflating.

Then, the screeching stopped altogether.

Nothing was there.

Ty glanced at his brother. Hen had watched the whole thing, a stunned look on his face.

Leaves of all colors sprinkled the street, like giant confetti. Ty sat in the middle of it all, wet leaves clinging to his jacket like papier-mâché.

"It's okay." Hen touched his shoulder. "It was empty. You were right. There wasn't a hedgehog there. It's okay."

Ty studied the mess, trying to find the right category for it in his mind.

"Come on," Hen said. "It's okay. Let's go home."

"You think?"

Hen walked his bike back to the house without another word. Ty trailed behind, studying the ground. He hadn't realized how many leaves were loose. Funny. People thought they were pretty, but they were dead. Death everywhere. Not just in neat piles, either. It was chaos. Multi-colored chaos. He couldn't wait to get inside. Outside was overwhelming sometimes.

Hen secretly called it Tyler's B mood. It often surprised him, but never scared him. Tyler just needed quiet time. Hen walked his bike home, checking back every few steps. Tyler moved slowly, but he was coming. They'd be home soon.

Hen propped the bike against the shed and waited for Tyler at the stoop. He ruffled Hen's hair as he passed. "Hey, little dude, how was school?" He grinned as if they hadn't been together on a bike adventure. As if Hen had just now gotten home. This, Hen knew, was also part of the B mood. Tyler forgot stuff.

Hen followed him in and got another surprise. Not a happy one.

Derek was there, sprawled on the couch as if he owned the place. Hen froze in the doorway.

"There's my Chicken. Bawk-bawk-bawk!" Derek flapped his elbows, laughing.

The hair on Hen's neck stiffened, like a porcupine when danger's nearby.

"Dude. Shut up." Tyler snapped at Derek. "Leave him alone."

Hen was okay to go all the way in, then, if Tyler was okay to stand up to Derek. But then they high-fived and Tyler fell onto the couch next to him.

That was always confusing. Of all the possible friends in the world, why would Tyler choose Derek?

With the front door shut, Hen coughed against the thick smoky smell inside. Not burny smoke. Perfumey smoke. No one was supposed to smoke in here. Hen shucked off his shoes and narrowed his eyes at Derek.

Derek slapped the couch. "Si'down, Chicken. *Rugrats* is on."

Hen hated *Rugrats*. Angelica Pickles was always up to no good. Wait until Tommy Pickles grew up. He'd let Angelica have it. She deserved whatever she got.

Derek had his arms over his head—pale dolphin bellies. His spicy deodorant mixed with the perfumey smoke, making Hen feel sick. Sitting in the middle, Hen felt split in two. Hot and cold, sitting between Tyler and Derek. Like a bad fever.

Hen kept tabs on the good guy. Tyler's B mood was not over. Hen could tell by the way he bit his nails, his knee fidgeting, wiggling the whole couch.

"I'll make you a new beaded bracelet at school." Hen wanted to make it better. "Just like the old one."

Tyler turned to him with a blank expression. Like he forgot who Hen was. Tyler wasn't snapping out of it. He needed quiet time. If only Derek would leave—

Bad guy knocked his knee into Hen's. "You gonna be a chicken for Halloween tonight? Come on, you gotta do it."

Hen ignored him.

"Yo, Chicken. Got yourself a girlfriend yet?"

Hen would rather sit next to Angelica Pickles.

"Chicken?" Derek sang. "I'm talking to you. HEY!"

Hen had to look at him then. His baseball cap was on backwards, and his stringy bangs came through the half-moon adjuster. His eyes reminded Hen of a wild dog's. Red and rimmed with black. Derek even looked like a meanie. He used to be burly and square and now he looked pulpy and soft. Fat, like his dad. Nothing like Tyler, who was long and lanky and all angles. Even though he ate like a Tyrannosaurus.

"Do. You. Have. A. GIRLFRIEND?" Derek shouted and faked sign language as if Hen were dumb.

"No."

Derek slapped his knee. "Well, shit, Chicken. We gotta get you some CHICKS!" A squeaky, girly giggle.

"How 'bout Roxanne Russo, Derek?" Tyler's laugh was bitter.

Derek tongued that weird patch of hair—like a square of Velcro—under his lip. He narrowed his eyes at Tyler. "How about Geraldine Greenbladt?"

"Ee-ee-hew!" Tyler snorted, kind of laughing. But his eyes were blank. Like someone had shut him off inside.

Then there was a knock on the door and Bernie Hubbard was inside the house, filling the foyer in his clumpy work boots. Hen could've squealed with joy. But something was missing. Bernie always had a smile on his face. Not today, though.

Hen's heart sank, realizing why. Something bad really did happen last night. To Miss Sally, Bernie's ma.

Bernie dropped his toolbox in the entryway, his face twisting like he smelled moldy cheese. "Thought I'd fix that window frame today." He pinned Derek with his gaze. "Check in on Hen."

"That's why we're here," said Tyler. "To watch Hen. Mom's orders."

"We?" Bernie asked. "Didn't know it was a joint effort. Don't you have school, Derek?"

Derek sucked air through his teeth. "Nah. Ty gets out of school, so don't I."

"Is that the way it works?"

"Yup. We're a package deal."

Bernie looked from Derek to Tyler, who shrunk into the couch.

"Hen's doing good," Tyler said meekly. "Right, buddy?"

Hen scooted to the edge. "We're watching *Rugrats*."

Bernie got a hammer from his toolbox. "I'll be in the kitchen fixing the frame." And then, "Hen, I could use a hand."

Hen leapt from the couch, even though he had no clue about how to fix a window frame. Turned out, all Bernie wanted Hen to do was hold the nails, hand them to him when he was ready.

"Don't know if you heard." Bernie started.

Hen tensed. *Please don't say it.*

"Ma's in the hospital. Miss Sally, to you, I guess."

In the hospital? The nail was cold and rough in his hand. Hen pressed his finger on the tip, hard. He was surprised it didn't make him bleed.

"Ah, a draft. Need some sealant." Bernie felt around the edges. He went back to his toolbox in the front room. Tyler and Derek now watched *The Jerry Springer Show.*

"You boys out last night?" he asked them. "Cabbage Night?"

Pause.

"Yeah." Derek sounded like he was stretching. "At my pop's place for a Reuben. Got the best Reubens, I swear."

Hen heard rustling from Bernie's toolbox.

"Yeah, they're some tasty sandwiches." Tyler did that snorting thing again.

Bernie's voice got loud. "Hey, you know my mother's in the hospital right now? Some punks broke in, robbed the place, and gave her a bruising. Pretty bad one."

Tyler's laughter dropped like a hot potato. Hen squeezed the nail into his fist, his insides squeezing together, too.

"So you can imagine I'm not in the mood for funny right now." Bernie shook his head. "Not that that was even funny."

Back on the step stool, Bernie squeezed the tube of sealant with shaky hands. That never happened with Bernie. His hands were always steady. Hen rolled the nail between his fingers. Felt the sharp tip with his thumb.

"She'll be okay, though. Right?" Hen asked quietly.

Bernie didn't answer. "Nail."

Hen handed it over.

Bernie hammered the nail in place, his jaw clenched tight. "I don't know, Hen."

Wait—what? The room swirled. Hen's head got dizzy but fear rooted him to the floor. Bernie didn't know? But...she had to be okay. They'd fix her in the hospital. She just needed to get better. And come home. They were in the middle of a chess game. It was Hen's turn. She'd get better. She had to. It was Miss Sally!

Hen stared at the linoleum tiles, tracing back in his mind what he'd seen last night. All those shadow blobs. It was worse than he'd thought. Not just a weird thing with scary noises. It was real. And it wasn't over.

Another knock at the door made Hen jump.

Bernie called to the front room. "You boys expectin' someone?"

What Hen saw through the window shook him to the core. It was too early for trick-or-treating, Tyler had said. It wasn't someone in a police costume. It was a real-life policeman.

Tyler's silhouette was backlit when he opened the door. Hen saw the full police uniform, from his shiny shoes to his dark sunglasses to the emblem on his cap.

"Tyler Trout?" After taking off his sunglasses, the policeman panned the room. His smile didn't seem happy, but smug. "Ah, Derek Hogg? Excellent. Two for one. Come with me, boys. We'd like to take you to the station for questioning."

Bernie hopped off the stool and brushed past Hen. "Hold up, officer. What's this all about?"

Hen scurried under the kitchen table to hide, moth wings in his chest.

The policeman's voice sounded harsh inside their house. "Bernie Hubbard? You're here too? Sorry, uh. I'm meant to take these boys in for questioning about the events that transpired last night."

"That was my ma's house," Bernie said.

"I know that, sir."

"You don't think these boys had anything to do with it, do you?"

"Mr. Hubbard, our job is to cross the Ts and dot the Is. They might have information that could help us. That's all."

"Tyler's mother will be worried. She's not back from work yet."

"No need to worry. Not yet."

"But—"

"I'm not authorized to discuss details. But this is standard procedure…"

They rambled on like voices from the radio, using big words Hen didn't understand. Hen let the words float away, and stared at the floor. Hen caught some crumbs with the pad of his finger. He flicked them across the floor like sleet pebbles.

In the front room, the radio voices shut off. Front door swished closed.

Bernie came back to the kitchen. "Well, your ma isn't gonna like that."

Hen's insides spun like he was on a carnival ride. Everything was mixed up. Tyler had gone with that policeman. When would he be back? In time to take Hen trick-or-treating later? Maybe Bernie would take him. Hen felt tears coming. The thought of candy made his belly sick. He didn't feel like dressing up in a silly costume, anyway.

Bernie finished fixing the window, sighing through his nose. Hen didn't move. He stayed under the table collecting crumbs, hoping Tyler's B mood didn't follow him to the station.

Trick-or-treaters long gone, Marcella finally found time to sit and process what Bernie had told her: Tyler was taken to the police station for questioning. That simple sentence boggled her mind. Did they really think he had something to do with what happened to Sally?

A dark mass of fear clogged her chest like a cement block. She bit a fingernail, trying to think around a growing headache. Sure, Tyler and Sally had their issues. But Derek was at the heart of it. More than once, Sally had warned her: "That Derek Hogg is bad news. Tyler will only find trouble with him, mark my words."

Marcella had to agree. The spawn of Leon Hogg never had a chance of being good news. But, geez, Tyler and Derek had been best friends since birth. He lived right next door. Was Marcella supposed to forbid the friendship? For what reason? Puberty? *Bah*, it wouldn't take anyway. Tyler marched to his own drum. That drum—offbeat as it was—had nothing against Sally. Did it?

She swallowed hard, mentally pushing down that cement block. Hen might know.

Just last week, while bringing laundry up from the basement, she'd overheard a conversation between them. "What do you do over there at Old Mother Hubbard's?" Tyler had asked, like he couldn't believe Sally was actually a good person. "Is she nice to you? She doesn't yell at you in that witch voice like she does to me and Derek, does she?"

"Be quiet, you hooligans!" Hen had cackled, mocking Sally.

Too shocked to intervene, Marcella had simply passed through with her overflowing basket. She'd stayed in her bedroom, folding towels and blue jeans, fuming silently. Now, she thought, she should've defended Sally, who was not only a neighbor and friend, she was Marcella's savior. They should all kiss her polka-dot socks. Bills were paid and food was on the table thanks to her babysitting Hen.

Tyler hardly appreciated his own mother. How could she expect him to acknowledge what Sally had done for them? Still, the idea that Tyler broke into Sally's house was ridiculous. Assault? Absurd! Attempted robbery? For what? Tyler had been working at Leon's Diner since last spring. He brought in money on his own merit. He didn't need to rob anyone, no less Sally.

The whole thing was just preposterous.

Yet, instead of taking Hen trick-or-treating, Tyler spent the evening at the police station. And he was still there. Being questioned. How did that happen? What if he needed legal counsel? She couldn't afford a lawyer. Bail? Oh, please. No. That darkness in her chest seemed to spread to her whole body.

She stared at her blank waitressing pad on the table, willing a plan to magically appear. To-dos she could check off. Steps she could take to save her firstborn.

"Tyler Trout," she said aloud, tripping over her tears. "What am I going to do with you?"

She tapped her pen onto the paper. The same pen she used to take pancake and onion ring orders five days a week, ten hours a day, so that she could feed her own children and buy them clothes. And shoes. The same pen she used to take notes as she read her ridiculous Marketing 101 textbook with the lightning bolt on the cover. She didn't know if she wanted to cry or hit something. She should've known, really. She should've known better than to try. Girls like her didn't get second chances at life. A dozen good decisions would never undo the big bad ones she made early on.

Why on earth would she study marketing, anyway? What good would marketing do? How would marketing help Tyler?

She gripped the pen with both hands, feeling like she might explode. How satisfying would it be to break it open, letting ink fly all over her sturdy, clean table? How right that would feel—

Rap-rap-rap.

Who could that be? Too late for trick-or-treaters and Bernie was at the hospital.

Marcella rewrapped her cardigan and squinted through the window at the familiar, oversized man.

Ugh. The darkness turned to nausea.

She opened the door but left the chain on. "What do you want, Leon?"

"Be a doll an' let your neighbor in."

"It's late. Go home."

"Aw, come on, Marce. Serious now. We should talk. Our boys are—"

"No," Marcella shout-whispered at him. "Not our boys. Never *our* boys."

"You know what I mean. Derek and Ty are in trouble. We gotta work together on this."

"Give me a break."

"Geez, come on. Lemme in? It's raining."

She undid the chain with a sigh. Leon stepped inside, still wearing his greasy apron. He helped himself to her fridge, grabbing two Miller Lites. He slid one to her, grinning like a rabid dog. "Wish you'd come back to work for me, doll."

"Ha." Never in a million years. Even though she had to drive thirty minutes to Ticonderoga for work now, she'd never go back to Leon's. He made her stepfather look like a hero. Leon would never again smack her ass as she carried a pot of hot coffee to the front tables.

He'd never lick his lips and call her *darlin'* in that syrupy, lewd voice in front of customers—folks from church, her son's teachers. He'd never again follow her out to the dumpster and insist on a kiss, petting her breast for a sickening moment. "Never." The word hardly conveyed her bitterness.

"What? I didn't treat you well?" He rubbed his distended, horse-like stomach. "You didn't make a fortune in tips?"

"Oh, please. You had me dress like a slut." She glared at him. "Treated me like one, too."

"Marce, Marce, Marce. You tortured me. You don't know what you do to a man!" His outstretched arms revealed fresh sweat rings. A rancid odor wafted across the room.

Marcella shifted in her seat, thankful for her thick cardigan. She tried to shake it off. "Are you here to talk about Derek and Ty or not? How we can help them? Something we can do?"

Leon's grin dropped. "Yah. 'Course. Damn kids. Yanno, I can't say I didn't think I was the cat's meow when I was his age, but damn Derek Hogg thinks the world begins and ends with Derek Hogg."

Marcella hid her surprise behind her beer bottle. Leon had always coddled his son unjustly—massaging excuses in his signature, aggressive charm to teachers since the boys were in kindergarten. Tyler was always left to suffer through detention alone.

"I tell ya, Derek didn't do that to Sal. No way. Even if she was an old bag that didn't do nothin' but yell at 'im and threaten to call the cops on 'im and think she was all in charge of the whole damn town."

Marcella straightened. "Wait. You're talking about Sally Hubbard, right?"

He rolled his eyes. "Yah. Old Mother Freaking Hubbard."

"Miss Sally is probably the kindest person I've ever met. She's taken care of Hen since he was born. If it wasn't for her—" Her throat caught. A wave of panic gave her a hot flash. Oh, no. What if Sally didn't get better?

Earlier today, she got a shock: Bernie told her Sally was in a coma. A *coma*.

Marcella shot up from the table. The linoleum tiles rotated

beneath her feet. For no good reason, she flung open the junk drawer and rifled through it. Bits of crayon, expired coupons, and unopened mail swirled through a sheen of tears. Tyler's report card from last quarter. Or was it last year? Didn't matter. Cs and Ds. Always Cs and Ds. At least he was passing. Right?

She shut the drawer, hopelessness pressing on her. "Don't speak of her that way."

Leon's voice got soft. "Hey, I'm not sayin' it doesn't suck. No matter who it is. I'm just sayin'. Derek wouldn't beat up an old lady. That's all I'm sayin'."

She leaned over the sink, woozy. "I know Derek didn't do it," she said, surprising herself. "Neither did Tyler."

"They ain't gonna take our word for it, are they?" Leon sounded scared. That was a first.

Marcella caught her reflection in the window. Tried to find Tyler's image through the glare, like she'd done just this morning outside Derek's car. That maternal instinct hit her like a shockwave. Where was her boy? Behind those moody, ice-blue eyes still remained that scared little boy. He was in there somewhere. She had to believe it. And he still needed her. Maybe now more than ever.

She spun to face Leon, folding her arms. "Why not? Why wouldn't they take our word for it?"

He gazed at her, his jaw slack and eyes half lit.

"Leon, you practically run this town. Every official goes to your place. You schmooze with all of them. You have them eating out of your hands. Why wouldn't they listen to you?"

She'd said the right thing. His thick face opened in a slow smile. His eyes gleamed. He puffed his chest. Drained his beer.

He nodded. A single, brisk nod. "You're right."

As wild as his mind could be, Ty couldn't imagine a situation that would land him in the police station—even for questioning. He knew he and Derek were in trouble, but he had a hard time pinpointing what he'd done wrong. Impossible images were stuff of nightmares. Had they gotten into his head?

That tingle of shame he'd felt earlier had to do with Hen's bracelet, didn't it? And he'd made amends today, with the bike ride. They had fun. Until the leaf thing. Damn. Ty didn't want to think about that.

He reached inside his kangaroo pocket where he'd tucked the book Mrs. Finley loaned him. He fanned the pages with his thumb incessantly, like a toddler with his blankie. He let Derek do all the talking.

"We went to Leon's for some food, and then went to the bonfire."

Ty's mind reeled. It kind of came back to him now. They had gone to the bonfire that night. Earlier. Ty had hoped Roxanne Russo would be there, wearing that high-necked sweater. She'd pass a joint with her glazed cranberry nails, smiling at him in that quick, secret way she always did. Like a wink. An invitation.

It wasn't an invitation, though. Not for him, anyway. And they hadn't seen Roxanne Russo at the bonfire. The night had gone a completely different way.

At the station, Derek said nothing of going to Miss Sally's—which they'd done. Or did they?

That's when it got murky.

Ty couldn't focus. That red eye on the security camera kept blinking at him, like it was sending a message. And the PA system in the station must've been on the fritz. It kept ringing static really loud all during the interrogation. Remnants of that whistling, screeching sound somehow formed into his name. He swore he heard it. "Tyler Trout" rang through the static, like someone was trying to reach him and had a bad connection.

After the twenty-question game with Officer Clapp, they got a stern warning that sounded more like a threat. It made Ty feel watery inside. Relief wasn't an adequate word for how he felt getting out of the station. He lit a cigarette as soon as his feet hit the pavement. The sky overhead was a foreboding opaque. Chalkboard black, a late-night, endless kind of dark. He had no watch. Morning was forever away.

Yet something heavy pulled him from that freedom. That familiar heat behind his eyes spread through his limbs. Derek standing next to him felt like a low rumble, a danger signal.

Fight or flight. He had to make a run for it.

"Where ya goin?" Derek called after him.

To Severance Beach. Ty just decided.

"C'mon. Let's get the hell outta dodge."

Ty winced. It was like Derek used one of those voice changers. He sounded like the officer. Like they had coached him there in the station. Ty picked up his pace.

"Where the hell you goin'?"

Distance grew between them. Not enough. Ty wasn't sure how much would be enough. He only wanted the lake. Not Schroon, the big one. But Paradox, the calm one. Home. He needed to be near it.

Breathe the air that came off it. Imagine himself as part of the Adirondacks that nestled it. Feel the water.

"Hey! What's your problem?" Derek's voice-changer voice was far away.

Ty threw on his hood, cinching it best he could. His eyes burned from the smoke. Derek kept on his heels, asking over and over in that voice-changer voice: *What are ya doin? Where ya goin? What're ya thinkin?*

He ran faster. Not fast enough. He tumbled to the ground. Smoke mixed with the kicked up dust and sand. Tiny stones poked through the knees of his jeans, jabbed the palms of his hands. He was down. Derek's footfalls clacked behind him like horses' hooves.

Gritting his teeth, he clenched his eyes shut.

"Screw off, Derek!" Ty shouted at the pavement in front of his face.

Then it all went silent. Slowly, sounds of Derek backing off came to, as he murmured a curse under his breath. Ty waited, squeezing everything shut. Shutting everything away. Until he knew Derek was gone.

Finally.

Behind him, Derek's truck revved and peeled away.

"Screw off." His voice filled the lonely street. He blinked. Snorted a laugh. It was over. His cigarette had fallen onto the pavement, still lit. His eyes cleared. The night was his.

Screw off, Derek. He chanted it over and over under his breath as he turned onto Alder Meadow Road. His Chucks crunched the sand and pebbles on the pavement. He jonesed hard for pot. Or the other thing. He searched his pockets, knowing they were empty but digging anyway.

As he walked, his anger toward Derek faded to a dull bitterness. Why did he get so mad? He was numb all over. Cold, too. He picked up his pace. One step after another. His knees ached from the running and the stones. Still, he kept going. He thought about hitch-hiking. His mother would have his head. Tonight, he had nothing to lose.

Cars were sparse at this hour. Especially on the back roads. When headlights cast his long shadow up ahead, he stuck out his thumb. Didn't bother to take off his hood, though, which didn't help. There was a reason Miss Sally called him a hoodlum. Couldn't think about that. Or her or Hen or Marcella, either. Or Derek, for that matter.

The car didn't stop anyway. He flipped them off as they passed. Whatever. He was almost to the lake anyway. He tossed his butt aside and that's when he saw it. Something by the road. What was it?

He blinked hard, rubbed his eyes. Yes, it was definitely there. He wasn't seeing things. A figure huddled by the side of the road. Dark clothing. Or wrapped in a blanket. Was it a shadow? No, definitely not a shadow. A person. A girl curled in a ball. Rocking. Distressed. What was she doing out here all alone at this hour? He could hear her crying. She was about fifty yards from him. Oh, no. He ran to her, panicked.

"Hey, you okay?"

Dizzy, he nearly tripped into her.

"Sorry. Hey, can you hear me?"

He took back his outstretched arm when she recoiled.

"Are you hurt? Do you need help? I can help you."

The hell he could. What could he possibly do? He had no car. He had no CPR training. He was as useless as a rat.

"Shit," he muttered, turning toward the road again. Now, the real panic set in.

But then another car came toward him. A miracle! Headlights poured over him. Heavenly lights. Ty waved his arms. Did jumping jacks. "Hey, stop! Help!" He shouted, feeling a sudden, inexplicable joy.

The car zoomed by—so close to the shoulder Ty nearly got sideswiped.

"What the heck?"

Quiet settled around him.

Too quiet.

Ty spun around, searching. What? It couldn't be.

She was gone. No crying girl in need of help. Not a trace of her.

He was alone.

"No, no, no." That whirring started in his chest again, like a spinning top. His breath caught. Tears pricked. He pulled at his hair.

His heart raced well before he started running. He ran anyway. He ran and ran and ran and ran until his legs shredded from fatigue.

He made it to Paradox Lake before dawn. Had he really been out all night? He had to calm down. Give himself some quiet time, as Hen called it. He went to the beach—no permit needed at this hour—and fell into the sand.

Breathe.

Inhale.

Exhale.

Okay. It's okay. It's okay.

The water, like black ink, seemed bottomless. The spinning top eased in his chest. Calm blanketed him as a line of sunlight crept over the mountains. As the sand warmed in the sun, cradling him, he fell asleep to the song of blackbirds.

Out of respect for the son, Officer Clapp allowed Bernie into Sally Hubbard's home, but not into the living area. The crime scene. Bernie wouldn't want to see it anyway, Clapp assumed. Families got touchy about that stuff.

To Clapp's surprise, Bernie was impressively clear-eyed, his questions careful and smart. He described his mother without the teary sentimentality Clapp found annoying. On the contrary, Clapp took a liking to the guy. So much that after they covered the nuts and bolts investigation stuff, Clapp felt drawn to hang around and chat it up. If Bernie was game.

He joined Bernie in the kitchen, and his stomach betrayed him with a hungry, rolling grumble. He craved a Leon's Reuben and had a hard time thinking of anything else. Maybe Bernie would join him?

"I can make coffee?" Bernie offered.

Clapp petted his gut. "All right."

The aroma of raw coffee grounds triggered another growl from Clapp's stomach. He paced to the other side of the kitchen to wait. Something on the floor in the entryway caught his attention: a rudimentary craft—a kid's token—of pipe cleaner and beads.

"Kids?" He raised his eyebrows at Bernie.

"Oh, that would be Hen's. Henry. Ma takes care of him after school. He lives next door."

Clapp widened his stance, tapping his gun belt with his fingers—his signature move. The coffee percolated. Clapp's mouth watered. He stared at the beaded bracelet smack-dab in the middle of the crime scene. Seemed depressingly out of place.

"Do you think...could I bring it to him?" Bernie asked sheepishly.

Clapp nodded once. "Don't see why not."

"He'll be happy we found it." Bernie folded the bracelet into his pocket and then went about filling their mugs.

The first, bitter sip scorched his throat. "Ah, good man." Clapp couldn't contain himself. He started to pull out a chair as Bernie inched toward the back door.

"I'd rather not hang here, if it's all the same to you."

"Right."

Bernie had a point. It didn't feel right to sit in the woman's kitchen as she sat in a coma. Clapp followed Bernie out. Steaming mugs in hand, they crossed the backyard to the small brown house next door. Bernie mumbled about helping out a single mom who lived there, a dopey grin taking up his face. They sat in her orange kitchen, which was comfortably sparse and smelled vaguely of lemons.

"Giants are kind of a mixed bag this year," Clapp offered, trying to make small talk.

"Yahp," Bernie said. "Don't think we'll be seeing them in the playoffs."

Clapp let out an extravagant sigh and rested an ankle over a knee. This day was turning out to be quite enjoyable. As he breathed in his next sip, the front door opened.

"There's Hen," Bernie said.

Curious, Clapp turned to receive him, expecting the usual child-like antics, though his natural instinct would be to ignore. For the second time today, he was taken by surprise.

The kid didn't run into the house, traipsing mud on the floor, demanding a sugary snack. No. This boy quietly removed his shoes and let his backpack fall to the floor in an absent thud.

"Hi there, Hen! How was school?"

The boy flinched from Bernie's animated voice. He stared at the men. His wise, hazel eyes seemed to have grown up without the rest of his body. He lingered in the foyer. The light shining from the window behind him made him appear almost saintly.

"This is Officer Clapp." Bernie's efforts felt painful. "Come in and say hello."

"Hello." Barely audible.

Clapp stared at the youngster. This certainly was an odd boy. He was at a loss as to what to say. Still, the boy's intense gaze made him want to say something. He cleared his throat. "You like guns, boy?"

Hen reared back, eyes wide with horror. Bernie scrambled toward the child, holding out the beaded bracelet. "Look what we found today."

When Hen didn't reach for it, Bernie's smile waned. "It's yours, ain't it?"

Hen's face blanched. His jaw clamped shut. He stared at it, his brow rumpled.

Bernie shook the thing in front of the boy, who reluctantly took it. "It was in Ma's house—"

The front door flung open then, and a gorgeous specimen of a woman appeared beside the boy, who was visibly relieved.

Clapp straightened in his chair, his senses perked. He'd seen this woman before. He once nearly ran into her in the plumbing aisle of Ames—a memorable moment despite the unfortunate fact he'd been carrying a plunger.

This woman. The one who turned every head in the Schroon Lake area. Heck, the entire Adirondack region at that. The one that looked like she'd been plucked out of a magazine, a cover girl come alive. He couldn't believe he sat in her kitchen. In her house. His tongue gripped the roof of his mouth as he flat-out stared at her.

"Hi, sweetie." She set a pale hand on the boy's hair. Clapp noticed she didn't wear a ring. He pushed his shoulders back.

The beauty looked from Bernie to Clapp, confusion crimping her flawless skin. He shot up out of his chair as if he'd been summoned by dispatch. "Hello, ma'am. I'm Officer Clapp."

"Oh," Bernie fumbled. "Clapp, this is Marcella Trout. Marcella, Officer Clapp."

Marcella. Beautiful name for a beautiful woman.

When she didn't shake his outstretched hand, he widened his stance and tapped his gun belt again. "I'm the lead investigator for the incident next door." His usual officious tone faltered. "Bernie here was—"

"What are you doing here?" Her words were clipped.

"As I said, ma'am, I'm investigating the incident that took place—"

"I heard what you said." She hugged the boy to her slender thigh.

A wave of jealousy coursed through him.

"I want to know what you're doing in my house," she said.

Bernie stepped between them. "He, uh, we were next door and it was..." The poor guy spewed nonsense. "We thought coffee. Something didn't feel right about, so, we came here and, ah, thought we'd be done before—"

It was clear as crystal. Bernie was in love with this woman. It was endearing, kind of. This average Joe-on-a-stick had no chance with this stunner. Clapp felt for the guy. Tried to send him a smile. All covert-like—

"What on earth is so funny?" Marcella's bold eyebrows darted together, narrowing on him. "Do you have any idea how traumatic the past forty-eight hours have been? For Hen?" Her almond eyes glistened with fury. The dimple on her chin trembled. She went on with her rant, her shapely lips pursing. Her delicate hand danced in the air with the authority of an orchestra conductor. Hot damn, she was gorgeous. He didn't catch one more word she said.

Silence. All eyes were on him. Even the boy's. Bernie had to translate. "She's asking you to leave."

Clapp nearly jumped. He turned on his heel to the door from which they came, realized it would lead him into the backyard, and pivoted back, stopping short. How to exit this house where he suddenly wasn't welcome? Never welcome. He would've laughed had his face not been burning with shame.

Marcella gestured to the front door—a ballerina's movement—flashing the pale skin on the inside of her arm. It was all Clapp could do to get outside before his ribcage imploded on his lungs and heart and whatever else was inside his chest.

Outside. Inhale the cool afternoon air. Replace his Top Gun shades. Finally able to walk to his cruiser at a healthy clip. Only then did his body finally relax enough for him to process what just happened.

No, it wasn't the woman. Sure, she was the most gorgeous thing he'd ever laid eyes on and he would fantasize about her all night and probably for the next several weeks. That wasn't what struck him, though, as he folded into the cruiser and settled behind the wheel.

It was the boy. Clapp took in a satisfied breath as he pulled away from the curb. Yes, he certainly wasn't an ordinary boy. That's for sure. When Bernie showed him that piece of garbage pipe cleaner with the beads. It was there in the boy's eyes. He knew something.

The beads were slick in his hand and Hen knew he was sweating. He squeezed them in his fist, squishing the pipe cleaner into a ball. Sitting at the kitchen table, ignoring his Goldfish after-school snack, he stared at his book about nocturnal animals wishing Miss Sally were around to read it to him.

Mom's voice reached through his gloom. "Oh, my goodness, Bernie. It's the hospital." Mom had the phone clutched to her ear. Hen hadn't heard it ring.

The next few moments were a blur. Mom and Bernie rushing around. Hen clambering into his jacket and shoes again. They hustled Hen into Bernie's truck.

"Where are we going?" He still held tightly to the beads.

"To the hospital," Mom said.

"We're going to see Ma. I mean, Miss Sally." Bernie almost choked on the words.

Hen pulled on his seatbelt and stared at Miss Sally's house through the window.

It had turned into something from a scary movie. Some kind of trick leftover from Halloween. Bright yellow tape made a big X over her front door. It trailed around the porch—a mummy's wrap. One loose ribbon flew in the breeze like a cautionary flag. It draped the three wooden steps Hen had climbed a zillion times to get into Miss Sally's home. The other day, he'd eaten an apple on those steps in the sunshine.

"I don't like that yellow tape," he said, a hollowness filling his chest.

"I don't like that yellow tape, either." Bernie's voice was so soft, Hen almost didn't hear him.

They seemed to pass by the taped-up house in slow motion. Hen couldn't look away. The robbers had taken something from him, too. His second home.

Hen had never been inside a hospital before. It wasn't what he expected. He always thought people got better there. It was where babies were born. A happy place. As soon as they stepped inside, he felt cold. Like the air conditioning was on too high. It smelled like vinegar. Nurses rushed around in cloud-colored uniforms, their shoes squeaking on the tiles. No one smiled. No one looked at him. The place seemed full of secrets.

Hen wanted to leave, but Mom held fast to his hand. Too tightly. She didn't let him push the elevator button, either. As it went up, Bernie mumbled into his hands. A prayer? His breath got gaspy and loud. Hen hoped he wouldn't cry. He'd never seen Bernie cry.

"Where is she?" Bernie asked the sky.

Mom took Bernie's hand and they walked in a three-part chain to Miss Sally's room. Hen stayed by the door while Mom and Bernie went to her bedside.

Hen wasn't ready for what he saw. As he stared, his insides trembled.

Miss Sally was so small in the bed. White bandages covered half her head. Her hair shaven off. One eye was huge and puffy and purple. The other, open slightly, an eerie sliver of white. Tubes came out of her nose.

He loved Miss Sally. He did want to see her. But he didn't want to see her this way.

The room was huge and echoey. Wires went from her chest to a beeping machine at her bedside—one that blinked numbers in lights, like the clock in his room.

Bernie folded over Miss Sally's bed and sobbed into her shoulder.

Hen went rigid with fear.

Mom gathered him in her arms. "Come on." She brought him into the hallway. "You okay?" She tried a smile, but tears trickled down her face. "There's a vending machine down the hall. Let's get you a chocolate bar."

His stomach turned at the thought of it. "Miss Sally's going to be okay, right?"

Fresh tears filled her eyes. She hugged him hard and whispered into his hair. "Oh, Hen, sweetie. We think she'll be going to heaven very soon."

Ty awakened with the book cradled to his chest like a security blanket. His sleep had been hard and dreamless. His back cracked as he came to. The sand had hardened beneath him, bruising his ribs.

Throughout his interrogation and then his long walk to the beach, the book was tucked into the kangaroo pocket of his drug rug. Ty didn't know why he'd kept it with him. He hadn't read a single word. And it wasn't until he faced the new light of day that he felt safe enough to read about the man who turned into a bug. He stayed there on the beach, reading, until the sun went high in the sky. It was slow going. That dude Kafka used some big words. But Ty got the gist.

Fascinated, haunted, Ty wrestled with conflicting emotions. Something about Gregor Samson's situation brought him comfort. He wasn't alone. Gregor had become imprisoned in a hard, scaly shell —his itchy, slick legs pilling the blanket.

Ty had also felt trapped in an exoskeleton of sorts.

Another part of Ty felt oddly violated. As if this author, this Franz

Kafka person, had insight into his psyche. Read his mind, or something. Exposed his secret.

The high sun told him it was past noon. He was mildly surprised no one had called him out for trespassing on the beach. Although it was off-season. He dug into his pockets again, a reflex. He was jittery, jonesing for something that wasn't there.

When he dunked his feet in at the shore, the cold went right to his bones and stayed there. He couldn't shake the chill after that. He pulled his hood over his ears. Sucked on his cigarette for warmth. Always chillier at the lake. The huge, auburn sun offered no warmth, like it had turned against him, too.

He didn't feel like being alone anymore.

Ty didn't try to hitchhike back home. He wasn't that far anyway. Still, he walked slowly, finishing the rest of his pack, stretching each cigarette a mile. It was meditative. Walking. Smoking. Everything else had fallen away. Even the girl. Or whatever. It seemed silly now. Trick of light or something.

No one was home when he got there. That was weird. He paced in the orange kitchen. Where the hell was everyone? Was Marcella pissed? Did she know he skipped school? Was she trying to find him? He thought of her searching for him at the station.

Oh, no. Maybe she saw Derek and cornered him and he told her—

What would he tell her?

This wasn't good. He was getting all angsty. He didn't like being in the house all by himself. That tingle of shame intensified. Not just about the stupid bracelet. It was bigger. Serious. It felt like he'd done something horribly wrong. Not just wrong—disgusting. Unspeakable. He couldn't shake the feeling. He felt excruciatingly hot, like his blood was set to boil. Guilt nearly swallowed him.

He stared out the kitchen window.

Rotting scum. I know what you did.

Slowly, he turned toward the voice, which had come from the living room. A few steps in, and he heard it again. Followed by laughter. Evil scientist laughter.

Then, a knock. Accidental, like a fall. Eyes on the coat closet as it flexed and bulged. A knee? Who was hiding there? Holy shit. Someone was hiding in there.

He clutched the fireplace poker and, holding it overhead, approached the closet. His heart roared in his ears.

"Say it one more time." His voice trembled. "I dare you."

Rotting scum. I know what you did.

Screw this. He couldn't stand it anymore. Ty flung open the door with a howl. *Whoosh.* He brought the poker down. Again. He kept swinging. He kept slashing.

Bwa-ha-ha-ha-ha. His blows were met with more laughter. Loud and relentless.

"Shut up, shut up," he repeated as he slashed down again. And again and again.

Boom. The laughter cut out. Everything stopped. Like a switch had flipped.

Ty studied the contents of the closet: summer jackets that had yet to be put away. The khaki trench Marcella used only in downpours. His and Hen's winter coats from last year. Snowpants. Black streaks— coal smears—marked each piece.

The fireplace poker clanged to the floor. Ty sank to his knees and buried his face in his hands.

What the hell? *What's wrong with me?*

He wanted to cry. Begged for tears to come. But everything was snuffed out. His emotions were so lost inside, he wasn't sure how to get at them. He shook, rocking and whining, wishing they would leave him alone.

He wasn't sure how long he stayed there, curled up in the middle of the floor.

At dusk, Marcella's Impala pulled into the driveway. His relief was profound. He ran out to greet them, a child again, his eager steps light.

Then he saw their faces.

He stopped. "Where have you guys been?"

Marcella went to embrace him. "Oh, Tyler."

He dodged her. "What's going on? What happened?"

Marcella looked away. Something was seriously wrong. A heavy silence came between them. Bird wings swatted at Ty's chest—his windpipe shrinking, narrow as a straw.

"What?" His voice was laden with attitude. "What?"

Hen appeared at his side. His huge eyes gazing up like twin, endless pools. "Miss Sally's going to heaven." He said it so simply, in the voice of an angel.

Ty's knees buckled and he fell against Marcella's car. "What did you say?" He clutched at his chest, tangling his drug rug straps in his fist. His throat filled. "No," he whispered. "No."

Marcella hugged herself. Hen reached for Ty's hand. "Tyler?"

Ty broke away, Hen's eyes too much to bear. He stumbled toward Miss Sally's house, but recoiled as if the yellow tape slapped him in the face.

CAUTION. DO NOT ENTER. CAUTION. DO NOT ENTER. CAUTION. DO NOT—

His breath cut off. He turned toward the backyard, his movements clumsy. He stopped near the bulkhead and retched beside it.

"No, no, no."

Snot and vomit drenched his jaw. He heaved again, and tasted ash. He crouched, hands on knees, until Marcella gently took him by the shoulders.

Leaning into her embrace, he imagined it was Roxanne's hair that tickled his face. His stomach settled somewhat.

Marcella led him inside, directly upstairs and into bed. She cleaned his face and dabbed his forehead with a cool, wet washcloth.

"My boy," she whispered. "My boy, come back to me."

She took off his socks. Fresh blisters throbbed when they hit the air. Fatigue overcame him, and he was nearly asleep as she covered him with his quilt.

Bernie held Ma's hand as she took her final breath. The room was stripped of beeping machines. The tubes removed from her body. Quiet. Still.

There hadn't been a final goodbye, she never woke up to tell him —even with her eyes—that she loved him, or how proud she was of him. The doctors and nurses let him stay there awhile, holding her hand.

He held on so tightly. His grief was so heavy he felt he'd sink into the floor.

He couldn't let go of her hand. When he did, the world would never be the same. He'd have to learn how to live all over again without her. Things wouldn't just look different; things would be different. All matter would transform, become undiscovered. Like artifacts. He would have to piece together a life for himself from the pieces. If he only knew where to find them.

"Ma." The word echoed dully in the empty room. Going forward, he would only use the word to talk about her, not to her. He would never call anyone else Ma.

He could've been angry—at the intruders, at the world, at God. He had no room in his heart for anything but sadness. Hours passed and his tears dried. When he finally let go, the tendons in his hand ached.

Bernie went to Marcella. He sat in her kitchen, content to do nothing and say nothing. For hours.

She fed him and gave him space. At night, after all were asleep, they sat quietly side by side. In the orange glow of her kitchen, he fought to ignore the auburn highlights shimmering in her dark hair and the way her chestnut eyes softened with specks of emerald.

Was it possible she grew more beautiful after Ma's death?

He knew how much she loved and relied on Ma. She had to be grieving, too. But Marcella surprised him.

After a healthy cry, she swung into action. She took care of him.

Over the next few days, she did so much. She set up an "in lieu of flowers" donation option that would go to the local Boys & Girls Club. When it was time plan the funeral, she wouldn't let him go into debt.

"What would your Ma say?" she'd said. "It doesn't matter what's on the outside. It's the inside that counts."

She sold her grandmother's curio cabinet and dining set, allowing her to cut back her hours at the diner in Ticonderoga. "We never really used it anyway," she'd said, her voice echoing through the now-empty dining room. "Who can afford that kind of sentimentality?"

A new kind of sentimentality afforded Bernie and Marcella a new chance, as they learned later in the Law Office of Greagh & Hochman where they met to review Ma's Last Will and Testament. Bernie assumed it was the fancy lawyer language that made it hard to understand.

It seemed Ma had set up a trust for Hen. Which meant, essentially, that Hen would be inheriting Ma's money. Could that be true?

Marcella cleared her throat and asked for a third time, "Would you kindly say that again in laymen's terms, if you would please?"

Lawrence Hochman seemed apologetic as he spoke. "Sally

Hubbard has listed Marcella Trout as executrix and Henry Atticus Trout as sole beneficiary, with a stipulation."

"Come again?" Bernie's cheeks burned. He couldn't possibly mean—

"I take it you've been together long enough, about seven years according to the dates referenced here. In many states, you'd be considered married under common law."

Marcella gave a nervous laugh.

"Although legally, in New York State, that doesn't apply, Sally Hubbard acknowledged your extended relationship as such. In regards to her Will, as long as your relationship doesn't change, the sole beneficiary will be Henry Trout."

"What do you mean 'if the relationship doesn't change?'" Bernie asked.

Mr. Hochman wore a strained smile. "In simple terms, if you two stay together, Henry Trout inherits Sally Hubbard's assets when he turns eighteen, which amounts to $1.3 million."

The pause that followed was thicker than Adirondack fog.

Marcella spoke in a thin voice, "And if we don't...stay together?"

"All funds will be donated to the Boys & Girls Club."

Bernie's breath stopped. He swallowed audibly.

Marcella turned to him, a glazed astonishment in her eyes. "Ma wanted us together?"

A question. A legitimate question. One that had already sidelined Bernie. Yet, it was the first time he heard Marcella refer to Miss Sally as "Ma." And she said "us" and "together." Bernie stared at her lips, willing her to say it again.

"Ma wanted us together," he said, breathless.

An abrupt knock and the door to Hochman's office opened.

"Mrs. Trout?" said Hochman's secretary. "You have a phone call."

Marcella's eyes left Bernie's. Too soon. "Me? Here?"

In a private conference room, Bernie stood by as she took the call. And his heart sank.

"Tyler?" she said into the receiver. She listened quietly for a few seconds, and then she folded, like her body cramped.

"I'll be right there." She hung up. "He's been arrested." Her voice faltered. "He needs me. I have to go to Justice Bowman's office. Right now."

The agony in her chestnut eyes, like a window into her soul, told him his love would never be enough to fix this.

Tap, tap, tap...

Hen sat on Mom's bed, knocking the plastic beads on his copy of *101 Facts about Nocturnal Animals*. The glossy pictures didn't interest him anymore. Getting a pet hedgehog seemed silly now. He closed the book, and got a whiff of Miss Sally—her Juicyfruit house, her plaid chair, her snickerdoodles. Open. Shut. The smell was still there. If the smell was still there, why wasn't Miss Sally?

How could everything change so fast? Just the other day they were playing chess. And then that awful thing and then the hospital and then she disappeared. Gone.

Miss Sally was gone.

She'd never come back? It didn't seem possible. Couldn't he run up her porch steps and the door would open to the Juicyfruit house? No. He couldn't. Her house was still wrapped like a neon mummy.

He sank into Mom's bed, swallowed by a black hole of fear. Was she really gone? Did she really die? His mouth went dry. Turning on his side, a single tear fell onto Mom's comforter. He held the beaded bracelet to his cheek, listening to the ping and swish of Tyler raking outside.

Since Miss Sally went to heaven, Tyler was in a constant B mood. When he wasn't sleeping, which was most of the time, he was scary quiet, plugged into music on his headphones and staring into space.

Today, though, Tyler was supposed to watch Hen while Mom and Bernie were at a meeting at a lawyer's office. Hen thought they'd do something fun together, like take a walk in the woods or build a hedgehog trap. But Tyler insisted on doing yard work, which was weird because he hated yard work. It was the only chore Mom gave him, but he never did it. He raked with all his might today.

From Mom's bedroom window, Hen had a clear view of Tyler in the yard. Hen told himself that's why he stayed inside. On any other day, he'd be out with Tyler—in his play tent or swatting trees with big sticks. Today, he only felt like lying in Mom's bed.

Hen was still there on Mom's bed when a policeman came to the house.

"Tyler Trout?" The plastic voice outside was familiar. It was the policeman who'd been here the other day with Bernie. The one who'd found his bracelet. What was he doing here?

Hen's ears grew four times their size as he crept beneath the window.

"Put the rake down, son."

"What?"

"It's considered a weapon. Put the rake down."

"Seriously? It's a rake."

"Down! Hands in the air! This is your last warning!"

Hen jolted. Tyler mumbled, a blunt edge to his voice, as the rake clanged to the ground. Hen dared to peek through the blinds, and at once wished he hadn't. The policeman pointed his gun at Tyler.

A gun! Paste filled Hen's mouth.

"You're under arrest. Anything you say can and will be used against you..."

Officer Clapp continued—like a robot—while Tyler raised his hands in the air. He slowly turned around and moved his hands behind his back, like he knew what he was supposed to do. Tyler kept his eyes on the ground. If he looked up, he'd see Hen.

Look up! Look up!

The policeman droned on, radio words in a radio voice, snapping handcuffs onto Tyler's wrists. Hen gasped, clapping his hand over his mouth. Tyler looked up then, and saw Hen through the window. The smallest shake of his head told Hen to stay quiet and hidden inside.

The policeman followed Tyler's gaze through the window. Hen froze. Oh, no. He was caught! He'd be put into handcuffs, too.

"Your mother home?" The question came out squeaky and high-pitched.

"No."

Back to the mean policeman voice: "How about the boy?"

A brief pause, and then Tyler shook his head.

The officer's pitch-black sunglass lenses must have shielded Hen. As they walked to the cruiser, Hen slid under Mom's bed to hide.

It took a long time for his heart to stop thumping.

Bernie arrived later. Maybe an hour. Maybe three. It felt like a lifetime under the bed.

"Hen?" Bernie's shoes tapped all over the downstairs. "You up in your room?"

The dust bunnies under the bed made the air tickly. Hen sneezed.

Taps got closer. And Bernie's feet appeared at Mom's door.

"Ah." Bernie's tip-tappy shoes hushed on the carpet. He wore dress shoes and light pants, Hen noticed. That was a change. Bernie always wore jeans and work boots.

The mattress sagged as Bernie sat at the foot of the bed. Hen tried not to sneeze again. A long stretch of quiet made Hen sleepy. He rested a cheek on folded arms.

Eventually, he heard Bernie's soft voice. "Sometimes I feel like hiding too."

Hen closed his eyes, sleep pulling him from what he'd seen—Tyler being taken away. He was drifting off when Bernie spoke again.

"Your momma's a real good woman. She'll take care of you always. Know that."

MARCELLA CLICKED in her lawyer-meeting heels to Justice Bowman's residence, yearning for her waitressing shoes. That urgent call from Tyler kept replaying in her mind.

"Mom, they arrested me." He sounded shockingly like his father. Then, back to her scared boy again, chasing the words with a butterfly net. "You need to be here. Please come."

"An arraignment," he'd told her. What a horrible word. Made just to intimidate the common people. That pre-law telecourse on the Coastal College flier she'd laughed off at first now seemed sadly relevant. Irritation drained through her as she pictured that infuriating Marketing 101 textbook. If she could, she would send a lightning bolt through every accounting spreadsheet on the planet for all it would do to help her family. *Bah.* What was she thinking, signing up for a marketing course? Did she really think she would have time to get a business degree in the midst of everything else? And now this.

An arraignment?

Whatever an "arraignment" was, Justice Bowman would clear it up in a flash. Why, though, was Marcella called in? Because Tyler was a minor?

No use trying to figure it out solo. Her mind ached trying to process the madness that had erupted in the past few days. To top it off, Mr. Hochman just dealt a bomb of a hand, reporting that Hen was named as Sally's primary beneficiary. $1.3 million? How on earth did Sally get all that money? And the stipulation—that Bernie and she stay together. Like, a couple. As if they'd ever been a couple.

If Mr. Hochman hadn't been so serious, she may have laughed.

After all, this was *Bernie.*

Bernie Hubbard had been a trusted friend since Hen was born. He had come to her rescue more than once. Marcella remembered holding her newborn at the hospital, scared and alone, wondering how she would swing raising two boys by herself. It was Bernie who'd collected them from the hospital.

"Ma sent me."

A man of few words, he'd driven the rest of the way in silence. He didn't try to stop Marcella from crying. Or insist things would be all right. The next day, Bernie came over with two boxes of diapers.

"Ma sent me."

The next day, formula.

"Ma sent me."

"Is there anything you do on our own?" she'd teased. His easy smile in response made her trust him. And that was that. But that was all.

Bernie drove her and Hen to his early doctor appointments. Bernie kept tabs on Tyler after he disappeared for hours on his bike. Bernie bailed out the water when her basement flooded. Bernie installed the chain lock on her front door. Bernie negotiated the impossible purchase of her trusty Impala. Bernie found that "wait-staff wanted" ad for that diner in Ticonderoga, which relieved her from Leon's payroll. And, best yet, Bernie convinced his mother to babysit Hen so Marcella could go back to work.

Bernie never once made a pass at her and Marcella never once wanted him to. He was plain pudding—the epitome of ordinary. The kind of guy no one noticed as he passed on the street. Balding, with washed out features, Bernie's best attribute was his smile. It extended to his soft brown eyes, and carved premature lines around his mouth. Reassuring. Safe.

Marcella sighed. All these years, she may have taken him for granted, sure. But to think of them as a couple? Marcella couldn't get her mind around it.

She could hardly try now.

Not to mention, she had written off men a long time ago. Since Hen's father went AWOL, she vowed the only men worth her spit were her own boys. So far, she'd kept that promise. No way in hell was she going to break it anytime soon.

What was worse, though—men or high heels? Her Achilles was raw and bleeding by the time she got to Justice Bowman's home office.

She'd been there before. A few months back, she brought a quiche pie after his wife Elyse's knee surgery. She'd never knocked on his office door, in the anteroom of their home. Part of her wanted to go to the front door like always. As a friend. To prove this was a social call. Not something legal and scary. But she took a deep breath and reminded herself to be professional. When no one answered the office door, she realized knocking wasn't necessary. Still, she felt like an intruder just walking in.

Inside, the room was lined with books and worn leather couches. Dishes clapped beyond the connecting wall, sounds of a dishwasher being emptied. The homey feel belied Tyler's horrific luck. Marcella's heart wilted. Her boy slumped in one of the oversized leather chairs, misery tainting his handsome face.

"Mrs. Trout," Justice Bowman said. "Please, have a seat."

Must be serious if first names were out the window. "Thanks, but I prefer to stand," she replied stiffly.

That smarmy officer—the one who she'd found in her kitchen that day—stood like a king's guard nearby. Too close. Tapping his belt incessantly. Officer Clapp, she recalled his name. Like the venereal disease.

Justice Bowman calmly explained why Tyler was being arraigned. Why did law officials use that nonsensical mumbo jumbo? It was worse than her ridiculous marketing textbook. The words swirled like noxious gas: Evidence...fingerprints...broken lamp. All pointed to Tyler Nathan Trout.

Marcella, lightheaded, grasped the desk. "Maybe I will sit after all."

Bowman gave her a sympathetic look. "Mrs. Trout, your son Tyler is a suspect in an extremely serious crime. Initially aggravated assault, this crime has become more severe since the victim—Sally Edith Hubbard—passed away as a result of the injuries suffered the night of October 30."

Marcella glanced at Tyler, who looked so small in the leather armchair. Shriveled.

Anger simmered. How could he speak like this about her son? Right in front of him! She clenched her jaw. "I thought you'd be able to take care of this, Carl. Surely, this is a terrible misunderstanding."

"Mrs. Trout—"

"Honestly. Fingerprints? She was our neighbor, Carl. Tyler could've been in her house on any occasion for whatever reason. She watched Hen every day. Tyler picked him up quite often. It's no surprise his fingerprints would be found there. I mean, come on."

Bowman blinked with deliberation, as if trying to summon patience. "Mrs. Trout, Officer, if you don't mind, I'd like to speak plainly."

Clapp finally stopped that annoying belt tapping.

Bowman continued, "In situations like these, where a very serious crime is being investigated, we hold these meetings—arraignments—to determine whether or not the suspect would have any reason to make a run for it. We consider the person's past, if he has a criminal record—which Tyler does not. We also consider if there would be any opportunity to go out of state, if they have strong connections to this area."

"Tyler's lived here his whole life," Marcella said.

"I know. I know." Bowman glanced at Clapp. "I'm sorry to bring this up, Marcella, but do you know where Tyler's father is?"

Thank goodness Marcella took that seat. The words "Tyler's father" sent needle pricks up and down her spine. She barely noticed he used her first name.

Tyler's father. Ha!

Marcella was suddenly twenty-one again, her stomach a hot-air balloon, lifting her into a world of disillusionment. A world with white picket fences and family dinners and T-ball and birthday parties. A world she'd hoped to share with Tripp Trout, a man who proved as absurd as his name. Tripp, at twenty-nine, had been more interested in guns and whiskey and bullfights than white picket fences. No less a wife and, God forbid, a baby. Tripp sensed that hot-air balloon in her heart and got spooked. Saw the end of his life, maybe. Needy baby, nagging wife, bills piling up. One good day at the horse races was all it took and he was gone. Just like that. Tyler was only three years old, too young to hold onto memories of him. She'd always thought that was a blessing in disguise.

Now she attended an arraignment for their son, whose eager eyes were full of hope and blue, blue, blue like his father's. Eyes that now begged, *Tell me about my dad*, as he'd asked countless times throughout the years.

"I don't know where he is," she told Bowman. It was sort of true.

"You don't know where his family is? Where he's from?"

"I do." Marcella pursed her lips. How much truth was required here? "Tripp was never close with his family." This was true. Emotionally, he wasn't close to them. Or anyone. Certainly, he'd never been close to Marcella that way. She felt her throat closing.

"Does it matter where his family lives?" she blurted. "It doesn't mean he's there, too. Who knows where he is?" Siberia, for all she cared. She tugged her skirt hem over her knees, fighting the heat in her face. That was all he'd get from her, period. Tyler wouldn't get any crazy ideas to start a scavenger hunt in Arkansas in search of his deadbeat dad. Especially now.

"Any interest in finding your dad, son?" Bowman asked Tyler directly.

Marcella started. What a jolt. How dare he manipulate the situation.

One glance at Tyler told her how dangerous that question really was. Her heart raced. "Tyler, you don't have to answer—"

Tyler nodded once, his ice-blue eyes filling.

She shot out of her chair. "Oh, no. Tyler. Come on." She couldn't help herself. "You don't want your father. You don't need him. We don't need him. We never have!"

She reached for him. She was enough, wasn't she? All these years, she had done it without Tripp-freaking-Trout. She'd worked so hard, saving every dime. Her voice got louder. "Tyler, really. Your whole life...who's been there when you were sick? Who rubbed your back for hours and sang you songs after a really bad night, huh? Who cooked for you, did your laundry, bought you clothes and shoes and everything you ever needed? It wasn't your father, I'll tell you that."

Justice Bowman stood. "Mrs. Trout—"

"Tyler, look at me!"

He did. And Marcella flinched. That stone-cold glare, so like his father's.

He was angry. With her? Her chest hollowed from shock. What had she done wrong? She was here to help him. Didn't he know that?

She sank back into her chair, feeling numb.

Bowman calmly stepped toward Tyler. "Do you have an idea where your father is? Has he been in touch with you at all? Sent birthday cards or—"

"Honestly, Carl. Must you torture the child?"

Bowman looked sharply at Marcella. "This child is accused of a very adult crime. In fact, he may be tried as an adult. Do you know what kind of prison sentence accompanies a verdict of involuntary manslaughter?"

Marcella's hand floated to her mouth. Manslaughter?

Tyler must not have heard. He was trying to find his father now. His words cut through her: "I think he might be in Arkansas." A student trying to please his teacher. "Right, Mom? Didn't you tell me his family was in Arkansas? He's probably there."

Oh, goodness. Had she told him? Her words ran together. "Probably not. I doubt it. He's probably in Mexico or something." Her lie painted her red, she was sure now.

Tyler shook his head, an *a-ha!* look lighting up his face. "No, no. You told me once he lived in Arkansas."

"When did I tell you that?" She hated herself for how nasty she sounded.

"A while ago. But I never forgot it." He added in a dreamy voice, "I've never been to Arkansas."

"And you're never going." Bitterness clipped her words. She had an urge to stomp her foot like a toddler. Now was not the time for Tyler to rebel. She was trying to protect him. Didn't he see that? Why couldn't he keep his mouth shut?

Tyler gave her his father's glare again. It blindsided her. She blinked at her son, hardly recognizing him.

The silence that followed weighed a ton.

Clapp tapped his gun belt.

Marcella turned to Bowman, heat creeping up her neck. "Mr. Bowman. Carl, please—"

He was making notes in a folder, the tab of which read: TYLER TROUT – MANSLAUGHTER.

Marcella felt hope spin loose like ribbon from a maypole. She might hyperventilate. It was ages before anyone spoke. In that maddening legal mumbo jumbo again. She only caught bits.

Due to the severity...state of mind of suspect...potential risk...suspect leaving the state...remain in custody...evidentiary hearing...whether he will be indicted...to the grand jury...

When Clapp snapped handcuffs on Tyler's skinny wrists, something snapped inside her.

"Wait-wait-wait a minute." Her voice rose. "What's this? He's coming home, right? He can come home with me, can't he?"

"I'm sorry, Marcella. I can't justify—"

"He won't go anywhere, Carl. He wouldn't do that." As she said it, her gut hitched. Tyler accepted the handcuffs too readily, like it was a game. His lips twisted in a cocky grin. He eyed Marcella as if to say, 'Watch this.'

Her stomach dropped, sickness filled it.

"He wouldn't..." She trailed off.

She had no idea what her son was capable of.

THE DINER'S bell triggered a Pavlovian sinking in Marcella's gut. Before she could turn back, Leon spotted her.

"Marcey-Marce, my love! Back to work for me, doll?" Leon winked, and mumbled to a customer who laughed into his napkin.

"Oh, please. No. Just hoped we could talk." Marcella made her way to an open booth, feeling Leon's eyes on her skirt. *Stay strong.* She was here for a reason. That reason involved Leon, regrettably.

Why wouldn't they listen to you? she'd said the night the boys were taken in for questioning. Hopefully, he still held the reins in this town.

The big oaf slid her a mug of black coffee and took a seat.

"What's up?" A toothpick clenched in his teeth.

"Really? You don't know? I'm here about Tyler. And Derek."

"Ah."

"Why else would I come here?"

He half-smiled. His scruff clicked beneath his hand. "What about 'em?"

Marcella blinked at him. "I just came from Tyler's arraignment. They wouldn't release him to me. They're holding him. Since Sally died, it's worse—the charges, I mean. Way worse. They're talking manslaughter." She could barely say the word.

Something crossed Leon's beady eyes. Compassion, perhaps? Marcella praised herself for coming. The unlucky truth? This slob of a man was her only real hope for helping Tyler.

He laughed, and she smelled raw onion. "This a joke?"

"No, absolutely not." Marcella forced a sip of coffee.

That lewd kink in his brow tormented her. Surely, he had to know that Tyler being charged with manslaughter meant about the same for—

"Hey, D!" he called, startling her.

What was he doing?

But then, a reply. An annoyed, teenage reply. The voice held the same cocky attitude she heard so often in Tyler.

"Yo, D!" Leon called again, his eyes not leaving Marcella's. "Derek! Come out here."

Derek appeared from the back kitchen, waddling in his loafy high tops and backwards cap, his attitude shifting from cocky to curious when he spotted Marcella.

What? Derek was here?

How many times did Pop call his name before Derek finally came out from the kitchen? It was a game he liked to play. See how many times the old man called him before losing his cool. Emerge just before cool is lost. For all Derek knew, Leon wanted him to haul in frozen patties or sacks of flour or whatever shipment came in.

Derek and his pop had an unusual relationship, if you could call it that. From his earliest memories, Pop had spoken to him as if he were a peer. No secrets—big or small. Derek had always known the truth about Santa Claus. He knew penny wishes never came true. He knew his mother died in a car wreck when he was two-and-a-half. He knew his father never loved her. He knew there was no such thing as heaven.

From age nine, Derek worked in the diner, mopping up the day's grease. Most nights he stayed until closing. Some might have said it was a crappy childhood, but Derek didn't think so. Someday he would own the place. It would be all his. And he'd be as powerful as his old man.

He rounded the corner chuckling to himself. And then he saw her.

Marcella.

He almost tripped on his laces. He had to consciously stay cool in his swagger as he approached her table, his heart racing.

"'Sup?" How hard it was to stay aloof.

"You know Tyler's mother, D," Pop spat. "Be polite and say hello."

"Hi, Mrs. Trout."

"Hello, Derek." Marcella hardened her stare. "Do you know where Tyler is?"

Not since he told me to screw off. "Not his sitter, ma'am."

Pop smirked. Marcella glared. Derek stood between them feeling like an ass. The last thing he wanted was to disappoint her.

Since losing his mother, Marcella was the mom he never had. Fed him hot dogs and macaroni on weekends, snuck sandwiches into his backpack at the bus stop. She taught him how to play checkers and Monopoly. In the winter, she'd take him and Ty sledding. In the summer, she'd let them run around in the sprinkler. She never forgot his birthday. Once when he was in first grade, his fever spiked and she held a cool cloth to his forehead as he shivered under a blanket for hours. He'd looked at her with bleary eyes and swore he saw a glow around her hair. A halo.

He tried again. "I don't know where Ty is."

Her voice shook. "He's been arrested. They're holding him. There's going to be a trial, I think." Angry tears slid from her wide brown eyes. "Derek, do you understand? Tyler can't come home. And you're loping around without a care in the world."

Derek cleared his throat, studied his shoes. "Sorry. Um, I think me and Ty are in a fight."

"What? A fight?" Marcella softened in an instant. "Oh, my goodness. What on earth happened?"

Pop's laughter sounded like he was gurgling marbles. Ignoring him, Marcella made room for Derek to sit. "Please, Derek. What happened? You can tell me."

Derek glanced at Pop for a microsecond. Marcella caught it.

"Leon." She smoothed her hair. "I just realized I'm famished. With everything that's happened today, I haven't had a thing to eat. Could you make me one of your famous egg-in-the-nests?"

After a pause, Pop knocked on the table. "Sure thing, doll."

"But I want you to make it." She gave a radiant smile. "You make the best ones."

Pop actually blushed. Derek fought a grin.

With Pop gone, Marcella took Derek's hand. "Go on. Tell me."

All those hard edges melted away. Derek yearned to curl up and cry in Marcella's lap, feel her slender fingers in his hair. Tell her everything. Let her make it okay.

He never wanted to be a bully. He never wanted to hurt anyone. Especially her.

"Go on."

Derek took back his hand. His shoulders shrugged on reflex. He heard himself say, "Wasn't me. Thought we were a team, yanno? But Ty, man..."

Her eyes dipped at the corners, softening him like butter on the counter. She loved him, didn't she? Like a son, one of her own. She'd love him no matter what, like a real mom. Didn't she? He gazed at her, searching.

The truth knocked against his chest, remembering, and the words choked out from that dark place he swore he'd never go. "We were scared. We were in there and...Ty, he. I dunno. It got outta control—"

"Where? Where were you?"

Derek reared back, catching himself. She didn't ask about that night. Did he want to talk about it? Confess everything? No. He couldn't go there. Not now, not ever. Put it back in the bottom vault of his memory. He reset his thoughts.

Marcella nudged him back on track. "Why are you and Ty in a fight, Derek?"

"Um, the police station. When they brought us in for questioning."

"Okay. In the station. Go ahead."

Derek sighed. It was a dumb story. Not even worth talking about.

"I dunno. They released us and I knew they were gonna release us. Wait. Ty's never been home since they brought us in for questioning?"

"No, he came home. Then Sally died and, well, they arrested him since. And they're holding him until the trial." She wiped her nose with a napkin. "But tell me what happened after they questioned you. You were together when they released you, right?

"Yeah, I guess Ty was still scared. You know how he gets sometimes. Not like regular scared, but crazy scared."

"I don't like that word. Tyler doesn't either—"

"I didn't mean crazy." He swallowed. "I meant, different. He sees things different. Sometimes he sees things that ain't there."

Out the window, the city bus passed. On its way to New York City. Why would anyone want to spend any time in a big city like that? He felt suffocated thinking of it. What would Ty do if he ever found himself in the city? Probably curl up on the corner. Just give into it. Let his visions take him to another place. Derek cringed.

Marcella took his hand again. Brought him back. "I know Tyler sees the world differently than the rest of us. He's always been sensitive."

Derek studied her. She didn't get it. How could she not know? "No, like..." What was he going to say? Something was definitely wrong with Ty. His mind was his worst enemy. He couldn't believe she didn't see it. Who was he to explain it to her? "Never mind."

"Okay." She seemed eager to move on. "You said Tyler was still scared after the two of you got released. I'm sure he was. So you got in a fight?" She stroked his hand with her thumb. It released a flood of emotion. He blinked back tears.

"Well, they released us and I started walkin' to the truck, yanno? And—whatever—Ty started walkin' the other way. Who knows where he was going? I thought he was confused. Like the whole situation knocked his brain for a loop or somethin'. Then I called to him. Nothin' bad or anything. 'Let's get outta dodge,' I said. I was gonna take him home but he kept walkin'. 'Where you goin'?' I said. I kept callin' after him, but he kept goin' the other way. And then he tole me to...well, he kept walkin'. He musta walked all the way back to Severance by himself."

"What were you going to say? He told you to—what?" She kept petting his hand. "It's okay. Tell me what he said."

He laughed through the flush of heat in his face. "Tole me to screw off. 'Screw off, Derek!' he shouted at me. Over and over."

Marcella nodded, her lips frozen in a mini-O. Then Pop brought her egg-in-the-nest and she let go of Derek's hand.

It had been days and days. Still, the shadows crept in to Hen's sleep.

...Two shadows. The Monster. And another. Small, soft, hunched over. Miss Sally? They faced each other, arguing. Something grew out of the Monster. A weirdly-shaped object. Heavy, by the slow way it swung around. Shadows splashed together. Now one huge, heaving blob, with sharp angles jutting out—a ball with spikes. It changed so fast. Like the darkness was trapped in a net.

"Put it down!" Miss Sally's clear voice. "Get out of my house this instant!"

Thump. Like something heavy dropped.

The shadow blob flung apart, like an explosion. Leaving only the Monster.

Another voice. Distant, angry yelling. Hen felt a chill, recognizing it.

No, no, no. Heart hammering, he ran, pumping his arms to go faster. He fell into his play tent and pressed his Spiderman hood to his ears. Then, a different sound—one uglier and more terrible than any he'd heard coming from Miss Sally's moments before.

A truck engine revving up. Not just any truck. A familiar junky, black Ford. Parked in front of Miss Sally's.

Now it matched up. Hen's brain clicked into gear. That other voice from the shadows? It went along with that truck, and belonged to Derek Hogg.

Fear gripped Hen's bones as he craned to see, to be sure. Yes, there was Derek—alone in the cab of his truck—pounding his fist against the steering wheel. Mad as heck...

SOMEONE SCREAMED. Shrill and high-pitched.

It was Hen. Hen was screaming.

He awoke panting. His heart thundering.

"Hey, now. It's okay. It's okay." Bernie hovered over him.

He blinked away the dream. But he couldn't shake the fear. He looked around, getting his bearings. He was home. In the livingroom, on the couch. As he came to, a streak of heartache broke through him. Miss Sally was dead. The Monster had taken her. The dark quiet still haunted him. Hen's chest rushed with heat.

"You had a bad dream, is all. You're all right." Bernie patted his shoulder like he was afraid Hen might break. He still wore his tappy dress shoes and button-down shirt.

Daylight came through the window. What was Hen doing on the couch? He wasn't even wearing pajamas. The house was real quiet.

"Where's Mom?"

"She, ah, should be home soon."

Hen sat up and rubbed his eyes.

"It's not all right," he told Bernie. In seconds, his fear turned to sadness, and he cried quietly, curling into himself.

"Not true. Everything's going to be all right." Bernie forced a smile, gave Hen's shoulder another pat, and sat in the armchair across the room.

Bernie. The one who has always fixed things. *Everything's going to be all right.* Hen stopped crying and took the beaded bracelet out of his pocket. Ran his finger over the beads. Red, blue, yellow, green. He squeezed them so hard they made marks on his palm. He did it in the other hand too, harder.

He knew what he had to do. "Where's Tyler?"

"Oh, he, uh…Why don't you ask your ma when she gets back?"

"The policeman came and took him away. He put handcuffs on him."

"Well." Bernie sat up a little. "You're right, Hen. Tyler's in a bit of trouble."

"Do they think he hurt Miss Sally?"

Bernie's eyes widened, but he sounded miserable. "I'm not sure, son. I think they might."

"No!" Hen smacked the couch. "He didn't! He didn't do it!"

"Hey, now. Hey, there. Let's not get all worked up."

Tears started as if a faucet turned on. It was coming loose. No stopping it. He had to tell him everything. "It was Derek," Hen wailed. "It wasn't Tyler. It was Derek."

Bernie moved in real close, looked around worried-like. "Now, don't go sayin' stuff like that, Hen. That's no good. You can't go accusin' someone of a crime. This is police work, Hen. They'll take care of it."

"It was Derek. He did it. I know it. I know it!"

"Hush, now." Bernie glanced out the window. Maybe making sure they were alone. "Okay, then. What makes you say it was Derek?"

Hen told himself to be brave. He took a big breath. "I was outside that night."

"You were outside?"

"I snuck out really late." Pause. "Mom was mad."

Bernie shook his head. "Oh, Hen. Why would you do that?"

"To look for Louis."

"Louis?"

"The hedgehog that's gonna be my pet."

A hint of a laugh. "Okay. You were out looking for a hedgehog, and—?"

"Noises came from Miss Sally's. Bad things were happening

inside. I saw a monster shadow through her window. And then in front of her house I saw…"

Bernie went a little white. "What did you see?"

"I saw Derek's truck."

Bernie huffed. "Well, see. Derek lives on this street. He's your neighbor, too. You're sandwiched between Ma's and Derek's houses, see."

"I know. But Derek's truck wasn't in front of his house. It was in front of Miss Sally's."

"Still. He could've parked there that night for some reason. It doesn't mean—"

"I saw him."

"What's that?"

"Derek. He was the Monster. I saw him leave Miss Sally's and get into his truck."

Bernie's face changed. His mouth opened a little. Hen could tell what he'd said was important. Maybe it could help Tyler? But there was something else in Bernie's face. It seemed like he was scared.

"Are you absolutely sure about what you saw?" Bernie's words were careful.

"I'm sure. I saw it."

Bernie sighed big. "Now, listen. I'm going to ask you an important question. Did you see anyone else? Or was Derek alone?"

"Just Derek. And he was angry."

"Now, how would you know that?"

"It was like he was mad at the steering wheel. He banged on it. Mad as heck." Hen added quietly, "I've seen him angry before."

Bernie rubbed his chin, like he was noodling something out. "You sure this wasn't a dream or nothin'?"

Hen squeezed his beads. "You don't believe me?"

"It's not that." Bernie's voice shook. "I mean, your ma wouldn't want you gettin' involved with this mess."

"But I was there when they came to Miss Sally's. A long time ago."

"What do you mean? Who came to Miss Sally's a long time ago?"

"Derek. And his father. They talked in the kitchen but I heard everything. I didn't want to listen but I couldn't help it. Miss Sally used her 'consequences' voice and they got really mad."

"What's that? Her 'consequences' voice?"

Hen did his best impression of Miss Sally: "'You can make that choice, Hen, but there will be consequences.'"

"Ah—"

"Consequences are always bad."

"She was always complaining about Derek's loud, late-night habits. That's probably what it was about. I'm not sure it has anything to do with—"

Hen smacked his knees, frustrated. "Derek and his dad are the only people on the planet who hated Miss Sally."

"Now, I agree with you on that. Why would anyone hate Ma, I mean, Miss Sally? To my mind, this is a break-in gone bad. Not a hate thing. But listen, this was a long time ago, you said, right?"

"After winter. Before summer."

"Well, it's unusual for fights to linger for months and months like that. Especially for Ma."

"But—"

"Okay, listen. Maybe I could do some investigatin' myself. In the meantime, let's keep this between you and me. Okay?"

Bernie went into the kitchen abruptly. Hen heard him going through some cabinets, mumbling something.

That wasn't how Hen thought the talk would go.

The room felt instantly cold. Hen hid under the fleece throw. Was it a mistake to tell Bernie? But he could fix it. Bernie fixed everything. Didn't he want to find the Monster? Didn't he want the Monster in jail, too?

Bernie seemed scared, though. Sad and scared and mad, all at the same time.

From the darkness of his fleece-throw tent came an image of Derek in his clompy shoes and backwards baseball cap, that perfumey smoke everywhere. His mean eyes tinged pink.

Bawk, bawk, bawk. How's my Chicken?

He was the Monster. Hen was sure of it. He had to go to jail. Not Tyler.

Hen felt tears come. If Bernie couldn't help, there was no hope. If Bernie couldn't stand up to Derek, who could?

What was it about Derek that made everyone afraid? Hen wished he were a grown up, big and strong. Derek would never hurt him—or anyone—ever again.

MARCELLA'S LAWYER-MEETING shoes weren't made for walking. She did a helluva lot of walking today. Albeit in circles—darn curlicues—for all the good it did Tyler.

She yanked off her stockings and stretched across the sofa, propping up her aching feet. Bernie had the good sense to put Hen to bed, thank heavens. All she wanted was sleep. The perfect escape. A deep, dreamless sleep that would go on for days or weeks or months. However long it took for Tyler to get untangled from this utter madness.

He was innocent. Why couldn't they all see it? The whole charade was like bad comedy. His fingerprints on Sally's end-table lamp? Come on! Who's to say he didn't touch her lamp when he picked up Hen one day? This was Tyler. He would never hurt a flea, no less a little old lady. They were so wrong it was stupid.

Bernie came down and sat across the room—averting his eyes, like, to respect her privacy. The quiet between them seemed charged. She glanced at her bare legs. Her skirt had ridden up to mid-thigh. Maybe she should have covered up with the throw? Oh, whatever. It was just Bernie.

"Oh, Bernie." She closed her eyes. "What are we going to do?"

No response.

Marcella swiveled upright.

They spoke in sync:

"Bernie—"

"Marcella—"

"Oh, sorry Bernie. You first."

He picked at his cuticles. "Hen, ah...I spent quite a lot of time with Hen today."

"I know. Thank you so much. How is he? Do you think he's doing all right?"

"Oh, I—"

"What a dumb question. Sorry. This is such a disaster. He adored Miss Sally. He idolizes his big brother. Of course he's not all right."

"About that..." He trailed off. He still couldn't seem to look at her.

"About what? Sally? Tyler? What?" She inched to the edge of the sofa. He clearly struggled with whatever he wanted to tell her. "Bernie, tell me."

"I'm not sure what to make of it. But Hen says he was outside that night. The night that Ma..."

Memories of that morning rushed to mind. Her pathetic attempt at studying for her telecourse in the wee hours before dawn while her baby was outside, shivering in a silly play tent. It was beyond embarrassing that Marcella could have allowed that to happen. "Well, he went out early in the morning. I went to wake him up and—"

"No, it was night. He was out all night."

"What? Out all night? Why on earth—"

"He wanted to catch a hedgehog?"

Marcella palmed her forehead, a familiar sandstorm of emotions cramping her psyche. Only one mattered, though. "Oh, how I love that boy."

"So. He was outside really late and 'parently he saw what happened at Ma's."

It clicked. Marcella gasped. "He saw?"

"Apparently so. And not only that..."

Marcella had stopped listening. Shock and guilt prompted her to move. She paced the living room, muttering to herself. "Oh, my goodness. He saw it happen? What's going on in his mind? Oh, my baby. He's so sensitive. This will stay with him for years. But, wait. If he saw, he must—does he know who did it?"

"Right. Well, he saw..."

"What?"

"He saw Derek Hogg's truck parked out front. He saw Derek leave Ma's and get into his truck, bang on the steering wheel, real angry like."

Marcella's jaw dropped, and then she clamped it shut.

"'Mad as heck' was how he put it." Bernie was looking at her now.

"Mad as heck," Marcella muttered, staring blankly at the fireplace. A heavy misery made her fold. "He's just a boy."

The house got real quiet. The radiator sputtered. Marcella felt her entire head swell with tears that wouldn't release. *My boy. My sweet, sweet little boy.* She fought an urge to run upstairs and bury her face in his neck. What she felt for him was beyond love. She wanted nothing more than for him to be safe and happy and feel loved. Yet, she wasn't paying enough attention to realize he'd been out all night and bore witness to something unspeakable. And now, losing Miss Sally and his big brother.

And the Hoggs were to blame?

A flash of anger spiked through her.

Bernie stood. "I know. And I told him we didn't want him involved in all this mess." He caught himself. "You wouldn't want him involved."

Marcella tried to summon those unwritten "To-dos." A mother's burden. Now was not the time to cry. Now was the time to take action. Be strong.

Her words had an airy quality not quite her own. "If he could help prove Tyler innocent, we might need him to be involved."

A sacrificial lamb. Hen's innocence in exchange for Tyler's freedom. It would be a deal with the devil. What did they call it—a Faustian Bargain? But it wouldn't be her soul she would trade. It would be Hen's.

Guilt stabbed. She felt queasy.

But, she reasoned, if Hen saw what happened, he was already involved. The gears were in motion. She couldn't protect him. She couldn't protect Tyler, either. Despair had invaded her home. She had no power against it.

Still, if those awful Hoggs were rightfully to blame, they must pay. Not her innocent, sensitive, frightened Tyler.

The room spun. The couch seemed a mile away. She ambled toward it.

"Maybe it wouldn't come to that." Bernie to the rescue. Hope glinted as she blinked him back into focus.

"When you went and talked with Leon..." His voice lilted, the question unnecessary.

Marcella slunk onto the sofa, feeling the weight of love and guilt and anger and hope all at once. Finally, she let herself cry.

"I don't think he can help us this time."

The next morning, Bernie treaded carefully to Marcella's front door. The dew had frozen on her driveway. Winter was already here. The cold air felt good, though. Each breath revived him. Or maybe it was the prospect of seeing Marcella. She had to leave for Ticonderoga shortly. He'd only see her for a few minutes, but every moment with her stretched long and deep, staying with him through the day.

This wasn't a social visit, though. He was here to help get Hen off to school.

"Thank you so much. You really have no idea." She smiled warmly at him. "Actually, I think you do."

"It's no problem."

"There's coffee."

They two-stepped around each other, swapping sides of the kitchen.

She kissed Hen's forehead as he ate his cereal. "Have a good day at school, sweetie."

She was gone before Bernie finished filling his mug.

Sitting with Hen, shame stung Bernie's insides worse than the scalding coffee he sipped. Only a few days had passed since Ma's death. He should have been grief-stricken. He'd learned yesterday that one hundred percent of her inheritance was going to a seven-year-old boy. He should have been resentful. But he wasn't. His mind was filled with thoughts of a future with Marcella. The idea made him almost giddy.

How could he be happy at a time like this? How could he be excited about the future without Ma in it? How could he accept so readily her gifting her estate—the value of her assets still astonished him—to Hen?

Ma's young beneficiary ate his Cinnamon Toast Crunch with impressive table manners. Never did Hen talk with his mouth full. He used a napkin rather than his sleeve. Always answered with "please" and "thank you."

Ma's influence. He could see why she'd been taken with the little guy. Hen had his mother's full red lips and a round softness to his face that begged for a cheek pinch.

Hen looked over his bowl at Bernie as if he could read his mind. His sullen hazel eyes tugged on Bernie's grief.

He got up to top off his mug.

Yet, if Ma had her wish, and Marcella's future included Bernie—which he so hoped it did—he'd be a father figure to this boy. At forty-six, Bernie had long ago given up the idea he'd have a family of his own. Not only could he possibly be father to Hen, but also to Tyler. The thought filled him with uneasiness. Pitcher frozen mid-air, Bernie breathed in the tangy coffee vapor and stared at a crack in the orange paint.

"Hearthstone" was the name on the paint swatch they'd used. Bernie had known after the test run in the pantry it wasn't exactly the shade Marcella had in mind. After the first coat, she'd insisted he finish. Perhaps she felt bad asking Bernie to redo it. Didn't she know he'd paint this kitchen a thousand times over for her? He'd do anything for her.

Bernie blinked at the crack, mentally noting to plaster it another day, and replaced the steaming pitcher.

Hen swung his feet back and forth as he spooned cereal into his mouth, and Bernie's heart swelled a bit. It dawned on him: If he were willing to do anything for Marcella, he'd do the same for Hen. Tyler, too. He could do it. He could be a good father.

"What should we do about it?" Hen's question startled Bernie.

For a fleeting moment, he thought Hen referred to the paint crack. Another sip. "What should we do about what?"

"About Derek. What we know."

Bernie turned on his smile. "I tell you what. How about if I pay a visit to Officer Clapp and inquire into the investigation?"

Retribution was the last thing Bernie wanted to pursue. He never liked Derek, sure. He did not want to start a personal vendetta on a hunch from a seven-year-old. Maybe his paternal instincts were kicking in, because he wanted to protect Hen from all this ugliness. In his heart, he knew Marcella felt the same way, despite what she said last night. *If he could help prove Tyler innocent, we might need him to be involved.*

Hen's voice almost sounded adult. "It was Derek. I know it."

"Well, if it was, the authorities will find out. They're already investigating. They are the experts here. They'll find out all the details of that night. Things we'd never even notice, they'll pick up. They've been trained. They do this for a living. They'll do the right thing."

"But they have Tyler. And that's wrong."

Bernie hid behind another sip of coffee, not knowing what to say. He agreed they were wrong to hold Tyler, but they must have their reasons. Soon, it will be cleared up for him. That was his hope, for Marcella's sake.

Part of him, though, wasn't sure what to make of Tyler and the fact that he may have something to do with what happened to Ma. Tyler was a bit of an enigma to him.

Couldn't say any of this to Hen, though.

Bernie glanced at the clock. "Come on. Let's get you to the bus."

Since Hen last walked to the bus stop, the leaf piles had been collected by the town.

That meant hedgehogs—maybe Louis!—were swept up with them. Into some leaf grinder thingy. Mulch maker. Hen's heart raced. No, no, no! He ran to where the biggest pile had been. Down on his knees, he searched the remnants for a sign. Louis?

He sobbed, inconsolable.

"I know you miss her," Bernie said. "I do too."

Bernie thought Hen cried for Miss Sally. That made Hen cry harder.

"Come on now. You don't want to get all dirty now."

Damp rings covered the knees of Hen's jeans. He brushed leaves off his coat. He remembered the leaf pile that upset Tyler so much, triggering a B mood. That was Halloween. Not too long ago. A handful of sleeps. Now everything was different. Everything changed so fast.

He trudged to the corner, smudging tears from his eyes.

"Did we time it right?" Bernie muttered. "Where's the bus?"

Hen was glad Bernie didn't ask what was wrong like so many grownups did. He breathed out little clouds, and watched them fade into nothing. He didn't think he could get any sadder.

"Why, hello there," a voice called. A policeman climbed out of his cruiser to join them. "How are we this morning?"

Hen inched closer to Bernie.

"Good morning, Officer." Bernie put a hand on Hen's shoulder. "Hen, you remember Officer Clapp?"

Hen recognized this man in uniform. Officer Clapp looked the same as he did in Hen's kitchen. The same as when he pointed his gun at Tyler in the backyard. It was like his clothes were part of his body, stitched onto his skin. Those pitch-black lenses still covered his eyes. It wasn't even a sunny day.

Why was Bernie being nice to this policeman?

Hen looked away, studying some leftover leaves in the street. Then Clapp squatted down next to him, his dark glasses right near his nose.

"Hey, boy. Too bad about your brother, eh?"

Hen saw his own reflection in Clapp's lenses. Contorted, like in a funny mirror. He shifted, and his head stretched into a pear shape.

Clapp took off his sunglasses. In one of his brown eyes was a speck of black, like a pebble in sand. Or a stain. These eyes saw bad things all the time.

Hen didn't want to be afraid. He looked right into them.

"Wanted you to know, boy. If you have any information, it's best you come forward and tell Officer Clapp now, you hear?"

Bernie started. "Officer, really. The boy's mother is—"

"I know your momma is real protective of you." Clapp kept talking to Hen. "She probably doesn't want you to get in the middle of all this. You don't want to see your brother go off and live in jail for a long, long time now, do ya?"

A gust of fear chilled Hen to the bone. He shook his head really fast.

"Didn't think so."

Now was the time. He needed to tell this policeman about Derek.

But he couldn't. His words wouldn't work.

He was locked in a face-off with the officer. The most frightening staring contest ever, looking into those brown-black eyes that saw bad things all the time. The black speck seemed to grow, spreading like an ink spill. Everything went fuzzy, and he leaned on Bernie so he wouldn't fall.

Bernie's voice was friendly. "Actually, Mr. Clapp, I was hoping to grab a few minutes with you about the whole business. The investigation."

"Oh?" Clapp stood, and it seemed Hen was off the hook. "And call me Rob."

"Rob. Thanks. Would now be a good time? Once Hen gets off to school? I'd like to keep the boy out of this."

Clapp glanced at Hen, replacing his sunglasses. "Learning a lot at school, are ya?"

Hen nodded.

"Bet you're a smart one." He didn't say it in a nice way.

The bus thundered around the corner. Hen pulled on Bernie's hand. He wanted to make sure Bernie would tell him about Derek's truck. Bernie was the grownup. He needed to do the grown-up things. What could Hen, a little boy, do to save his brother? Would anyone believe him, anyway?

Bernie patted Hen's back, sending him toward the bus. "Have a good day at school, now."

Hen forced a shaky breath and climbed onto the bus. Officer Clapp's words echoed in his mind. Tyler couldn't go to jail. He wasn't the Monster.

Hen fell into the seat next to his pal Murphy. Out the window, he followed Officer Clapp with his gaze. He walked side by side with Bernie toward the cruiser. Bernie was talking, his lips were moving. What was he saying?

Tell him! Tell him!

Bus door thumped closed.

Bernie and Clapp smiled at each other. Clapp buddy-punched his shoulder. Like friends.

"Police car. Cool!" Murphy said, leaning across Hen.

No. Not cool. Not cool at all.

The bus rumbled away from the curb, and Hen craned to see.

Now Bernie headed back toward Miss Sally's house. Officer Clapp was just a shadow in a police car. Another monster shadow. The one that took Tyler away.

Bernie was wrong. This policeman wouldn't help them. No matter what Bernie said to him.

There had to be something else Hen could do. There had to be someone Hen could talk to. Someone bigger than Bernie, or Clapp, or even Mom. Hen squeezed his eyes shut to think harder than he ever had before. There had to be someone out there who could save Tyler.

"I was a cop for Halloween." Murphy nudged Hen's arm.

Hen tried to think about all the people he knew in town. Big, important people.

"What's the next thing?" Hen asked Murphy. "Like, after a cop."

"After a cop?"

"I mean, if a cop was in trouble, he wouldn't call the cops. Who would he call?"

Murphy shrugged. "Probably a lawyer."

Hen's mouth fell open as he remembered Mom's meeting just yesterday.

"Or a judge," Murphy said. "A judge is the mack-daddy of it all."

Hen's thoughts raced.

"But how boring would that costume be?" Murphy laughed.

Hen felt himself smile, as a germ of a plan took seed in his mind.

Ty lay on the cell cot at the county jail thinking about his dad. He'd imagined a whole life for him. Actually two lives. In the first, he lived alone in Arkansas as a cattle rancher, where he spent all his days outside. Far away from any arcade or post office or supermarket. He'd come home late at night. He'd guzzle a beer and grill a slab of steak. Fall into bed in his undershirt. Sleep like the dead.

The second imagined life was better. Ty and his dad lived together in a log cabin on a lake—a lake not unlike Paradox Lake. Each dawn they'd canoe to a rocky cove to bass fish. Every afternoon they'd return with a bouquet of slippery creatures, delighting Marcella who'd have spent the day working in their vegetable garden. Hen collected worms alongside Marcella, waiting to be old enough to join his big brother in the canoe.

Hen was always in the picture even though he had a different father. Didn't seem right to exclude him. Roxanne Russo would be there too, somehow. He was still trying to figure out how to fit her in.

If he focused hard on these scenarios, he could blank everything else out. In a way, being in a cell was easier than being out in the world. There were clear boundaries. Black and white. Things didn't transform before his eyes. There wasn't room.

Except at night.

Nighttime was kind of sketchy. Last night, his cot became a life raft, floating in the open sea. The rocking soothed him at first, but then became violent. Sharks circled. The room sloshed and undulated around him. The sharks didn't quit. He woke up in a pool of vomit.

He tried to shut that out too. Kept thinking about Dad.

By the time Marcella visited later that morning—dressed in her waitressing uniform—he'd all but convinced himself that his *father* was on his way. Dad would figure out this mess, come to his rescue. Ty believed it with everything in him.

Marcella's pained expression snapped him back to reality.

Which sucked.

She kissed his knuckles across the table. A dozen times or so. Quick, silent kisses. Rubbed them in like lotion. She put on a brave smile, and he saw new wrinkles in her face. Around her lips and eyes. Lots of thin lines. It hit him like a cold shower. She was getting older. It was like he'd missed something. Made him sad.

"Have you spoken to a lawyer yet?" she asked.

Ty withdrew. "Gerrity? More like he spoke to me."

"You've got to trust him. He can help you. It's his job."

Ty wanted to laugh. Trust him? Gerrity ate breakfast every morning at Leon's Diner. He looked through Ty as he spouted legal jargon Ty neither understood nor cared to know.

Marcella hugged herself. "Derek says you're in a fight."

Ty shrugged.

"From what he said you were pretty angry with him."

Another shrug.

"It doesn't take a genius to figure out he got you into this mess. Right?" Marcella checked the door. "Tyler, we're going to figure this out." She tapped the table with her fingernail. "Hey, look at me."

He did. Her eyes looked sore, like she'd been crying all night.

She took his hand again. "I want you to know. There is nothing you could do that would ever make me stop loving you."

Pressure built behind his eyes. Something bloomed in his chest and he thought he might burst. It wasn't fair, to have this kind of love from someone like his mother. He didn't deserve it.

"I didn't do it." It was his voice, but it wasn't his voice. It was from another dimension. Metaphysical stuff.

His thoughts went to the book where the bug crawled out of the man's head on the cover. He hadn't finished it yet. He was only a few chapters in but he felt like he got what he needed from it. Like he could write a paper on it, even. But where did he leave the darn book? Mrs. Finley would be pissed if he lost it.

"I know."

"What?" He'd forgotten what they were talking about.

"I know you didn't do it."

Tears spurted. His mouth stuck open. Had he lied to his mother? Did she know?

The UFO camera perched in the corner of the room. Its red eye blinking at him. They watched his every move. He sobered in an instant. Wiped his eyes dry. They kept tabs on him in the cell. He played a good game there, outwitting them by keeping still. Still as a statue. Trying not to blink his eyes. Even when he went out to sea.

In this little box of a room—the visiting room—he was supposed to talk. People always tried to get him to talk. He clenched his jaw, glared at the thing. They tracked everything—his mouth, his pulse. Like a lie detector test on crack. He wouldn't fall for it.

Marcella followed his gaze to the camera. "It's okay. Standard stuff. For your safety."

Ty nodded. But knew better. He eyed her askance. Maybe she worked with them too? He carefully let go of her hand.

Her brow knitted together. "Promise me you'll talk to Mr. Gerrity."

"What should I tell him?"

She opened her mouth in a kind of laugh. "Tell him the truth. That should be easy, right?"

"Easy." The red eye winked. Sweat gathered under Ty's arms.

Clapp barged in then.

Marcella stood, making a barrier.

To Ty's surprise, his mother did the talking. "Officer Clapp, may I have a word, please? In private?"

A NERVOUS THRILL went through Clapp as he closed the office door. Marcella's perfume filled the room, like exotic fruit.

"Can I get you some coffee?" He coughed away the high pitch of his voice.

"No, thanks." She stood with her arms folded and hip kinked. Fighting position. "Could you explain to me, please, why Derek Hogg is not under arrest?"

"Ma'am, if you'd have a seat—"

"Thank you. I'd rather stand."

He gave her his best grin, the one that made him look like Mel Gibson. He half-sat on his desk, going for the casual vibe. "Ma'am, this is police business. No need to worry your pretty head over it."

"Excuse me?" Redness crept up her neck. A natural blush to her cheeks. Made her eyes glisten, even as they glared. "No need to *worry*? Sir, my son is in custody. He's being accused of a heinous crime he did not commit."

"I understand you're upset—"

"Upset? You have no idea." She took a breath. Her chest lifted with it. His eyes reflexively went to her breasts. "Officer, why is my son sitting in a jail cell while Derek Hogg is hanging out at Leon's Diner?"

Clapp tapped his gun belt. "I don't see what one has to do with the other."

"Oh, please. You honestly don't believe that, do you?"

"Ma'am—"

"Please stop calling me that."

"Marcella—"

"I don't want you calling me that either, if you don't mind."

"Mrs. Trout?"

"Fine."

"Mrs. Trout, the investigation is still underway. I understand your eagerness to obtain information. See, I'm not in a place to disclose alibis."

"Alibi?"

Clapp gulped. He'd said too much.

"Derek has an alibi?"

He glanced at the door, wiped the corners of his mouth.

"What on earth is Derek's alibi?"

Sweat broke out. "Okay, listen. This is not usually done. I don't, uh, I'm not supposed to. Um, I can't say."

Marcella leaned over his desk. His eyes grazed the constellation of freckles on her chest, her olive skin kissed by the sun. The shadowy warmth of her cleavage...

He was baking in his uniform. Cologne-scented steam emitted from his collar. Too spicy. Too much. Queasiness made his knees buckle. Or something did. He wiped the corners of his mouth again, wondering how the saliva got sucked from it. He searched for his sunglasses. Did he leave them in the cruiser? Damn. He had to get away from this woman.

"Tell me, officer." All her edges softened. Her voice was like Kahlua and milk. "Please tell me. What's Derek's alibi?"

She rested her pale, slender arms on his desk. Her eyes had him. Like sugar-coated almonds. He couldn't break away. Her full lips shimmered pink. Those sexy freckles. He could lick them. He trembled with desire.

"He was at Leon's, all right? He and Ty went there for a late dinner. Ty said he had to run an errand. So Derek helped his dad close while Ty borrowed Derek's truck."

Clapp tore his eyes from her.

"An errand? In the middle of the night? What kind of errand?"

"That's approximately when the...crime occurred, ma'am. I mean, Mrs. Trout."

Marcella's forehead crinkled. "Derek doesn't let Tyler drive his truck. He certainly wouldn't let him take it on his own to run a so-called 'errand' in the middle of the night."

"Well, it seems on this night he did. Must've had a change of heart." He tried to smile, but her eyes went so cold it spooked him.

"I have reason to believe it was Derek in his truck that night. Alone. Running an errand." She crossed her arms again. "Pretty good reason, in fact."

Clapp huffed, recalling what Bernie had told him. "Yeah, well. I don't think the word of a seven-year-old is going to hold any weight in court. Especially if it conflicts with the word of a well-respected grown man."

She stepped back, her face smoothing. Perhaps stunned. "A well-respected grown man? Who's that? Who vouched for Derek's alibi?"

That was easy. Clapp shrugged. Gave her the Mel Gibson. "Leon, of course."

Six months earlier
Spring 1991

"You don't touch that shit, D, you get me?" Pop told Derek for the hundredth time. They sat at a booth in the dim light of the closed diner. "Anything that goes up your nose is coming out of our wallet. You do the runs, you'll be rewarded. You steal from me, you're out on the street."

"I got it, Pop."

"That truck you drive? That belongs to me. That's for family business, D. Understood?"

"I know. I got it."

Pop's warnings weren't necessary. Sure, Derek liked a good high as much as the next guy—a clean high. Beer was decent if he stuck to a few, but he didn't like being out of control. Sloppy. He never got to the point where he couldn't drive. No freakin' way. He stuck to weed. It was easy. Kept him alert. Never had power over him.

They had this in common. Pop didn't touch the hard stuff, either.

Derek admired that about the fat cat. He did get sloppy with his beer, though. Too often.

Cracking open a new Bud, Pop slurred on about the past. "When I was a kid, I wanted to be a contractor."

Derek nodded dutifully. He'd heard this story before.

"A builder," Pop went on. "Work outside all year long. Cigarette in one hand, hammer in the other. Lunch in the shade. Never have to wash your hands." He sniggered. "Hated that about helping my pop, your granddaddy, at the diner. Wash your hands every two seconds. Before cracking eggs, after cracking eggs. Before filling ketchups, after filling ketchups. I swear I grew up hating soap."

Derek's lip curled. "You still hate soap, Pop."

Big guffaw. Pop slapped the table. "You're right!" He guzzled some, then swung his eyes around the place. "D, this will be yours someday, you know."

Derek puffed his chest. "I know. I'll do right by you, Pop."

"You will. I know you will. I don't have to tell you how important this place is. All those customers lined up at the counter every morning? They're not only here for the grub, you know. No matter how good the corned beef hash is." He knocked on the table. "Pay attention next time. You'll see the mayor here talkin' with newcomers from the city, mill workers and, yup, construction guys." He nodded, eyeing Derek. Testing him.

Derek raised an eyebrow. "So?"

"They're not just here eatin' breakfast, see. They're parts of a whole."

"What do ya mean?"

"They're here to build somethin'. They, each of 'em, are like blocks. Means nuthin by itself, but together, ya got somethin'."

Derek squeezed his beer can, denting it. His strong hand versus the weak aluminum. He could build something with these hands. He had plans for this place. Once it was his, he'd change everything. Pop got it off to a good start, but Derek had bigger things in mind.

He caught his reflection in the window and spun from it, pressing his thick back against the cool glass. He drained his beer and crushed the can all the way. It felt good.

Pop was still at it. "So, them's together? Ya got somethin'. Whatcha got? This town. They all make up this town where we live. They decide whether the Strand will be fixed or torn down. They decide if the school gets textbooks. They're talkin' about a huge town hall expansion with a new library and everything. You see what I'm sayin'?"

Derek nodded, feeling a soft spot for Pop, who could never have been a contractor. His grubby, grease-stained hands could never have built anything. The physical labor would've given him a heart attack. Derek smiled to himself. Pop needed him. Derek was his number one asset.

"We've built something here," Pop said, almost to himself. "This town would be nothin' without us. You get it?"

Derek took a mental inventory. Closing chores rolled through his mind like movie credits. The floors had yet to be mopped. The stove scrubbed, the bathrooms sanitized. It would be nice to have some help.

Now was a good a time as any to ask. "Hey, what about hiring Ty to help close the place? You know, for the summer."

"Ack. I dunno. I know he's yer pal, but he seems out of it lately."

"What do you mean?" Derek's ears perked. To say Ty was "out of it" was an understatement. But Derek wanted to hear it from his old man. Confirm Derek's instincts. Ty had some sort of mental problem.

"I dunno, D. I'm no freakin' psychic or whatchamacallit. Probably hormones anyway."

Ty's problem had nothing to do with hormones. But Derek found himself nodding.

"Yeah, fine," Pop said. "Ty can help out for the summer. Minimum wage, though. He gets no more."

"Thanks, Pop." Derek sighed. Ty was not his problem to fix. Getting him a job would be a help, maybe. Nudge him into reality a little more.

He tossed his empty into the slop sink and grabbed the mop, his steps lighter. He'd be done in a jiffy. Soon, he wouldn't have to do it at all.

Pop's belch echoed across the empty diner. "Hey, remember, D. You gotta make a run for me on Thursday. They expect you in Rensselaer eight pm sharp."

"I know. I won't forget."

"Grab me another one?" he called from his seat.

Derek was on his own, again, to close the place. "Sure thing." *Drink up, Pop. I got this.*

It was already happening. He could feel the transfer of power. The diner was as good as his.

TY WAS psyched when Derek asked for company on the drive down to Rensselaer. Motion was good. Sitting in Derek's truck was good. Ty zoned in on the tactile stuff. The seat's hard, cool leather through his T-shirt, the carpeted steel beneath his Chucks, the vibration of the wheels against the highway.

He didn't care how far it was. Or why they had to go there. Something about an errand for Leon. It was a Thursday night. They'd be back late. He'd coast through tomorrow. One more day until the weekend. Sleep was overrated anyway.

Their favorite station played Guns N' Roses, Pearl Jam. Good stuff. One song after the next, Ty rocked against the passenger seat, eyes closed, living in the music.

Less than an hour into the trip, the car radio went to static. No reception.

"Ack." Derek shoved it off with his fist.

Silence was no good. Ty felt the passenger seat close in around him. Out the window, the trees blurred into what looked like wet sand at low tide. Tidal tracks. Like a wet giant's claw marks. Tearing long divots in the grainy earth.

He held his breath.

They were just trees.

The tree line broke and the nearly-full moon blazed against the darkening sky. It was dusk—a dangerous time. Ty's chest tightened as a face appeared in the moon. Laughing with a gaping smile. Squinting eyes darting at him. Ty cracked his knuckles. The sound was huge.

"Man on the moon," he mumbled.

Derek didn't hear. He smacked the dash. Ty jumped.

"So, I got it all set up," Derek said, businesslike. "You'll start at the diner in June. Closing shift."

"Why?"

"You want to mow lawns all summer again?"

"No. Why June?"

"That's when school's out, nerd."

"Why can't I start now?"

Derek shrugged. "Guess you could. Long as Marcella don't mind you workin' late." He lit another cigarette. Offered one to Ty. Sulfur from the match filled the car. In the next moment, the driver's side window was open. White noise and wind swirled in his ears. He tried to get the music back, but it was gone. He forced himself to think of something happy, like Roxanne Russo.

"If there was one girl, who would it be?" Ty shouted over the wind.

Derek cranked up the window. Smoke trickled from his upturned lips. "Cindy Crawford."

"No, dude. Serious. Someone we know." He took a long drag. It never seemed like enough.

"I dunno."

Smoke curled, hung in the air. Ty closed his eyes before the smoke grew into something. *Count to ten. Open. Deep breath.* He focused on the fiery tip of his own cigarette. "What about Roxanne Russo?"

"Been there. Done that."

A buzz in his ears. He couldn't have heard right. "What?" The word was a breath.

Smoke was everywhere. His eyes stung. The last bit of daylight outlined the mountains in the distance. Mosquitoes splattered the windshield. Their green, slimy innards smeared against the glass.

Been there? Done that?

Ty trembled. A hot, wet blanket covered his head and shoulders. "What did you say?"

Derek threw out his butt and rolled up his window.

Ty's fingertips went numb. The hum of the wheels against the pavement ground in his ears.

Splat. Another mosquito. Smeared alive. He could literally feel its pain. Alive one second, dead the next. Guts spilling onto the glass.

Ty's chest was being pinned. A panic attack?

Been there? Done that?

"What do you mean?" Ty's voice wavered.

"No big deal, Ty."

"No big deal?" Ty whined, tearing away from the dead bugs to study Derek's profile. Partly shadowed, the line of his flat forehead bumped out to a simple nose. His meaty neck gave a false promise of strength. That square under his lip needed grooming. Stubble grew in thick around it, like he was fully a man. He'd gone and left Ty behind.

What did Roxanne see in him?

Fidgety now, Ty felt his virginity stink on him. His vision blurred and his palms got sweaty. "When the hell did this happen?"

Derek cracked his neck, kept checking the rearview as if they were being trailed. Were they? No. The road was dark.

Ty threw out his cigarette, wiped his hands on his jeans. Derek and Roxanne? Together? He didn't hear right. It didn't happen. No way did that happen.

"Derek. Tell me. When did you and Roxanne..." He couldn't even say it.

"It was, ah, I gave her a ride home that night after Don's party."

Don's party. Two weekends ago. Maybe three. Ty remembered that night. She sat next to Ty on the floor. Glazed cranberry nails passing him a joint. That quick, secret smile. Derek wasn't even in the circle. He didn't even like her. She didn't like him. She couldn't.

Ty swallowed bile. "You didn't give her a ride home that night. You gave me a ride home, asshole."

No response. Derek steered with one hand, drummed the stick shift with the other.

"Don't lie to me." Ty hated how he sounded. He couldn't help it. He was drowning in lava.

Derek sighed, annoyed-like. "At the party, she asked me to come by her house after I dropped you off."

"She did? When? You weren't even with us."

"I dunno. She kinda grabbed me on the way to the bathroom."

"Grabbed you?"

A laugh. "Kinda."

Ty's blood boiled. "You're such a prick. What happened when you got to her house? Weren't her parents home?"

"She snuck me into her basement."

Ty's eyes pinched closed, trapping the heat and the tears and the disturbing images that came rushing at him. It didn't match up. Roxanne and Derek—their bodies didn't fit together. That wasn't how it was supposed to go down. His fleshy lips slobbering all over hers? Disgusting. Gag reflex-worthy. "She musta been totally smashed."

Derek whapped his chest. "Screw you."

Anger boiled from the depths of his spine. He snapped, "So you dropped me off and went and porked Roxanne? Just like that?"

No response. Lava was everywhere now. Filling his chest and his ears. He thought he'd explode. He locked his hands together, prayer-like, and squeezed hard.

"Are you guys dating now?" Ty squeezed his eyes shut. His head hinged open. A bug crawled out.

"Dating? Come on. What do you think?"

Ty's voice was high and whiny and on fire. "Why not, though? Why aren't you her boyfriend?" He sounded pathetic. Desperate. Jealous. But he couldn't stop.

Derek shrugged. "Maybe I don't want to be."

"Maybe she doesn't want to be seen with your fat ass."

"Whatever." Derek punched the radio dial and a trace of a song came through static. Something Marcella listened to. The unmistakable voice of Annie Lennox.

Derek fumbled with the tuner until it came in clear.

"Didn't know you liked the Eurythmics." Ty sneered.

It was quiet for a while before Derek answered. "Maybe you don't know me as well as you think you do."

Maybe I don't want to know you anymore. Ty's thoughts roared in his mind. He forced his eyes out the window. He needed a serious distraction from the sudden gash in his heart or he might puke all over Derek's truck. He zoned in on the street signs. Almost there.

It was Ty's first trip to Rensselaer. It had been eons since he'd been to the tri-city area at all. He'd built it up in his mind, though, as a big metropolis. Weird that it looked like any other northern Adirondack town, aside from the graffiti and traffic and the occasional hobo on the street. But right now he was too pissed at his best friend to care about the tri-city area. It didn't matter what Rensselaer had to offer. They could be going to Mars for all he cared.

Derek's truck was poisoning him. He had to get out of the lava. When the truck pulled to a stop, he poured out of the seat. Out of habit, he walked alongside Derek. With each step, though, he fantasized about the different ways he could hurt him. Make him bleed.

They went up the deserted drive that led to a rundown two-story house. The ramshackle house could've been in Schroon Lake or Severance or any other upstate town. Broken windows revealed grimy curtains, unhinged gutters hung like broken limbs.

The place looked abandoned.

"No one's here," Ty said.

"Shut up."

Worn wooden steps creaked underfoot to the front door. Four rusty bicycles were stacked against the foundation.

"What's with the bikes?"

Derek glared before knocking twice, hard. "No license. How you get around?"

They waited. Ty glanced back at the truck. Weighed his options—go back to the lava or stay with his asshole-best-friend?

The front door opened as if by itself. No one was there. Derek stepped in. Ty hesitated.

"Maybe I'll wait in the truck."

"Whatever."

Then Ty was inside too. The house was dark save for a purplish glow coming through a bed sheet tacked to the doorway—a sheet dotted with pink flowers.

"Stay here." Derek went through the floral bed sheet.

Ty didn't dare move. The weed smell masked the odor of mildew. Ty's stomach heaved.

Hurry up, Derek.

Laughter from the kitchen. Ty clenched his teeth to keep from moving. He stared at the flowery bed sheet. Did Roxanne have sheets like that?

"Sit down." The words vibrated near his left ear. He turned toward them, expecting to see nothing, assuming his mind played another trick. But—holy shit—someone was there. He had a thick beard, though he couldn't have been older than twenty-five.

"Sit," he said. This time, Ty had read his lips and knew the guy was real. He palmed his chin, tugged at the fine hairs that grew there.

The man sat on the marshmallow couch. A numbing sensation crept up Ty's neck, as if both arms had fallen asleep and the tingling traveled up to his brain. He fell into an armchair nearby.

The bearded man didn't speak as he retrieved a wooden box from under the coffee table. His motions were deliberate and businesslike as two lines of white powder formed on the glass. Ty stared, disbelief starching his eyes. Only when the man cleared his throat, Ty realized he was handing him something.

A pen.

Relief pumped the room like Vegas oxygen. Must have been a trick of light. Those weren't lines of white powder. That stuff only happened in the movies. It must have been some sort of receipt. While Derek collected the goods for the diner, Ty had to sign for them. That's it.

Ty nodded, taking the pen in its chopstick position, ready to give his John Hancock.

But the pen was hollow in his hand.

"Hurry up," the bearded man ordered.

More laughter from the kitchen. The empty pen trembled in Ty's grip. He glanced at the sheet and its flowers electrified by purple light. He yearned for Derek—his asshole-best-friend—like a child yearned for his momma. At this moment, he didn't care about whatever happened or didn't happen with Roxanne Russo. Derek would help him out of this. He'd know what to do.

Sweat trickled near his ear. Deep breath. That mildew smell disappeared. Incense too. He couldn't smell anything. Like his nose stopped working. The bearded man spoke again. Ty didn't hear any of it. His ears stopped working too. It didn't matter. None of it did. Derek and Roxanne, this bearded guy, the white stuff on the table. A weird out-of-body thing happened, like he was floating, watching it all from above. Aha! It was a movie after all. Those were lines of coke. Ty almost laughed. Was this even real?

Dude tapped the table, impatient, and Ty looked over at him again. More closely this time.

Wait. Bearded dude wasn't a dude, but a bear. A brown bear! His thick, dark beard covered his whole body. He sat upright and talked somehow. Talked nonsense. Bear talk.

Now, Ty couldn't help laughing.

Okay, Bear. What do you want me to do? Snuff this up my nose? Will that make Bear happy?

"Let's go," Bear growled.

Ty understood that. Everything snapped back. Smells were everywhere, suffocating him. No more laughter from behind the flowery sheets. The quiet was loaded. Lava churned in his gut. Everyone waited. Derek was waiting. For him.

"Whatever." Ty leaned down and sniffed the shit up his nose. Just like he'd seen in the movies.

Thanksgiving 1991

In the backseat, Hen clapped his backpack straps together, excited for the day. Mom finally agreed to take him to see Tyler in jail. She drove while Bernie sat in the passenger seat of her Impala. The air was sharp between them, even though they weren't talking to each other.

"Can we open the window?"

"It's only forty degrees outside, Hen," Mom said. "I'll turn off the heat."

"Supposed to get cold this weekend," Bernie said. "Real cold. They're talking about snow."

Mom sighed. "Wouldn't be the first time we've seen snow in November."

Why did she sound so unhappy? It was Thanksgiving. They were spending it with Tyler. They had turkey subs with cranberry mayo and a jug of apple cider. Mom even bought little napkins printed with horns of plenty.

She seemed sad, but gave *him* a pep talk. "Let's stay positive for big brother, okay? Let's not worry him about anything. Smile. Tell him a joke. What do you say?"

"Okay."

She parked near the brick building. Hen skipped to the glass doors as if it led to an arcade. Inside, heat hit him like a wave. A door opened down the hall, a swish of movement, shuffling feet. Tyler?

Tyler!

His brother entered a room across the hall without looking at them. He held his hands behind his back.

Officer Clapp, behind him, paused to wink at Hen. His dark sunglasses were propped on his cap, covering the police emblem. Hen shuddered. Seeing Officer Clapp reminded Hen of where they were. He was suddenly afraid of what he might see.

IN THE SMALL, windowless room, Ty sat at the narrow table chewing on a hangnail. The UFO camera's red eye lit up, staring him down. He refused to look up. Clapp said he had visitors. It would be Marcella, of course. Still, he held onto a sliver of hope his father would come through the door.

A tap on his shoulder. Ty yelped, his heart racing. What the—?

"Hen?"

"Tyler!" Hen threw his arms around his brother's neck. Ty unclasped them, removing an albatross.

He blinked at his little brother, a knot forming in his chest. "What are you doing here?"

"Happy Thanksgiving!" Hen sang, smiling big.

"Is Mom here?" Ty craned to see out the opaque window. His heart pounded.

Hen nodded. "We brought turkey subs. And apple cider."

"You shouldn't be here."

Hen's grin wouldn't quit. "I figured it out. I need a bucket. And cat food."

"Cat food?"

"Tyler! For the trap."

"What?" Ty went rigid. They were listening. He had to be careful.

"A trap," Hen called more loudly. "To catch a hedgehog."

Red eye blinked. They won't understand. He looked right at it. "He's just a kid." Red eye winked out for a long beat. An answer. They were suspicious.

Ty's voice shook. "Talkin' 'bout trappin' a hedgehog. An animal. Not for mean reasons. For a pet."

Hen looked up. "Who are you talking to?" He spotted it. "Oh. Hi, there!" He waved both arms.

A flash of red. "Hen, stop it. What are you doing?"

"Saying hello to the camera."

Sweat broke out. Not good. "No. No camera." They wouldn't like this. It was supposed to be hidden. Secret. They've been exposed.

"Yeah. Right there." Hen pointed. He actually pointed at it.

"Stop it. Just stop it." Ty was scrambling. He had to get Hen out of here before he did more damage.

"Why?" Hen stopped pointing, but he still stared at the red light, which had stopped blinking. It was a solid red. Angry, like a siren.

"Hen, please. You have to leave."

"Leave? We haven't even eaten yet. I told you Mom brought turkey subs and apple cider."

Ty got up—a sudden flash—clanging the table. "Mom? Are you out there?"

Clapp appeared in the doorway. "Easy now, Tyler."

"Can you get my little brother out of here?"

Clapp looked confused. "Your family is here to visit you."

"Is my mom out there?" He tried to push past Clapp, which was like trying to push past the Incredible Hulk.

Clapp shoved him back into the room. "Sit down, Tyler. She's on her way in. Bringing in quite a feast for you."

Hot tears started. He glanced at the red eye. Still angry. Always on. And there was Hen, staring right at it. "No, no, no."

"Don't do anything stupid, now. This is supposed to be a nice, family visit."

The room was unbearably hot. Ty couldn't get any air. The red light buzzed. They were really going to let him have it. He had to get out of here. If Hen wouldn't leave, he'd have to. Desperate, Ty tried to squeeze between Clapp's shoulder and the doorframe.

"Mom!"

"That's it." Clapp folded Ty head-first onto the table and cuffed him behind his back. Everything turned sideways. Ty felt the table cool against his cheek. Hen cowered on the other side of the small room.

"I'm not making a run for it. I want to talk to my mom!"

Clapp pinned his torso with a sturdy forearm. Ty shut his eyes, blocking out the sideways world. He couldn't block out Hen, though, who'd curled himself into a corner, spikes out.

"Tyler, I'm here." He heard her voice before she appeared, grocery bags in tow. "What on earth is going on?"

"Tried to escape, Mrs. Trout." Clapp still held him down. His cheek mushed against the table.

"Escape? I highly doubt that."

Bernie came in. "Hey, Rob? Ah...that's a bit extreme, don't you think?"

Everything shifted into focus. Ty got handcuffed in the visiting room while his baby brother cried in the corner. Clapp hesitated, then keyed the cuffs loose. Ty scrambled back to his chair. The red eye winked, aloof. If he could find his tears, he would've cried openly. In front of everyone. But his insides had completely shut down. At once, he was overcome with fatigue.

His words were warbled. "Why did you bring Hen here?"

"He wanted to see you. Tyler, it's Thanksgiving."

"He's not supposed to see this." Ty couldn't tell Marcella about the UFO camera, either, he knew. Misery filled him.

"Tyler, please—"

"I don't want him here. I don't want him to see this."

Marcella spotted Hen.

"Oh, no. Hen. I'm sorry." She went to him. "Bernie, will you take him back to the car?"

It took ages for them to leave.

Red eye stared.

At some point, Clapp left too.

Red eye blinked.

Marcella sat across from him. Her lips moved, but he couldn't hear what she said.

Ty's eyes burned. He pulled on his hood. He couldn't look at the UFO camera. Shame colored him. It was all a giant misunderstanding, but they wouldn't see it that way. They heard "trap" and made all kinds of assumptions. He was trapped now. No making up for it. It was so hopeless. They had heard everything. And they still listened.

"Did something happen?" Marcella's voice rang clear, like they'd switched the volume back on.

His eyes went wide.

"Is there anything you want to talk about?" Her tone strained with worry.

"No."

On the table, someone had scratched *Prick* into the linoleum. Could they see that too? He tried to smudge it out with his thumb, but it was etched. Permanent.

"I'm sorry I brought Hen here," she said softly. "I was—we were hoping to share a meal with you. I guess I'll leave you your dinner. Is there anything I can bring you? Anything else you want?"

He looked at his mother, sober now. "Dad?"

Confusion flitted over Marcella's face. "You—you want me to call your father?"

"Does Dad even know I'm here? Does he know I'm in trouble?"

A sigh. "Tyler, it's not that simple."

"He's my dad. He's got a right to know what's going on."

"Tyler, honey." Her voice caught. "I don't think you'd be happy with the outcome if I called him. I want to save you from—"

"You asked me if you could bring me anything."

"You want your father...to come here?"

Ty nodded. "He's my dad."

A laugh fluttered out. "Tyler, you can't really call him 'Dad.' Has he really been a father to you? I mean, Bernie is more of a father than—"

Tyler narrowed his eyes. "Bernie's not my father."

She sniffed hard. "Bernie has been there for our family since Hen was born. He would do anything for us. He's a good man."

That *Prick* etching shouted at him.

"Bernie's not Hen's father, either." Ty crossed his arms. "Find my dad. Please. Tell him I'm here. Tell him I want to see him." He stared her down. "Please."

"Okay. Fine." She pinched her lips like she did when she was upset.

Ty nodded, hiding his face from the camera. He made it better. He could feel it. Giving them something else to work on. They'd forget about Hen's trap. He could hear their tiny gears spinning inside, behind the red eye. This would keep them busy.

Minutes ticked by. Maybe hours.

His mother was still there.

"I love you," she said, as if trying out the words, which were absorbed into the reprocessed air and sucked up into the UFO.

They took that too. They had dibs on everything.

Marcella would rather eat a worm sandwich.

She stared at the phone, the dial tone buzzing her hand. It wasn't going to dial itself. She knew she had to push the dang buttons.

Meep, meep, meep—

The dial tone switched to alarm mode.

When she hung up, she expected relief. No such luck.

When did she last talk to Tyler's father? The thought of him made her insides quiver. After all this time—nearly two decades—he still had a hold on her. He took up space inside her, carved a place for himself there. A rat in the wall. He shouldn't matter. He shouldn't even be a thought.

They'd met line dancing at Raul's Rodeo in Ticonderoga back in

'73. Marcella had gone with another waitress from the diner, Darlene, for Ladies Night two-for-one drinks. The place was mobbed with costumed cowboys in novelty bandanas and pointy boots. Wide-brimmed hats on the most dedicated phonies.

The band was one of those scaled-back miracles—just three instruments and vocals for a big sound. The guitarist was tall. His thin, sinewy body mismatched his square, superhero jaw. Under the stage lights, his eyes sparkled a bright blue and his grin flashed whiter than a movie star's. He crooned into the microphone, his lips caressing it, seducing it. He moved his hips slowly behind his guitar. Sensual. Made love to it.

When the band took a break, he smoked sulkily by the payphone, James Dean style. Marcella swayed next to Darlene on the dance floor, but couldn't look away from him. His eyes were hungry on her.

When the track switched, he was there. Encircling her with his strong arms like he'd done it a hundred times before. His warm body sheathed in denim and smelling of Jovan Musk. With their hips locked, he sang into her ear, his bright blues glistening in the strobe light. She'd never seen eyes like that. He twirled her, dipped her. Her laughter filled the space between them.

"Oh, my," he said, as if he'd bitten into a perfect cut of steak. "God is good."

His sharp blue eyes cut to her soul. Three margaritas didn't have anything on this guy. She sobered in a second. His intense gaze was like a sponge.

"What do they call you?" he asked.

She hesitated.

He didn't. He leaned in to taste her. He kissed her neck, his full lips tugging the tender skin there, sending a tickle through her body. She went limp in his arms. No man had ever made her feel like that before.

Do that again.

When he kissed her neck a second time, she pressed against him. She couldn't get close enough. Everyone on the dance floor disappeared. Just the two of them under the lights. She wanted to kiss him for real, and pulled him to her. Never had she been so bold. But he was ready. Their mouths were like magnets for each other. His tongue played on her lips and danced across her teeth. He cut away too soon, spinning her around, and then caught her close. Her breath stopped. When he traced a finger across her V-neck top, nearly touching the top of her breasts, she thought she'd never breathe again.

"Marcella," she finally said, though names seemed superfluous now.

"Marcy." As if he already owned her. "I'm Tripp." It could've been anything, but it was that ridiculous name. She barely heard it.

He'd grabbed hold of something inside her. Pried her open and climbed inside.

And there he stayed. Even though she hadn't seen him or spoken to him in years. He still remained.

And now she was calling him.

For Tyler, she told herself. This was for Tyler.

His voice was groggy, as if he'd just woken up.

"It's me," she said, knowing.

"Oh, my." As if he'd bitten into a perfect cut of steak. "Marcy."

Her stomach went wiggly and her feet itched. Her kitchen linoleum became a dance floor. His brilliant blues gazed at her, disco lights pulsing and flickering behind him. His sure arms hugged her close, their hips locked...

She should hang up.

She pressed the receiver to her cheek.

"What do you want?" His words were clipped. That snapped her out of it.

She stood tall, stomped her foot lightly. And wiped the smile from her face.

"It's Tyler."

December 1991

Thick snow—slush farts, as Hen called them—obscured her windshield as she drove to Port Henry Amtrak. Dark as pitch at five pm, thanks to Daylight Saving Time. She parked with a view of the arrival platform, kept the heat and wipers on. Headlights off.

And waited.

The wipers were hypnotic. Put her in a trance.

Tripp had accepted her offer without hesitation. He may have agreed without her paying his fare. She'd expected a battle. But no. It was suspicious how quickly he got from Arkansas to the Adirondacks. Had he been waiting for the invitation all these years? Marcella shook the thought. He wasn't here to see her. She bit her lip. That shaky, upside-down feeling told her he wasn't exactly here to see Tyler, either.

"Man of mystery." Her voice was hoarse.

She cleared her throat, sure something was stuck there. She hadn't brought water, and now she felt she might choke. She turned off the heat.

Platform was still empty. Where the heck was he? Train should have been there already. She forced a deep breath. A bellowing whistle signaled the train's approach. When its doors opened, it was like opening floodgates. Passengers disembarked. They lugged their bags to the parking area. Things busied around her. Still, no sign of Tripp.

Safe inside her dark, warm car, she had an urge to make an escape. What was she doing, anyway? Why did she agree to this?

In the next moment, she panicked. Where was he? Did he miss his train?

The platform lights were bright and bare. The crowd dwindled.

Maybe he waited under the awning? She flashed her headlights.

There. He emerged from the snow mist like a spirit. His cowboy hat moved as if disembodied under the platform lights.

"He still wears that thing?" she said aloud.

Across his shoulders, he carried an enormous canvas bag—a dirty laundry sack or a body bag. He paused, kinked his hip. Damn, he still looked good in jeans. The hat's broad rim tilted and his face came out of its shadow, searching for her past the falling snow. His free hand, gloveless, clenched to keep warm. His mouth was slightly open, vulnerable. She felt a trace of warmth for him, like pulling an old file.

She flashed her headlights again. And rummaged in her purse for a mint.

"You'll have to find me. No way am I getting out in this."

He sauntered toward her car.

She steeled herself as he approached, a sinking feeling in her stomach. The steering wheel was hard and cold in her hands. She crunched her mint and checked her lipstick in the rearview.

"Oh, Marcella. What are you doing?" She adjusted her scarf. "And why are you talking to yourself?"

The passenger door swung open, sending a gush of snowy air inside.

"Oh, my." His once-liquid baritone sounded gravelly and aged.

She refused to smile at him. "Hello, Tripp."

He slammed the door, shutting out the outside world. The silence was too intimate.

"My, my Marcy."

"I'm not your Marcy." She meant to be firm, but it came out high-pitched. Almost flirty.

He slung a large duffle bag into the backseat as if to shrug. "How about some grub, Mount Marcy? I'm starving."

Mount Marcy—both a noun and a verb, in his mind.

The steering wheel was like her tether to the earth. "Don't you want to see Tyler?"

"Now?" He cracked his neck. "Can he join us for eats?"

Her jaw dropped. "Join us? He's being held, Tripp. I told you his situation over the phone. After his just cause hearing, they're holding him until the trial."

"Damn." Too casual. "Welp, still starving. Pull in at Leon's, would'ya?" Reclaiming his role, making demands, expecting her to blindly obey.

Not this time. She gritted her teeth and kept her eyes on the road. By the time they got to Schroon Lake, though, her stomach was growling.

"Fine. But then we need to get home to my little guy."

"Oh, right. The little guy. What's his name again?"

Marcella hesitated. "Henry. We call him Hen."

"Hen." Tripp soiled the name.

Leave my Hen alone.

She said nothing as she pulled into the parking lot. Leon's Diner neon lit up her windshield. It offered a good look at Tripp, in profile. The double chin as he studied his train ticket, the slack around his strong jaw. Secretly pleased, she checked herself. After all, she'd aged too.

They walked toward the front door together, couple-like. Tripp held it open for her.

"Go ahead." Marcella waited, shivering, until it fully closed again. That gave Tripp a head start and—she saw now—an advantage. Tripp went directly into the bowels of the diner where he high-fived

Leon as if they were old buds. Which, of course, they were. Marcella slid into an empty booth alone. Why hadn't she hit the drive-thru at Burger King or a quick pit stop at Stewart's?

Being at Leon's Diner with Tripp was like entering a time warp. Tripp was a regular back then. Mostly in the back room doing who-knows-what. It probably wouldn't be long until the good ol' boys hid back there again. For old time's sake.

A steaming mug of coffee appeared in front of her.

"Thanks," she told the waitress whose nametag read "Blondie."

Through the order-up window, Tripp bear-hugged Derek. The three of them—Tripp, Leon, and Derek—gurgled with secretive laughter. Bile filled her throat. She willed him to look at her. Once again, she was ignored. As she predicted, they retreated to the back room. And she was alone, waiting. Again.

Turning to the window, she saw her reflection in it. Melting snow made wet streaks on the glass, stretching her reflection into a ghoulish image. A stinging memory came flooding back.

They'd been married only a few months. Tripp had left home without his favorite belt—the one with the longhorn buckle. A helpful, doting wife, she'd trailed him like a lost puppy. Sniffed him out where she wasn't welcome. At Raul's. In the back room. Playing cards.

"There you are," she'd said, saddling a chair behind him.

No answer.

Maybe he hadn't heard?

"Hey, babe," she tried again, nuzzling his neck.

His body went rigid.

A catcall from across the table had made Tripp come to. He flinched away from her, ducking toward his cards. He shuffled his hand, lay a chip down, made his play.

He was busy. She carefully detached from him, detonating a bomb. She draped his belt over his chair back. While his cigar-smoking neighbor made his move, she leaned close to Tripp's ear, and pretended not to see his jaw clench.

"I brought your belt," she whispered, sure he'd be glad.

Tripp's glare scalded her. It was fleeting, but it stung. The heat stayed with her out to her car, throughout the drive home.

All night, she'd stewed. As dawn opened, she couldn't wait any longer. She went back to Raul's. Stomped to the back room with resolve. "Tripp, I want to talk to you."

Cigar guy rolled his eyes at her. Tripp ignored her.

"Hey, I'm standing right here. I need to talk to you."

No response.

She welled with rage. "Tripp, talk to me!"

God knows what possessed her to grab his arm. She did feel that way—possessed. She would not be ignored. She had to talk to him. She needed reassurance. Proof of love. Right then. She yanked his elbow so he'd face her.

Her efforts were futile. Laughable. He flicked away her hand like it was a beetle.

"Tripp!" Her voice was ugly and unfamiliar.

"What?" He might as well have spit on her.

She steadied her voice. "I need to talk to you. Please."

"You need to talk to me?" He barked a laugh. They all laughed. Cigar guy and the rest of them. Howling at her.

Shaken, she'd made it back to her car and back home. How dare he dismiss her like that? Humiliate her! She tried to reason around it. A dirty look. Some harsh words. Laughter. It couldn't have been that bad. Right? But something had happened that night. He'd frightened her. She never quite got over it.

Now, alone at the booth in Leon's Diner, the coffee cup shook in her hand.

Blondie set the check on the table. "Sorry. I gotta go. Not suppose'ta close. Derek was gonna—"

"It's okay. Go ahead." Marcella reached in to her wallet, strangely impassive about money. After paying Tripp's fare and now dinner, she was spent.

She helped herself to a glass of water, and—on autopilot—grabbed a dishrag. She wiped down all the tables and counters while Blondie finished with the last customer. Why was she doing this pro bono crap for Leon? Where the hell was Tripp?

This was not happening. Not again.

She ventured to the back room to see.

The three of them, together. Each holding a Bud Light. Derek a part of it, like one of the guys. They laughed. No cards or gambling or girls or heavy booze. Just laughter.

Still, it was too much. Tyler sat in jail while they had a freaking party.

"What the hell is so funny?"

"Marcy," Tripp said, rubbing his crotch.

Leon sniggered, his eyes half-mast.

Derek stood between them, puffing up. "Y'all are a bunch of pervs. This here woman's an angel and as long as I'm breathing, no man is going to do her wrong."

A few beats of silence, then unadulterated hilarity.

Marcella, both touched and sickened by what Derek said, pulled him into the bright light of the dining area.

"What are they up to, Derek? I don't think I have to tell you Tripp is not here on vacation."

"Yes, ma'am. I gathered that. Let's just say, Tripp and Pop are smoothin' out some unfinished business."

"What does that mean? Tripp was never involved in the business of this diner."

Derek tried to hide his laugh. "No, ma'am. Not about the diner, pacifically."

"You mean: specifically?"

"Right. Pacifically."

"What, then?"

"Afraid I can't tell ya." Derek's grin was too wide. To her horror, he had the nerve to giggle.

Marcella leaned close to his face. "If this has anything to do with Tyler, anything you're not telling me, you are in big trouble, young man. Do you hear me?"

"Has nothin' to do with Ty, ma'am. Promise." That cocky grin.

Tripp came over, and draped his arm around her. Her knees buckled under the weight of it. "My Marcy." He eyed her breasts.

She shoved away from him. "I'm not your Marcy. Don't call me that anymore."

She stomped outside, through the snow towards her Impala.

How did it come to this? How could Tripp's presence help anyone, no less Tyler? That boy had no idea what he asked for. She flicked her hand at the diner. Tripp should just stay here, with Leon.

She froze in her tracks, panicking a little. Oh, no. That wouldn't work.

She needed Tripp on her side. Leon couldn't get his hooks in him. Turning back, she opened the diner's door and called, "Tripp, your ride's leaving."

Her car seat had turned to an ice sculpture while she'd been gone. Her teeth chattered as she started the engine and turned on the heat. "Come on, you pain in the ass."

The car was so warm by the time Tripp came out, she'd almost fallen asleep.

Tripp slid into the passenger side as if he'd done so for years. And now she'd take him home. Where she'd have to host him. Cook breakfast for him. Introduce him to Hen. Maybe even Bernie. Ugh. The couch was already made up with sheets and one of Miss Sally's quilts. Tomorrow, she would take him to see Tyler.

This had better be worth it. He'd better come through for his son. For once.

He closed the passenger door, caging them together in her car.

"My Marcy—"

"Don't call me that."

A few beats. He waited for her to look at him.

His eyes caught the light of the diner, and shone a blue brighter than an Arkansas sky. Tyler's eyes. Tears threatened and she turned away.

"How can you not be my Marcy? You look exactly the same. As beautiful as that night we met on the dance floor."

Marcella said nothing as she pulled out of the parking lot. She felt his eyes on her.

Tripp serenaded her softly as she drove. The chorus of *Danny's*

Song filled the car in the same warm-honey voice she remembered from long ago.

That song. That song. It had been the soundtrack of their courtship and the early days of their marriage. All her worries about their finances and their future would melt away whenever he sang her that song. As long as he loved her, it would be okay. She believed him.

Marcella kept her eyes on the road, praying they would stay dry. The last thing she wanted was for Tripp to see her cry.

BIGFOOT'S feet stuck out from the throw, off the couch and onto the end table. Hen stopped in his tracks, half way downstairs. A strange man—a giant—slept on their couch? He hunched down, peering through the wooden spindles. The throw looked like a napkin for as much as it covered him. He wore a white T-shirt and red striped boxers.

Hen's belly rumbled, and the man stirred. When he stretched, he filled the room. His jaw was box-shaped like Tyler's. When he opened his eyes it was like headlights turned on. His bright blue eyes matched Tyler's, too.

Oh.

This was Tyler's dad.

His yawn sounded from a bullhorn. As his jaw shrunk back to a box, he noticed Hen.

"Hey, there. You must be Henry. Or Hen, I guess."

Hen nodded, gripping a spindle.

"Well, come on down here then. Gotcha a present."

Hen didn't budge.

"Come now. Don't be scared. I won't bite-cha." When Hen still didn't move, he said, "I'm Tyler's daddy, see. Nothin' to be 'fraid of. I'm family."

"You're not my dad."

The man scratched his head, ran his fingers over the bare spot.

"Nope, I'm not. You're right about that." He laughed a little. Hen wasn't sure why.

Mom's slippers swished in the kitchen, and then she was frowning in the doorway. She spoke to Tyler's dad. "You're awake."

"Just tryin' to make a friend here." He gestured to the stairs.

"Oh, Hen." She brightened in an instant. She came over and lifted him off the steps like he was still a toddler. "Good morning, sweetie bug."

He nuzzled into her hug. She smelled like Mom. That orange blossom lotion she liked to wear. She wore her uniform, which meant she'd be leaving soon. Hen worried she'd ask Tyler's dad to take him to the bus stop.

She finger-combed Hen's hair. "Hen, this is Mr. Tripp. Say hello."

Tripp, like when you fall over something? "Hello."

"I was just tellin' little man here I got a present for 'im. But he wouldn't come down. Spooked or somethin'." He dug into his huge duffle bag that sat open in the middle of the room, clothes spilling out. "Here we go."

He held up a green, fuzzy thing—like a giant raindrop—attached to a tiny chain. In Hen's hand, it was soft, with little bumps inside, and something sharp on the end.

"Ya like it?" Tripp leaned closer.

"What is it?"

"Rabbit's foot."

Hen blinked at it.

"You know, bunny bunny hop hop? A rabbit. That's the foot of a rabbit."

The foot of a rabbit? Hen stared at the man named for falling over something, his mouth open in shock. It dropped from his hand, landing near his feet. He squirmed from it.

"It's a good luck charm." Tripp dangled it in the air. "Carry this with ya everywhere, you'll have good luck."

When Hen didn't take it, Mom did. "Thank you, Tripp. How thoughtful." She didn't sound thankful, though. She must not have liked the rabbit's foot either.

"Ya like it?" Tripp grinned hard.

"The bathroom's upstairs," Mom said. "Why don't you get cleaned up while I give Hen his breakfast?"

Tripp kept staring at Hen. "He's got your eyes. Tyler got mine." He winked, and put on his wide cowboy hat. His outfit was funny: a T-shirt, red-striped boxers, and a cowboy hat.

Mom brought Hen into the kitchen. His cereal was already poured.

"His daddy around?" Tripp's voice followed them.

Mom tried to whisper. "Excuse me, Tripp. That subject is forbidden around here. Especially coming from you. That is none of your business."

Tripp didn't try to whisper. "Thought the kid might be in need of a daddy man while I'm here."

"Hen's doing fine. He's none of your concern."

Hen dug into his cereal. Floorboards creaked in the next room. Mr. Tripp sounded like he was stretching again. Mom looked in his direction.

"What?" The man's voice was smiling.

"Nothing." Mom turned toward the sink.

"Nothing you haven't seen before."

Mom cleared her throat. "After I put Hen on the bus, I'll take you to see Tyler. Then I have to go to work."

Hen felt mixed up inside. He was glad Mom would take him to the bus. But he wanted to see Tyler. He pushed away his cereal bowl. "Can I go see Tyler?"

His mother wasn't listening. She loaded the dishwasher, fast. Almost throwing the dishes in. Did he make her mad?

"Why does Mr. Tripp get to go and not me?" But he didn't say it loud enough. Mom didn't hear.

Hen didn't like what happened at Thanksgiving. Hen promised to be better next time, but Mom had been firm. Hen wasn't going back anytime soon. Something about Tyler not being ready. It didn't make sense. They were brothers. They shared a room at home. Why would Tyler need to get ready to see Hen?

It wasn't fair. If Mr. Tripp and Fall—who killed harmless bunnies for their good luck feet—was spending time with Tyler, why couldn't he?

MARCELLA HAD NEVER SEEN Tyler grin so big. He and Tripp hugged like old high school pals, slapping each other's backs.

"You're here." Tyler gazed dreamily at his father. Marcella swallowed her envy.

The trio sat around the small table, the *Prick* etching facing Tripp.

"Got somethin' for ya." Tripp retrieved a crinkly bag of spicy barbecue pork rinds from inside his jacket. "Merry Christmas." He tossed it like a football.

"Wow. Thanks so much, Dad."

Marcella winced. *Dad*. And pork rinds? Really? What kind of idiotic gift was that?

"Got a joke for ya," Tripp said. "So, what do you call a camel with no humps?"

Ty laughed as he blushed. "I know this one. *Humphrey*."

"Nope. You call him 'one unlucky bastard.'"

They laughed in sync. Marcella groaned inside. Completely inappropriate. Why should she be surprised? He was performing for his son, but he was a bad actor. He used to do it all the time at parties. Sure sign of nerves. Most people thought he was charming. Ring leader. Life of the party.

Tyler was charmed, too. He didn't talk much. Just sat and grinned. A huge grin—that unceasing frown Marcella had chalked up to teenage angst flipped on its head. Relaxed and happy, those brooding lines across his forehead gone kaput. That darkness in his eyes brightened. Between the two, she was blinded by the blue sparkle in the room. A mixture of disgust and pride kept her from chiming in. She settled to be an observer, her insides at war.

"Those were the days." Tripp referred to his defunct country music band. At least he had moved on from dirty jokes.

Tyler interrupted. "I've always wanted to play guitar."

Marcella's eyebrows shot up. Tyler always wanted to play guitar? He never once expressed an interest in being a musician. Not that she could afford lessons. Still, where did this come from? She tried to hide her surprise. Didn't matter. No one paid any attention to her.

"I'll tell you what." Tripp clapped his hands, rubbed them together. "Let's bust you out of here and I'll get you some lessons. Better yet, I'll teach you myself."

Her jaw dropped. *Bust you out of here?* Did she hear him right?

"You will? You think you can get me out of here?"

No way. Her son would not suffer from Tripp's empty promises. "I don't—"

"Any son of mine is destined to be in a band. It's in your blood." Tripp yanked on his belt loops. "Besides, I've been told I have a gift for teaching."

She hoped he saw her eye roll.

Tyler latched on. "My best friend Derek wants to play drums. We could get our own band together."

"Derek? You mean, Leon's Derek?"

"Yeah. Derek Hogg. He's my best friend. Has been since forever." Tyler sounded like her little boy, and Marcella felt her heart breaking. Yes, his best friend who has completely thrown him to the wolves. Weren't they in a fight?

"Interesting." Tripp stared at the *Prick* on the table until his eyes glazed over.

Marcella bit back a sudden, uneasy feeling. "We should get going."

"I have the perfect name for it." Tyler's grin hadn't quit.

Tripp started. "Huh? Name for what?"

"For the band."

"Right. The band." Tripp's eyes narrowed and refocused on Tyler. "Whatcha got?"

Tyler glanced up at the security camera. "The Ex-Convicts."

They laughed like a couple of intoxicated teenagers. When Tripp reached over the table for a high five, Marcella's chest constricted. As their hands touched, something broke inside of her. She'd lost control. Her son was almost unrecognizable.

"Tripp? We should get going." She caught herself reaching for him.

He ignored her. She wanted to scream. *Look at me.*

Tripp didn't. Of course, he didn't. Marcella felt a corner of her heart crumble. It dawned on her. He never really saw her. Her chair squeaked back. "I'll wait outside."

Clapp lingered in the hall. He didn't wear his sunglasses or cap or even his holster. He folded his hands, suppliant. This was new.

"Mrs. Trout?" His voice had that strange lilt to it. He gave her his trying-too-hard smile.

"Yes?"

He seemed lost for words. Redness crept up his neck.

"Officer? How is the investigation going?"

He snapped back to his haughty self. "Ah, right. Fine."

"Anything leading to Derek Hogg?"

"I'm not at liberty to say ma'am. Mrs. Trout."

"Still." She *tsk*ed, disappointed, and spun on one heel toward the exit. She'd wait for Tripp in the car. A biting wind fought its way in with the door cracked open. Over the gust, she heard Clapp's mewling voice. "Was hopin' to see your boy, Henry, today."

That stopped her. She stared back at him.

"Why—" she caught herself.

Clapp gave her a wry smile. A warning, maybe.

Her head spun, her protective instincts kicking in. She wanted to go to Hen right then. Take him out of school just to hold him.

"Keep your distance, Mr. Clapp." Her voice shook.

He winked. "Call me Rob."

"No, thank you."

Breaking eye contact, she pushed the glass door shut, creating a barrier between them. She walked swiftly to her car, the head-to-toe, blood-to-bone chill having nothing to do with the cold, December Adirondack air.

December 1991

Bernie had been avoiding cleaning out Ma's house, though Clapp had given him the all clear over a week ago. It made him physically ache. The thought of stuffing her belongings into boxes, organizing clothes and shoes for Goodwill, sifting through her file cabinet to reconcile any unpaid bills...

Today, though, he needed a distraction. Since Marcella had invited Tripp into her home, he would rather do anything than see them together. What if Tripp tried to rekindle their romance? He didn't know much about their history aside from the fact that he'd left when Tyler was still a toddler.

Tripp's visit was for Tyler, Marcella insisted. Bernie had no choice but to believe her. Maybe Tripp could help Tyler. Besides, he would never stand in the way of a reunion between father and son. If his own father had paid proper attention while he was a boy, maybe he'd have turned out different. Stronger. More assertive. He'd never know, though. For his entire childhood, it had been just him and Ma with his father swirling somewhere in the background. Working. Always working, too busy providing for his family to be bothered having a part in it.

Where did this sentimentality come from? In the wake of Ma's death, he thought about his father. Bernie hadn't thought about him for decades. Not since the cancer took him when Bernie was still a young man. At least he went quick. Ma had taken comfort in that. He didn't suffer long.

Bernie supposed he was glad his father didn't suffer long too, though he never gave it much thought. Strange that memories of his father crept into the forefront now. They seemed to be a physical barrier as he stepped into Ma's living room.

And then, thoughts of his father vanished as traces of Ma's life hit him like a tidal wave. Her favorite plaid chair, her knitting basket, framed family photos from years past, the chess set stuck mid-game.

A deep sigh escaped him as he cautiously made his way through the small house. Being in her bedroom was almost too much to bear. There, the frozen-in-time items that marked her sudden passing— the novel on her nightstand bookmarked a third in, her half-used makeup on the vanity, the dry cleaning ticket for her favorite wool coat—those things nearly broke him.

He was supposed to pack this stuff away and...do what, exactly?

His throat clogged. Ma would never be here again. Without her, all this stuff...was just stuff. Did any of it matter? Why not toss it all? Burn it. What good was it anymore without Ma?

He was already overwhelmed.

The kitchen was safer. Silence crowded around him as his eyes panned the room. It looked as if she'd just stepped out, leaving dirty dishes for later. At the base of the sink, mold grew at the bottom of a soup bowl. On reflex, he went to load it in the dishwasher, and was hit with a waft of rotten vegetables. His eyes watered and he bit back tears. Ma was gone, and this mess was in her place. The world seemed so cruel and unfair at that moment he wanted to run away and cry. But he had work to do. He squirted some Cascade and hit start on the dishwasher.

Amazing what a little button could do. Its methodical churning filled the awful silence a bit. The kitchen—the whole home—felt warmer. Steam-heated. Bernie took his first full breath all day. Inexplicably, he no longer felt like crying.

As a boy, he had always been comforted by the sound. At night, he'd toss and turn in his small bed trying to sleep until he'd finally hear the hum and swish of the dishwasher. It told him Ma had closed up the house for the night, with nothing left to worry about. He was safe.

One particular night, a nasty cough had kept him awake long after the dishwasher cycle ended. Kept Ma awake too. "My heart hurts," he'd said. She knelt at his bedside for ages, rubbing Vicks VapoRub on his chest. He hadn't remembered falling asleep, but slept soundly—the weight of her palm assuring him, healing his heart— even after she'd gone to bed herself.

The dishwasher clicked into another cycle, bringing Bernie back to the present. He opened a cupboard and marveled at the tower of dishes inside. Ma had enough to set a king's table. Packing it all up seemed impossible. He might need Marcella's help for that.

Spare bedroom was probably the next-safest spot. Ma kept her important papers in the file cabinet there. Manila folders organized in an orderly left-middle-right tabbed pattern, labeled by her small, curlicue cursive. A surge of affection rose up. Maybe look at these later? He closed the drawer. The canvas bin atop the file cabinet looked much less intimidating.

What he found inside the bin surprised him. Made him smile. Keepsakes: personal letters and cards Ma had saved, Hen's crayon drawings. The Mother's Day card he'd given her last spring caught his eye, with its butterfly design in rose-colored glitter. But there were two of them. Did he send her two of the exact same card?

Opening one, he recognized Marcella's handwriting.

In my heart, you will always be my mother. In my heart, you always have been. Thank you for loving my Hen.

His heartbeat thundered in his ears. The card went hot in his fingers as if it were electrified. He knew Marcella loved his Ma. Reading her words, written by her hand, he nearly choked with emotion. Dropping the card back in the bin, he sank onto the bed. His face fell into his hands. He felt smothered by grief.

Here he was in Ma's house, surrounded by her belongings, and his heart was full with love for Marcella. Her voice, her orange-blossom smell, her image affixed in his mind like a recurring dream, making everything in his Ma's house look strange.

He loved Marcella. Had loved her for years.

What he felt now was new.

Fear. Somehow, fear played over everything. Ma had been the glue that kept them together. Despite what she'd requested in her will—that they become a couple, officially—he wouldn't want Marcella that way. To be forced. Coerced. He'd want it to be her choice. And now, Tripp was here. Would she take him back? The idea made him nauseous. The fear that he might lose her was painful beyond words.

He searched the room for something to distract him from that fear.

In-Box

A mesh bin atop the dresser held the businesslike label. Business, he could do. To bury that nagging worry in his gut, he dug into it. Envelopes. Bills. Stuff that needed immediate attention.

Shoot.

With a heavy sigh, he shuffled through the unmailed letters and bills and to-do lists, trying to prioritize. When he saw the sealed envelope addressed to Leon's Diner, he paused, his anxiety turning into curiosity.

Why would Ma be sending a letter to Leon?

LATER THAT NIGHT, when Bernie knew Hen would be in bed, he ventured to Marcella's. She hadn't asked him to babysit Hen, so he assumed she was home. Unless she left him with Tripp? A sudden protective feeling for Hen surprised him. If he dug deep, he'd realize he had always been protective of that child. Since before he was born, even.

Hen's father left when Marcella was still pregnant. It still miffed him how two men could be so daft that they'd walk out on the most extraordinary, beautiful woman in the world. And yet, they did. Tyler's and Hen's fathers, both. Bernie had missed Tyler's early years, but not a single day went by that he wasn't there for Marcella once Hen was born. It struck him now how attached he'd grown to the little guy. What if he lost both Marcella and Hen? He couldn't fathom it.

He knocked lightly on her door.

To his relief, Marcella's voice called, "It's open."

Tripp's blanket and stuff were still in the front room, his makeshift bed on the couch, the freshly rumpled sheet and bed pillow. More relief. How would he feel if Tripp and Marcella shared a bed? He shuddered as he worked his way to the kitchen, where he found her.

She raised her beer bottle with a half smile. "Help yourself."

With his beer, he sat at Hen's place—his usual seat occupied by her bare feet.

"Been a while, Bernie."

"Seen more of Hen than of you lately." No hint of complaint in his voice.

She shifted and tucked her toes at the edge of Hen's seat near his thigh. They were like tiny ice cubes, her toes. It was an automatic thing, on her part, finding warmth for her toes. It meant nothing beyond that. He could tell by the absent way she studied her beer label. His thigh could've been a couch cushion. Still, a jolt went through him. Never had he been in contact with her like this. He forced himself to stay seated while his heart raced.

Why not me?

He thought about collecting her feet in his hands. Massaging them. The idea of touching her bare feet—skin on skin contact—paralyzed him. He didn't budge. The chill of her toes went straight through his jeans.

"Is he here?" He nodded to the couch where Tripp slept.

Marcella shook her head. "What's up?"

"I, uh, found something at Ma's. Can't really make sense of it. Wanted to talk to you about it."

"Oh?" She put her lips to her bottle but did not take a sip.

He got the letter from his shirt pocket. As she reached for the envelope, her feet dropped to the floor. His jeans held a chill from where her toes had been.

"It's addressed to Leon's Diner." She furrowed her brow. "The return address—Hubb Corp. I don't understand."

"Ma meant to send it." He pressed a callous on his hand. "I opened it."

Marcella's wide eyes reminded him of Hen's. Bernie felt a pang of guilt, bringing this to her, as if she were a helpless child in his care. But they were in this together. Ma had made sure of that. He watched her read the letter he almost knew by heart, her lovely, tired eyes roving the words.

She was quiet so long, he thought it best to clarify. "It's an invoice for nine hundred dollars, plus late fees."

"Owed to Hubb Corp? Is that—"

"Hubbard Corporation."

"You?"

"Not me. Ma."

"What's this money for? Why would your Ma be charging Leon almost a thousand dollars?"

"This wasn't the only one. It was a monthly thing. Ma kept records."

"Rent."

"Right. For the diner."

Marcella's jaw dropped. "For the diner? Sally owned Leon's Diner?"

"It seems she owned the building, not the business."

She shook her head. "Did you know any of this?"

"No," he whispered, betrayal settling like a dark cloud. He'd grown up ignorant of the family business. His father had made sure of that. Only after he graduated high school, his father let him in, offering him a job as property manager for his multi-family complex in Lake George. "One of my endeavors. One that will keep you respectably busy," he'd said. Bernie had known not to ask questions, and conveyed proper gratitude. For his entire adult life, he'd been property manager there. His father had been right. It kept him busy. When his father passed away, he assumed any other assets were liquefied and given to Ma. He had no idea about Leon's Diner. Why would Ma keep this from him? How much had Ma been involved in his father's business?

Marcella seemed as puzzled as he. "Sally was the landlord? Leon Hogg was her tenant?"

"Not was. Leon Hogg is a tenant, who owes a boatload of rent to Hubb Corp."

Marcella pinched the paper, visibly processing what Bernie just told her.

He cleared his throat. "That's not all I found."

He slowly reached into his shirt pocket as he recalled what Hen had told him. Long ago, Miss Sally using her 'consequences' voice with Leon and Derek Hogg. And whatever she'd said had angered them.

Turns out, Leon Hogg did have a reason to be angry with her. Good reason. Good reason for a long, hard grudge in fact. On the table, he put the other envelope addressed to Leon and waited for Marcella to read for herself.

Her voice was breathy with shock. "An eviction notice."

"Hey, Dad, you okay?" Ty's voice scratched the air.

Tripp seemed different this visit. He'd come in every day since his arrival to Severance. Every time wearing the same hat, the same denim shirt. His scruff had grown into an uneven beard. His fingernails bitten to the quick and he couldn't seem to keep still.

His eyes darted around the room. "Listen, you and me. We're gonna start our own band, right? What's that catchy name you got goin'?"

"The Ex-Convicts." Ty was less confident now.

Tripp barked a laugh. "Yah, yah. That's great. And your friend, your buddy there, Derek? He's gonna do drums. I got it now. Sure." He drummed the table with his pointers, hummed an unrecognizable tune. "You know that song?"

"No." Tyler felt an inexplicable dread.

"You don't know that song? Man! That's a damn shame. What the hell do you listen to, then? How the hell are we going to get a band together if we don't even listen to the same music? I bet you and Derek listen to that bullshit rap. Am I right?" Tripp leaned in close. It smelled like he hadn't showered in days. "You listen to that garbage, don't you? LL Cool J?"

Ty wished there was room to back away. "Some Public Enemy."

"Yah. Losers. All of 'em." Tripp's eyes flitted across Ty's, and his face softened as if a vacuum had cleared his thoughts.

Ty glanced at the UFO camera. The red eye had blinked out. Stayed off a few seconds. Panic shot through him. So focused on the UFO camera, waiting for its red eye, he jumped when his father clutched his hand. Red eye blinked on. Dad had triggered it. Ty's lungs shook, waiting for the next signal.

It came from his dad. "It's okay. They can't hear if we talk quiet."

Ty's ears went hot. The earth came to a standstill.

"What did you say?" he whispered. Did Dad work with them? Had they sent him here?

"Hey, listen." Tripp grinned crookedly at his hands.

Ty couldn't stop staring at the UFO camera. A thick paste filled his chest.

"Ty, hey buddy. I'm talking to you. Forget about them."

"Okay." Ty forced himself to look at his father, who maybe wasn't really his father. They may have sent someone who looked like his father to get information. Or, more likely, they had gotten to him. Hired him as a spy.

Tripp went on. "I was hoping. You know your friend Derek? I need his help."

Ty snapped, alert. "Derek? You need Derek's help?"

"Sh-shut up." Tripp checked the UFO camera, then the opaque window. "Sorry. Shush, okay? Okay. Yes, I need your help. I want you to talk to Derek—"

Ty's laugh was all nerves. The red eye blinked. He saw it from the corner of his eye. They were listening. He stared at the camera, enunciating his words, as if reciting them from a teleprompter. "Dad, I can't talk to Derek—"

Tripp slapped the table. Then he did something truly shocking. He pointed a finger directly at the UFO camera.

"Stop it!" he shouted at the red light. "Stop with that inane cryptic bullshit. I need to talk to my son."

Ty froze. His insides swirled while his outsides went still.

Tripp shook his head, annoyed. "Damn codes. Think I can decipher them? What? Am I supposed to be some kinda engineer? Why did they pick me, huh?"

Ty couldn't blink. He couldn't believe what he heard. Dad *did* work for them. He was being forced to. Coerced. Blackmailed, maybe. They sent messages through him. To get to Ty. Panic fluttered in his chest, but he worked hard at keeping still. Poker face. Don't let them see you squirm. Don't let them know they've gotten to you.

Tripp's face turned beet red. He ranted, spittle foaming in the corners of his mouth. "I need Derek's help. Leon has shut me out, the bastard. Freaking guy doesn't have any respect for history. Damnit. I'm his friend. Have been for years! I'm back. You'd think he'd—"

"Dad." Ty used his on-stage voice. They were listening. He had to be careful. "I don't know what you're talking about."

Tripp's glare chilled Ty. "Don't play dumb with me. You're old enough. You didn't get in here by being a freaking goody-goody."

Ty swallowed that thing in his throat and leaned back in his chair. For the first time, he wished Clapp would interrupt and tell his father he had to go. He didn't dare look at the UFO camera anymore. Too dangerous. Tripp must've felt it too.

"Forget them!"

On his feet, Tripp came between Ty and the camera, blocking their view. Ty's heart seized. He bit down, clenching every muscle in his body. They would punish him later. And his father? This was a serious violation. Tripp couldn't hide from them. Didn't he know that? He would be severely punished. There's no telling to what extreme—

"Let's work together, now, kid." Tripp leaned into Ty's face. He kept his voice low, but was it low enough? "You know what I need. I need what you need."

What? Ty asked with his eyes, a little afraid of the answer.

Spit flew from his mouth with a word Ty never thought he'd hear his father say.

"Blow."

MARCELLA'S DOOR FLEW OPEN. A rifling through the duffle bag in the front room, and she knew it was Tripp. Chewing a thumbnail, she threw a cautionary look at Bernie.

"This is bullshit," Tripp mumbled. "This whole town is still bull-shit. No wonder I left."

The air thickened with tension. Bernie hid the documents in his shirt pocket just before Tripp stormed into the kitchen. He looked wild and unhinged, his hair static frizz without his cowboy hat.

He raged. "Nothing has changed. All a bunch of pansies!"

"Be quiet!" Marcella smoothed the air with her hands. "Hen's sleeping."

"I don't know who he thinks he is, but this is absolute crap!"

"Who?" Her defenses kicked in. "I hope you're not talking about Tyler."

Tripp pulled at his thinning hair. "No, I'm not talking about Ty. Although he didn't help none either."

"What do you mean? Who's wronged you now?"

"Damn you, Hogg." As Tripp dove into the fridge for a beer, Bernie got to his feet.

"How 'bout I go?" he whispered to Marcella. "I'll be right next door."

Two men's footsteps sounded in sync—one to the front door, the other to the kitchen table. As Tripp sat, Bernie shut the door behind him. The sound made Tripp start. "What the hell? Oh, that guy was here?"

"Bernie. His name is Bernie."

Tripp scratched his chest. "Didn't even know he was here."

"He's a good man, Tripp."

"Yeah, but is he sleepwalking?" He chuckled and sucked on his beer. His eyes floated to the ceiling. The anger had faded. His lips moved, as if he were talking to a ghost. It was eerily familiar. Tyler had the same habit. Talking to the sky.

She put away the memory.

Curiosity got the best of her. What had Leon done to offend him so much? "Tripp, what happened with Leon?"

He glared. "I can't believe all those years you workin' there. You had no idea."

"No idea about what?" She was a terrible liar. Her pulse raced. Why did Bernie have to show her those documents?

He coughed, mucous caught. He rolled the white marble on his tongue. "What went on in the back room."

In the back room. Her stomach dropped. Tripp certainly wasn't referring to the dozen times Marcella had been groped back there. Leon would trail her when she'd go for a fresh roll of tape or napkins or whatever, and he'd lock them in the small room alone. Pawed at her with his grubby hands. She'd shove him away, hiss at him to stop. He'd laugh, like it was all a harmless game. Sexual harassment, it was. She knew now. Illegal, for heaven's sake. And she was too weedy to do anything about it. What would Tripp have done if he knew? Or would he have even cared?

"What about the back room?" She tried to sound bored.

He swallowed more beer, taking the white marble like a pill. He scanned her from head to toe, objectively, without a hint of lust. It was so unlike him, she felt uncomfortable.

"Maybe you can help me," he finally said.

"Help you? With what?"

He looked away. "Get me some blow."

She croaked. Time to educate him about sexual harassment. "News flash! You and me? Off limits. Nothing's going to happen. Never. I made myself crystal clear well before you got here, Tripp. When we spoke by phone—"

Tripp laughed, threw his head back.

Oh, the gall. "What? What the hell are you laughing at?"

"I'm not askin' you to blow me, unless you wanna." He leaned toward her. "I'm talkin' about cocaine."

She stared back at him, perplexed. He could've easily mentioned the Kuiper belt. "Cocaine?"

"Mount Marcy, my Marcy." The back of his hand caressed her cheek. Her skin went hot under his touch. And those eyes, they pierced her. She filled with that fizzy, carbonated feeling—yet tinged sour—like skunk dressing. She smacked his hand away.

"How sweet you are." He sat back. "And so naïve."

Naïve? "You have some nerve—"

"Pretty and dumb." He laughed. "The way God made 'em for us."

"Shut up, Tripp." She seethed.

"All those years workin' there, you really didn't know?"

Anger simmered. "I have no idea what you're talking about."

His laser blues shocked open. "News flash!" he mocked her. "That diner is just a front, babe. A cover. Leon's business is illicit, under the table. Little packets of white stuff. That's what happens in the back room."

Something swirled, obscuring her retinas, blocking her ears, attacking her senses. "What?" she managed, shock and disbelief making the word inaudible.

Explanation over, he was back to his mission. "Use your girly wiles. It'll be easy. Give Hogg a little romp-n-roll if you need to, I don't care. Just figure it out for me, will ya?"

Marcella shook herself alert. "Are you kidding me?"

Tripp rolled his eyes. "Here we go."

"What you're asking me to do, Tripp, is illegal. What the hell? Are you really that thick?"

Tripp shot out of his chair. "Forget it. I'm outta here."

"Oh, the drama. Where will you go? It's late. The whole town is closed for the night."

"I'm not talkin' right now. I'm talkin' I'm out. Leavin' town."

Marcella folded her arms. "Really?"

He pointed to the sky like a freaking astronomer. "I want out of this hole. ASAP."

"What about Tyler?" She raised her eyebrows. That would get him.

"What about him? Ain't my problem. Never was."

Marcella's arms dropped to her sides. There it was. Her intuition confirmed. Tripp was never interested in helping Tyler. She tensed with anger. "Why did you come, then?"

He stopped. His glare like a knife. That old fear roared back, and she flinched as if he'd struck her. She fought against it, but crumbled inside. Who knows how long they stared at each other? Her limbs went cold as heat filled her.

Finally, without another word to her, he stormed to the front room where his clothes and crap lay sprawled all over her living space. He mumbled one curse after another as he packed his bag.

She tiptoed to her bedroom, and prayed he wouldn't hear the lock click into place. Or the rush of tears that followed.

MARCELLA TOOK Tripp to the train station the next morning after getting Hen off to school. As she drove, snow flutters dotted the gray sky as if it hadn't made up its mind to storm. Loosened milkweed, aloof.

She and Tripp were silent en route. The silent treatment had been in effect since his outburst the night before. Still, as she'd pulled up to the train platform, she thought they'd say goodbye.

Tripp heaved his duffle from the backseat and shot out of the car without a word, pressing his cowboy hat onto his head.

She watched him go, slightly stunned. He was going to walk away? Just like that?

White dots of snow freckled his hat as he sauntered blithely, his duffle over his shoulder like a sack of potatoes.

She waited. He'd turn around to wave goodbye. Any moment now.

Or not.

When he ducked into the station to buy his ticket, it hit her. She'd never talk to him again. Or see him. She gripped the wheel, fighting an urge to go to him. Make things better. Apologize.

For what? Why was she such a flimsy, desperate weed? Ugh, she disgusted herself sometimes. Besides, he was the one in the wrong. He left Tyler. Yet again. Selfish ass that he was.

It took less than ten minutes for the train to arrive. That hard nut in her chest tightened as Tripp boarded without hesitation. No wave, no look back.

"Good riddance," she spat.

Rails squealed. The train rasped into motion. As it picked up momentum, steam shooting from its horn, Marcella felt something slip away. The train careened into a valley and disappeared into the lower Adirondacks.

Falling against her seat, she stared at the platform, now deserted. Her breath came more easily.

Then, oddly, she laughed. She laughed and laughed, feeling lighter every second. Oh, the relief! Her chest opened with it. The car windows fogged with it. She laughed until tears gathered. She wiped her eyes. A song of a sigh filled the silence. She cracked a window and the rush of cold invigorated her. Like her car had an infusion of oxygen.

She was free.

Six Months Earlier
Spring 1991

Meep-meep.

After finishing his joint in his truck, Derek honked outside the Trout home. It was a humid Friday night. Sweat gathered under his arms. Had to get the AC checked.

"Come on, Ty."

He hadn't called. He assumed he'd hang with Ty like every other Friday night. Not sure what exactly they'd do. Smoke another joint. Grab some grub. There was a bonfire later. Roxanne might be there. That wouldn't suck. Even if she wasn't there, it never hurt to drink a few Buds in the woods.

Suddenly Marcella—not Ty—leaned into the passenger-side window. She wore a white blouse that fluttered in the wind, and Derek saw the lace trim of her bra. Her dark hair blew into her face. She gathered and held it by her neck. Derek took off his cap and ran a hand through his own hair. She smiled, and Derek noticed she wore lip gloss.

"It's Hen's birthday."

That's all she needed to say. Memories came swirling: Marcella home from the hospital with this tiny bundle wrapped like a baby mummy. She dressed in white too, for weeks after, as if she were marrying the thing. He'd never seen someone so smitten about a blob that did nothing but slobber and poop and cry all the time. Even after the baby's dad left, her love for that blob made her glow. Made her love stronger with him gone. She held the baby all the time. They were stuck closer than if he'd still been inside her. They meandered around the house like that, all white robes and blankets. A big, fluffy cloud.

"Ah." Derek nodded, understanding. Ty couldn't come out.

"How are you doing, Derek?" Marcella smiled brightly.

Derek squirmed, tongued his soul patch. He couldn't remember the last time Marcella talked to him, no less asked him about himself. "Aw'right, I guess."

"Staying out of trouble, I hope?" She winked.

"'Course."

"Are you still working at the diner?"

"Yah." A dumb question maybe, but he didn't care. Weird that Marcella would be asking, though. Didn't she know Ty worked there too?

"Tyler says you have a girlfriend?" Marcella's smile changed. Was she teasing him?

Now he was sweating. "Nah, not really."

She glanced back at the house. "Well, we're going to Flanagan's. Hen likes their mac-n-cheese almost as much as he likes mine. Would you like to come?"

"Who's going?"

The head tilt always got him. "Is that a polite question?"

A half-hour later, Derek found himself at Flanagan's, sitting across from a plate of chicken wings. And none other than Old Mother Hubbard.

"It's customary to wear sleeves in a dining establishment," she told him, her bird-like eyes peering over her reading glasses.

If he could've sneered at her, he would have.

"Didn't know I was comin'," he mumbled, jittery from his joint. Or nerves.

It was true. He didn't know he was coming. And it wasn't his fault. This old T-shirt with the cutout sleeves was the only clean shirt he could find in his house this morning. The over-bright restaurant felt like an interrogation. He considered putting his cap back on.

As if she read his mind. "At least you took off your baseball hat. There's hope after all."

Derek gritted his teeth, his appetite lost. He was dying for a cigarette. Ty had already torn into the platter of wings, and he noisily slurped sauce off his fingers. Derek drank his iced tea, and searched the room for an escape. Something to save him from this neighborhood witch. It baffled him how Ty tolerated her presence like he did. Marcella pretty much kissed her wrinkly ass. And the kid, Chicken, thought she was love in a biscuit.

Hen, Marcella, and Bernie were engrossed in their own thing at the other end of the table, leaving him with Ty—who was, as usual, stuck in his own head—and Old Mother Hubbard, the witch.

She dipped celery into blue cheese. "So tell me. What are you up to, Derek?" Nothing about her tone was friendly.

He shrugged. "Nuthin'."

"No? Helping your dad at the diner a lot? Are you involved in all aspects of the business or only the food service part?"

Ty karate-chopped his hands. "He's a food processor. Chop, chop!" His voice was too loud. "He's got style, though. Ask Roxanne Russo."

Derek rolled his eyes.

"Don't you have aspirations, Derek? You don't want to be a slave to the diner all your life, do you?"

For real? The diner was the hub of the whole freaking town. He was proud to work there. It would be his someday. "What's wrong with the diner?"

The waitress served a second platter of wings along with Hen's mac-n-cheese. Then, a cup of chowder for the witch, who dropped her oyster crackers in one by one. They floated and bounced like moorings in the lake.

"Where were you and Ty planning to go tonight?" she asked.

Ty perked up. "Hey, isn't there a bonfire later?"

Derek nudged him with his knee. *Shut up.*

The witch cackled. "Oo-oo! Nothing like drinking beer and building a huge fire in the woods. Very responsible."

Ty laughed, and the witch smiled at him. Actually smiled. She had never—not once—smiled at Derek. He knew he shouldn't care, but it pissed him right the hell off.

Marcella called from the other end of the table, "Derek, aren't you hungry?"

Derek obediently picked up a wing. He ate it absently, not tasting it, making it last until Ty finished the rest. Finally, Hen's peanut butter pie came with a big candle in it. While everyone sang Happy Birthday, Derek felt the witch's eyes burning his skin.

What? he asked silently, scowling at her.

I'm watching you, her eyes told him.

He refused to let her get to him. She thought she had all the power in this town because she was a stupid watchdog nag, but she didn't.

Pop did.

ONCE A MONTH when produce was delivered, Derek played hooky to help Pop with the heavy lifting. This month it fell on a Monday, the only day the diner closed. Pop went about administrative stuff, like bills, while Derek brought in the crates.

Pop squinted at a letter. "This is getting out of control."

Derek set the bag of potatoes atop the box of cabbage. "What is?"

"All these years, I been payin' more rent than any business in town. All to Hubb Corp. They don't have no office. Return address is a PO Box. Phone number gives me some mechanical voice askin' me to leave a message."

Derek was used to Pop's outbursts about rent. "Yah?"

"And then this letter comes in. From a lawyer. Hochman. Comes in here for a blue-cheese burger nearly every week."

"I know 'im."

"Letter says I gotta hand over my balance sheet, tax returns, and payroll detail. Required by law."

Derek paused. "That's odd."

Pop's neck was so red it was like a volcano about to erupt. "More than odd. So unfair, it's an outrage. You weren't here last week when this examiner guy came by. Checked the electrical to see if we were up to code. Threatened to shut us down if we don't comply with his demands." He tore the letter in half.

Derek thumbed his belt loops. "Damn."

"Yeah, damn it all to hell and back, I say. Woulda cost a fortune to do everything he asked for."

"Where's it comin' from?"

"Tole you. Lawyer named Hochman. He eats a—"

"No, someone hired him. Who does he work for?"

Pop knocked on the table. "Let's pay a visit to Hochman and find out. Right now."

In less than thirty minutes, they sat across from Lawrence J. Hochman, Esq. Derek's worn flannel and grunge jeans seemed ratty against the studded leather armchair.

Hochman did not seem like the kind of man who liked surprises. He fidgeted at the opposite side of his desk. His satin tie dazzled against his starched white shirt. He yanked at his cuffs, stretched his arms, and yanked at his cuffs again. The law seemed to emanate from his pores. Derek wasn't sure he trusted him.

"What can I do for you?"

Pop tossed the letter onto his desk.

Hochman barely looked at it. "Did you have a question about something?"

"Who the hell is Hubb Corp?"

"Excuse me?"

"Oh, Larry, cut the crap. You eat at my place every week. Be a pal and tell me what the hell's goin' on here. I shell out more dough to this company—freakin' crazy high rent for this area—and I dunno who the hell they are."

"They'd like to remain private about the matter."

"Screw that."

"Mr. Hogg, please—"

"They can't 'remain private' when they send all these suits over who force me to spend money for no good reason. I have a right to know who's behind all this."

Mr. Hochman donned his reading glasses and studied the letter.

Pop paced the room, fury stinking off him.

Derek tried a gentler approach. "We want to do the right thing. What do they want?"

Mr. Hochman softened. "She just wants everything above board."

She. Derek's ears perked. He kept his voice level. "Above board?"

Sigh. "It's a basic consideration, really. It's important to Mrs. Hubbard that any business under her roof is a respectable one."

As soon as he said her name, he must've realized his mistake. The air in the room vanished. The bookshelves grew to the ceiling. Silence rang against the books, the gold etching on the spines pinging.

Derek fell back against his seat.

Pop's face blanched. "What did you say?"

Mr. Hochman folded and unfolded the letter. Dropped his readers. Sweat gathered on his forehead. "Well. Um."

"Sally Hubbard?" Pop was either pissed or in awe.

Derek's fists clenched in his lap. Old Mother Freaking Hubbard. The neighborhood witch. Always yelling at him and Ty. Tattling to Marcella. Threatening to call the cops on them. Derek's blood boiled.

Hochman tapped the letter against the desk. "Yes. Not that it matters, really. It's not who that's important, but what. Hubb Corp— the entity—is who you are dealing with...through me."

"Sally Hubbard lives two doors down from me."

"Still, it would be prudent to address any communications through this office."

Pop snorted. "That's not very neighborly, is it?"

Derek had to smile. Now Hochman's face went white.

THE CHESSBOARD STRETCHED BETWEEN THEM, a few pieces left on the squares. Some pawns, his bishop, her queen, both their kings.

"You're a smart boy. You're learning to read already. You can learn this game easily. And it's good for you. It exercises your brain." Miss Sally beamed at Hen.

"Like, jumping jacks?" Hen giggled.

"Not exactly like jumping jacks. But you don't want your brain to turn to mush. So you have to use it. Find new challenges to keep you thinking. Keeps you fresh. Look at me. I'm an old lady. But because I like to play Scrabble and chess, I stay sharp as a tack."

Phone rang. When Miss Sally went to answer it, Hen yawned big. It was his turn, but his brain was sleepy.

"Your mom will be here soon," Miss Sally said after hanging up. "Do you want to finish tomorrow?"

"Okay." Hen curled up on the couch, snuggling Miss Sally's afghan. A gurgle from his stomach. He was hungry, too. So many things: snack, sleep, Mom. But his eyes were closed already, and sleep came for him.

Rap, rap, rap.

It wasn't Mom's knock on the front door. Hen perked awake. The afghan fell as he sat up.

Miss Sally padded in her polka-dot socks to open the door. Hen craned to see that meanie, Derek Hogg, and his father on the stoop.

"Took you long enough. Come on in. I just put on some tea." Miss Sally stepped aside.

Stunned, Hen stared at the two Hoggs, who were too tall and fat for Miss Sally's fancy living room. Leon's apron was dirty. Derek wore the same backwards cap. They smelled like cigarettes and bacon. All wrong. They didn't belong.

Leon followed Miss Sally into the kitchen, but Derek stayed behind. Hen's belly went shaky.

"Well, if it isn't Chicken man." Derek licked that lip patch of hair, his whole tongue out in the open. Hen ducked inside the afghan. Derek chuckled. Who knew at what? It felt like it took a year and a half, but Derek finally followed his dad.

Hen didn't want to listen to the grownups in the kitchen. But he couldn't help it.

"I'm here on a business matter." Even Leon's voice was fat.

The fridge opened and shut.

"You drink Bud, right?" A can opened with a pop. Miss Sally was hosting them? "How about nachos, Derek? Used to be your favorite."

How did Miss Sally know Derek's favorite anything?

"I'm good," Derek mumbled.

"You're good? Does that mean you're not hungry? I don't believe it."

Why was she being so nice to them?

Chips fell onto a plate. Microwave beeped on. The smell of melting cheese made Hen's stomach lurch.

"This is unnecessary, all this stuff." Leon sounded annoyed.

Miss Sally's voice was sugary. "I'm your neighbor. And your landlord."

What was a landlord?

"Yeah. Hubb Corp. That's you, right?"

"It was my late husband's company. And now it's mine. So, yes. Hubb Corp is me." Hen could hear her smiling. He would bet a hundred dollars the Hoggs weren't smiling.

The kettle whistled, and Hen followed her in his mind: getting her favorite mug from the cupboard, placing a licorice spice bag inside, pouring the boiling water. Now smells of black licorice mixed with melting cheese. They didn't go together.

"Please, sit."

Ceramic platter tapped onto the table. Chairs scraped the linoleum. Slurping beer, sipping tea. Finally, nachos crunching. *Mmmmm...*gooey cheese over warm chips. Hen's mouth watered.

A knock on the table from Leon's big knuckle. "I gotta ask you to stop sending over those officials, ma'am. They're nothin' but a pain in the ass." Pause, then softer: "Sorry."

Miss Sally laughed a little. "I'm sure they are a pain in the ass. Okay, no more officials."

Leon cleared his throat. "And I wish…I mean, I'd appreciate it if you wouldn't keep raisin' the rent. But keep it, yanno, even with other places, like local commercial properties. Bonnie's Boutiques on the other side of Main doesn't pay half what I do."

"Okay."

"Really?"

"Yes. That's fine."

Hen had heard Miss Sally use that voice before. *You can make that choice, Hen, but there will be consequences.*

Consequences were never good.

More crunching. More slurping. Finally, Miss Sally's voice came again, this time like a siren. "I'm glad you're here, Mr. Hogg and Derek. Because I've been wanting to talk to you about something I haven't yet shared with Mr. Hochman."

"Oh? What's that?"

"And I don't intend on sharing it with Mr. Hochman, unless this conversation doesn't go as planned."

"What's that? I don't follow, ma'am. Sorry."

"Mr. Hogg, Leon's Diner is a Hubb Corp building. I need to know that your restaurant is your sole means of income in that building."

"Sole means of income?"

A sigh. "I've had a suspicion for quite some time. I'm too old and stubborn to turn a blind eye anymore. As we get older, our principles are all we have left. So I can't ignore it. It's about time I do something about it."

A big, heavy pause. No more nacho crunching or beer slurping. Just tea sipping.

"I'm running an investigation on the property, Mr. Hogg."

"How?" Leon spluttered. "Who?"

"It's an entirely covert operation. You won't know it's going on at all. Although it would certainly help your case if you would release your balance sheet and the other documents Mr. Hochman and I are asking for."

"Oh."

"We can keep it between us, keep it simple," she sang. "If everything comes out on the up and up, you won't have to worry about a thing."

"You mean, rent going up?" Derek sounded like a child. "Stuff like that?"

"Oh, Mr. Hogg. If my people find anything illegal going on in my building under your supervision, rent will be the least of your problems. Trust me."

Radio voices went on, raging louder. Leon cursed, raised his voice. Derek yelled at him. Yelled at Miss Sally too. Hen's insides got all tangled up. A chair fell to the floor. Clatter of ceramic. Big noises. Like panic after an explosion.

Hen pulled the afghan tighter around him. He looked out the crocheted holes to see them leave, finally. They grumbled out like angry trolls.

Sleep was far away now. He couldn't shake Miss Sally's consequences voice. She'd given them a warning. Something bad was happening in the diner where his mother used to work. Miss Sally planned on finding out. Then, there would be consequences.

And Leon was mad as heck about it.

December 1991

Marcella had had her fill of lawyers' offices. The décor in Mr. Hochman's had felt like a dusty museum. Light years away from where they now sat in Mr. Gerrity's office, which was white and modern with a distinct sterile feel. It seemed to match how she felt these days—numb.

She and Bernie sat in plastic chairs that looked like flying saucers. The Hubb Corp documents Bernie had found lay dog-eared like curled bark on Gerrity's metal desk.

Marcella observed her son's appointed lawyer, trying to get a sense of whether he could do the job. He looked like he had brio enough. Strong, like a wrestler. Was there any tie left to knot after looping around his thick neck? His lion's mane of graying hair was combed neatly back. She could see it. Gerrity-lion wrestling through prison bars to free Tyler, superhero-style.

"Thank you for squeezing us in today, Mr. Gerrity. And thank you for all the hard work you're doing for Tyler." He'd better be working his ass off for her son.

He nodded to Marcella, impassive.

Why wasn't he reading the stuff she brought? She waved her hand over it. "Here are the documents I mentioned in my message."

Mr. Gerrity scanned the papers faster than a photocopier. He tossed them down too quickly. Dismissively.

He must not understand.

"Mr. Gerrity, these letters are from—"

"Hubb Corp. Yes, I can see."

Still didn't get it. "Hubb Corp, as in Sally Hubbard."

Bernie cleared his throat. "Ma owned the building where Leon's Diner is. He's been paying her rent for over twenty years."

Mr. Gerrity tapped a gratuitously thick pen on the desk, making the papers dance.

"One is an eviction notice," Bernie went on. "He'd fallen behind on his rent."

Mr. Gerrity's deep breath inflated his bulky chest. "All right. Mrs. Hubbard was Mr. Hogg's landlord. Mr. Hogg had been negligent on paying rent. These are common issues we find with tenant situations. I don't see what it has to do with the incident involving your son, Mrs. Trout."

"No, see, it absolutely has to do with it. And this *incident* does not involve my son. That's the point. He's innocent until proven guilty."

"My apologies, Mrs. Trout. As you know, I'm representing your son in this case and—"

"Right. That's why we're here." Her hands shook. She knotted them together. "Couldn't it be seen as motive, Mr. Gerrity? I mean, if Leon owed all this money to Sally Hubbard and wasn't able to pay?"

Mr. Gerrity nodded rhythmically as he spoke. "Mrs. Trout, I understand you are eager to find your son innocent. Please know that I'm doing everything in my power to achieve the best possible outcome. At times like these, family members often grasp at straws—"

"Grasp at *straws*?" She gripped the sides of the chair. "Mr. Gerrity, I don't—"

He stopped her with a short salute. "Mrs. Trout." He checked his oversized watch. "I'm sorry. I have an appointment."

"Hold on." Bernie raised his voice. Almost aggressive. "Marcella has other information that might be helpful."

Bernie encouraged Marcella with a look. For a moment, she went blank.

"Oh." She tumbled over her words. "Yes. Right. There's something else. We have reason to believe. Actually, we know—and our source is good—that Leon has been using the diner as a cover for a...drug operation." She hesitated. She'd never said the word aloud. "Cocaine."

The pen tapping stopped. Mr. Gerrity stared at Marcella, unblinking.

She went on. "Yes. It's true. Leon has been selling cocaine from the back room since...forever. This changes things, doesn't it? This makes it an 'uncommon tenant situation,' to use your phrase. Am I right?"

Mr. Gerrity bit the inside of his cheek. "It would." He gathered the letters carefully now. "You say your source is reliable? Who is it?"

Oh, crap. Marcella shot a desperate look towards Bernie, who nodded like this was all peachy keen. Who was she supposed to name? Tripp Trout was as reliable as a Chance card. Not an option now, anyway. That chapter was closed. His train was long, long gone, thank goodness.

She had to focus. Who could she list as a reliable source for Leon's illegal drug sales? Who would cooperate? By now, the entire town might be complicit. Maybe even Clapp, that randy officer. Collusion would fit nicely with his Napoleon complex.

Then, an idea.

She turned from Gerrity's intense gaze. "Bernie, Hen's still waiting in the lobby. Would you—" She didn't have to finish. Bernie left to take care of Hen.

Back to Mr. Gerrity. Deep breath. She pressed her thumbnail into the pad of her index finger. Focus.

"I worked for over ten years at Leon's Diner, sir."

Mr. Gerrity narrowed his eyes. "You are the reliable source?"

"Yes, sir." It's just a white lie, Marcella told herself. This was the kind of thing a mother did for her son.

"Over ten years, you say?" Mr. Gerrity twisted off the pen cap and scribbled on a legal pad. "And you were aware of these goings on the whole time?"

She looked right into the lion's eyes. Even as she squirmed in her chair. "Maybe not at first, but yes. Pretty much."

Just a white lie. Anyone in her position would do the same thing.

Gerrity dipped his head, a nod. Scratched onto his legal pad. "I'll need someone else. You're too close to the defendant. Can you get me another source? Someone who'd be willing to be a witness if and when this comes to trial?"

She deflated a bit. "Is that really necessary? I mean, as a former employee, I—"

"You're the defendant's mother, Mrs. Trout. If this is true, we need a more objective testimony."

Marcella swallowed what felt like a tennis ball. Couldn't name another waitress. No one was stupid enough to stay very long. Or, maybe Leon made sure no one stayed. Who could she name? Who else would know? Besides Tripp...

Oh, Tripp. Marcella could only think of Tyler's deadbeat father. Dread filled her.

No. No way was he coming back. Never. Over her dead body.

"You have someone in mind?" Gerrity must've seen it in her eyes.

"Well, yes. But he wouldn't work either."

"Who?"

"Tyler's father."

"He's the only one who can corroborate this story?"

Marcella bowed her head. "The only one I can think of."

Gerrity pursed his lips. "Well, keep thinking. But, regardless, we should give it a try. Especially considering Tripp Trout has been an *estranged* father for the duration of Tyler's childhood. My gut tells me we'll need him for other reasons anyway. Can you assure me he'll be here for the trial?"

No. Please, no. That worm sandwich was downright tantalizing now.

Ugh. Tripp would have to come back. And she'd have to convince him.

"Yes," she said miserably. "I'll do my best to make sure he's here for the trial."

THE LOBBY of the lawyer's office reminded Hen of the hospital. All starchy and cold. Hen was surprised Bernie came out from the meeting without Mom.

"She'll be right out," Bernie said. "How 'bout we wait in the car?"

Hen was relieved to leave the lawyer lobby.

On their way to the Impala, Officer Clapp appeared like a magic trick. His dark sunglasses hid his eyes. Hen froze. And squeezed Bernie's hand a little harder.

"Hi, there, Officer."

Why was Bernie always so friendly to this policeman?

"I told you to call me Rob." He grinned with all of his teeth. "Just wanted a few words with the boy, if I might."

Bernie shuffled a little. "Mmm... Aren't you supposed to do that sort of thing with a parent around? His ma will be right out."

He chummed Bernie's shoulder. "Ah, no worries. This isn't official. Off the record, let's say. Besides, you said yourself that you're his guardian."

"Still, I don't feel right about—"

"Hey, Bernie." Officer Clapp did that low voice thing grownups did for secrets. But Hen heard, always. "I appreciate you helping with the investigation. I know you want to find answers as much as I do."

Bernie looked sad. Like he'd given up.

The policeman crouched down to Hen's level. His words were sharp. "I know you got something to tell me, boy. Now's the time to come clean. Before lawyers make it all messy and complicated. Come now. Tell Officer Clapp what you know."

Officer Clapp took up all the space around him. Not a policeman, a cyborg. Half man. Half machine. Hen's mouth went dry.

Then Officer Clapp did a strange thing. He took off his dark sunglasses and smiled. Even tilted his head—something Mom liked to do. He wasn't a cyborg after all.

"There, there," he said. And Hen realized—oh my gosh!—Officer Clapp held his hand. Kind of shaking it, like grownups do. The staring contest was still on, it seemed. That black spot stole his attention.

"Yeah? What do you say, boy?" Clapp's eyebrows went up.

Hen felt very important. "That night...Derek's truck was parked out front. Derek Hogg."

Bernie sighed big behind him.

"Good boy," Clapp said after a moment, in a tone that asked for more. He seemed almost disappointed. "You're right, too. Derek Hogg's truck was parked outside Miss Sally's house at the time of the incident. How smart you are! You probably knew that before we did. You should work for us."

Hen felt very, very important. "And then I saw Derek get into it. In the driver's seat."

Clapp seemed less excited now. Bernie had already told him all this. "Are you sure it was Derek getting behind that wheel?"

Hen nodded with his whole body.

"It was dark. Sometimes your eyes trick you in the dark."

Hen remembered his book. "Not if you have night vision."

Clapp laughed in a not-so-nice way. "And you don't have night vision. Neither do I. Neither does Bernie here. So you can't be sure it was Derek Hogg in the truck. Now, what else do you know about that night?"

"No. I *am* sure. I know it was Derek. I know him. I knew him my whole life. He walked side to side on the way to the car, like a gorilla. And he punched the steering wheel, angry-like."

Clapp sighed again. Then he gave a too-big smile. It didn't fit what they were talking about. He looked like a scary Halloween clown.

Hen tried to pull away, but Clapp held tight. "Now, now. Don't you have something else to tell Officer Clapp?"

His face was back to straight lines. Serious eyes—the black speck menacing. A black hole.

Clapp leaned in closer. "Want to tell me about these beads?" His whisper was laced with a bitter odor of coffee.

Hen's stomach turned. He'd forgotten he'd been wearing it, the beaded bracelet Bernie rescued from Miss Sally's house. He'd meant to give it back to Tyler on Thanksgiving.

Everything had gone wrong that day. The grimace on Tyler's face when he saw Hen. Tyler squirming on the table, calling Mom over and over. And then Clapp barging in. Pushing Tyler down. Hen had curled into a corner, shaking like a wet dog. Scary and messy stuff Hen didn't like to remember. He didn't like the way Clapp handled his brother. Tyler cursed and screamed and didn't sound like his brother at all, but creepy and mean.

Why did you bring Hen here? Tyler had shouted at Mom.

The worst part was the hard shell Hen felt forming around his heart as he cried in the corner. Tyler had barely talked to him. He wouldn't even look at him.

Why had his brother rejected him?

And now this policeman asked about his beaded bracelet.

"No," Hen said to Clapp, surprised at his own voice. Like a grownup's.

"Really? There's nothing you want to tell me about these beads?"

The world went still a moment.

Caw. A crow hopped on the wrought-iron fence near the lawyer's office—as big as a chicken and jet black. Hen shivered.

Clapp wouldn't let up. He leaned closer, and the crow flew off. "It sure seemed like you had something on your mind when Bernie here gave these beads back to you. After we found them at Sally Hubbard's home."

Miss Sally. A bad feeling trickled to the surface.

Hen shook his head. *No!* Tears itched his cheeks, but he didn't dare move to wipe them away.

Clapp's movements were quick. The black speck blinked out a moment. And Clapp had the beaded bracelet in his hand. Hen rubbed his wrist where it had been.

"I'm going to hold onto this. When you decide you want to share what you know with Officer Clapp, have Bernie here bring you down to the station. Maybe we can go get an ice cream down at Stewart's after."

Hen held his wrist as Clapp stuffed the beads into his uniform pocket. Hen's hand was free now, hot and moist from Clapp's.

"Rob, honestly," Bernie said. Finally. "I think that's enough. His ma should really be here—"

"Right." Clapp tapped his belt and fake laughed. "No worries. It's all good."

"Sorry, Rob. I mean, he's just a boy. You gotta talk to Marcella about all this."

"My pleasure." His voice peaked and dipped like an opera singer's.

Bernie led Hen away from Clapp, and Hen felt lighter. Lighter still when he heard Mom's voice calling after them. "What's going on here?"

Everyone seemed to be happy to see her, not just Hen. All Clapp's hard angles fell away. Bernie's smile was back. Mom made everything better. She rushed over and tugged on his knit hat, and he could smell orange blossoms through the cold winter air. He didn't care about the beads anymore. All he wanted was to get away from Officer Clapp. And go home.

"Have a nice day, Mrs. Trout." Clapp replaced his sunglasses and smiled sideways at Mom. "See ya, Bernie."

Mom turned to Bernie. "What was that about?"

Bernie rubbed the back of his neck. "I think we might need to have a talk with Hen."

HEN WAS IN TROUBLE. Something about the beaded bracelet. He

stared at his hands in the backseat of Mom's Impala as they drove home.

"Why would he take something like that from a child?" Mom asked Bernie.

"We found it in Ma's house, after." Bernie tried to whisper.

"Right. He'd left it there. Couldn't find it. He was all stressed about losing it. I'm sure he was glad you found it for him."

Putty filled Hen's ears. Truth was thick. Mom had no idea he'd given it to Tyler that night. It wasn't his beaded bracelet Bernie found. It was Tyler's. Should he tell her?

"That's the thing," Bernie said. "He didn't seem glad when I gave it back to him. More like scared."

"Well, considering the circumstances, I can't say I blame him."

Hen felt hot all over. Didn't they know he was right here, in the backseat? He hated it when grownups talked like he wasn't there. Or didn't understand.

"Still, Clapp thinks it's a clue or something. The bracelet. You might want to talk to Hen about it."

Mom found Hen in the rearview. Gave him a bright smile. Hen looked at the blur of trees out the window. Kept staring until he felt the car pull into his driveway. He'd been so eager to get home. Now he didn't know what was in store.

Minutes later, Hen sat across from Mom in the orange kitchen. She'd asked Bernie to go. Tyler was still being held at county jail. So much quiet filled the house. It seemed sad.

"Hen, let's talk." Mom used her no-nonsense voice. Her wide eyes waited for something.

Hen's stomach went fuzzy. He didn't feel like talking. He didn't know what she wanted him to say. The kitchen warmed like an oven. Sleep tugged at him.

Yawn.

A glass of apple juice appeared before him.

"Why don't you tell me, Hen? About the beads?"

Hen's heart picked up and he wished Bernie had stayed. He sipped his juice, coating his upper lip with stickiness.

Mom was extra patient. She undid her hair clip and dark curls fell, making shadows on her face. Everyone thought she was beautiful. Hen did, too. But right now, with her stern face, shadows made her look mean. She waited, but the words were scared right out of Hen.

Mom's smile was tired. "It's me, sweetie. You can tell your mom anything."

He coughed a little. "I don't want to."

"You don't want to tell me?"

Hen shook his head.

"Why? Why don't you want to tell me?"

Hen stared at her. She had all kinds of feelings in her eyes. Anger and fear and hope and sadness. Hen could feel all of them too.

"Are you afraid you're going to get in trouble?"

After a beat, Hen nodded.

"If you tell me the truth, you won't get in trouble. Understand?"

Hen just stared.

Mom stared back, serious-like. "The truth is always better than a lie, even if you think that lie will save you from getting in trouble. Always tell the truth."

His eyes stung. "I don't want to tell you."

"Tell me. Tell me the truth, Hen. I promise you won't get in trouble if you tell me the truth."

Hen looked at his hand that Clapp had held. He rubbed the spot on his wrist where the beads had been. How smooth they were. How easily they slipped off his hand. And now, they were in Clapp's pocket.

That Thanksgiving memory didn't let up—Tyler's body pinned by Clapp's Popeye arm. Tyler's face twisted, his eyes moving over Hen as if he didn't see him. Or didn't want him anymore.

Tears sprang to his eyes. "I gave it to Tyler."

"What? You gave it to Tyler? What-what did you give him?" Mom took Hen's hand. Her cool touch took away Clapp's heat.

"The beads."

"I don't understand."

"That night. Before."

"No. You left them at Miss Sally's. Remember? We were looking for them before we left that day. You couldn't find them and I said, 'Don't worry. We'll get them another time.' Remember?" A laugh fluttered out, but her cheeks went pink.

Hen stared, confused. Did she not hear him? "But I did. I found them. Before we left."

"No, no." Her voice cracked. She fanned her hands as if to catch it.

"Yes, I did. I wanted to show you. But you were talking to Miss Sally so I put them in my pocket. When we got home, I went upstairs and gave them to Tyler. He put it on. He was wearing it."

For a moment, no one talked. Mom looked like something hurt inside. "He was wearing it?"

"The beaded bracelet. He was wearing it that night. That night when Miss Sally—"

"No, no." She paced the kitchen, smoothing her hair back into its clip. "It can't be that bracelet. Bernie says that he and Officer Clapp found it—"

"At Miss Sally's. After."

Mom shook her head. Like she didn't want to hear. A blunt, bitter laugh. "That can't be. How would it end up back at Miss Sally's? How—?" She froze. She gazed out the window at the giant willow tree.

She had finally heard him. She clapped a hand over her mouth.

"Oh, no. Oh, please no."

She rushed to Hen and wrapped her arms around him. She held him a long time. When she straightened, tears had wet her whole face.

"Hen, listen to me. This is important. Okay?" She gripped his shoulders. Her low voice cracked with her crying. "If Officer Clapp asks you about that bracelet again, you have to tell him that you lost it that day at Miss Sally's. And you couldn't find it. You didn't find it. Okay?" She shook him a little. "You lost it at Miss Sally's. You did not find it. You did not see that bracelet again until Bernie brought it to you later. You hear me?"

Hen didn't say anything. He didn't blink. He didn't move. Fear made everything stiff.

She kept squeezing his shoulders like juice would come out. "Promise me you will tell Officer Clapp you never found the bracelet. It never touched Tyler's wrist. Okay? You need to promise me. Hen? Do you understand?"

A big feeling built inside him. "But—"

"What? But what?" Her voice was harsh. Her hands trembled. She let go of him and shivered. Wiped tears from her cheeks. Softer now, "But what, sweetie?"

"But that's not the truth."

HEN COULDN'T SLEEP. That big feeling wouldn't quit. Mom's words pinged around in his mind: *Always tell the truth.*

She insisted he tell her the truth. Promised he wouldn't get in trouble. She was right. He didn't get in trouble.

But then, it got confusing. She acted weird. He'd never seen her so jittery. Then, she made him promise to lie.

Promise me you will tell Officer Clapp you never found the bracelet. It never touched Tyler's wrist.

His stomach got all twisty. Why did she want him to lie? Just because Tyler wore the bracelet that night didn't mean he did anything wrong.

Or did it?

He pictured Tyler wearing it. He'd given it to him that night.

Tyler wore it that night. It was found in Miss Sally's house. But Tyler wasn't there, Derek was. Maybe Tyler gave Derek the bracelet.

Why would he do that?

Maybe Derek took it from him. That's the kind of icky thing Derek would do. For fun. Take things from other people and laugh about it, especially if it came from Hen. That must have been it. Derek stole the bracelet and had it that night when he went into Miss Sally's house and did a very bad thing.

Was Tyler there too?

No. No. No.

Maybe Derek left it there on purpose to get Tyler in trouble. Make it seem like Tyler did that very bad thing, not him. But Tyler didn't have anything against Miss Sally. Hen knew that for sure. She annoyed him sometimes, but he didn't have any reason to do a very bad thing. Not like Derek.

Derek had all the reasons to do a very bad thing. That day she made them nachos, Miss Sally had warned them there would be consequences. Leon had been angry. Derek had been angry. Mad as heck.

Still, something didn't sit right in Hen's belly. He wished he'd never made that beaded bracelet in school. He wished it never existed. Hen tossed and turned so much that night, it was like a giant eggbeater had gotten to his covers.

Maybe Bernie could help.

THE NEXT MORNING, Bernie walked Hen to the bus stop. It was the last day of school before Christmas break.

Hen tugged on Bernie's hand until he looked at him. He took a big breath and asked his big question.

"What is truth?"

"Whoa. What is *truth*?" An awkward laugh. "That's kinda deep."

"But what is it?"

"Like, what does the word 'truth' mean?"

"Yeah." By the time they reached the corner, it had started to snow.

"I guess it's what's real. Like, facts."

Hen held out his mitten to catch the snow. A perfect snowflake landed. He could see its lacy design. "Like, what you know is real?"

Bernie sniffed hard. He didn't wear a hat or gloves. "Well, it's like this. It's snowing right now. That's a fact. I know it. You know it. We see it and feel it and smell it. It's real and true."

"Truth."

"Right." Bernie rocked back on his heels, smiling outside and in.

More snowflakes fell on Hen's mitten. So many that he couldn't see any lacy designs. Just a clump of snow.

"What about Santa?"

Bernie's smile disappeared. "What about him?"

"Is he real?"

"Well, now, Hen. Of course he is." Bernie eyed the empty street.

"But I've never seen him."

Bernie sucked the inside of his cheek. "Well, it's like this. Sometimes truth is tricky. Sometimes truth is what we believe is real. Even if we don't see it or feel it or smell it."

"What if some people don't believe?"

Bernie grinned. "Maybe they're lyin' to themselves."

Hen let the clump of snow fall from his mitten. It landed by his boot, mixing with the fresh snow. He couldn't see where the clump began and ended.

"What about God?"

After a pause, Bernie cupped Hen's shoulder, looked him right in the eye. "Now, son. God is definitely real. That's the truth."

He waited until Hen nodded before straightening. Snow had collected on his thin hair. The tops of his ears were bright pink from the cold.

The bus rumbled in the distance.

"So, truth is what we know is real, but also what we believe is real?" Hen wanted to be sure.

Bernie sighed. A cloud cone shot from his mouth. "I know the bus is coming. And it's about time 'cause I'm about freezin' out here. That's the truth."

HEN'S SEAT on the bus, the one he shared with Murphy, seemed bigger than usual. And quiet. Like it was protected somehow. A bubble.

"Do you know what truth is?" Hen asked him.

Murphy giggled. "What do you mean?"

"Like, truth. What's true and what isn't."

"I don't know what you're talking about." Murphy made a face.

"Like, Santa and God and stuff."

"What? Santa and God and stuff? You don't make any sense."

Hen bounced through some bumps in the road. He was a little afraid to ask, but wanted to know. "You don't believe in God?"

"'Course I do, you boob." Murphy's cheeks got red, embarrassed-like. "Santa's another story."

"You don't believe in Santa?"

"No. Only boobs believe in Santa." He turned away, breaking the bubble.

"Maybe you're just lyin' to yourself," Hen said, but Murphy didn't hear.

Hen spent the rest of the ride working it around in his mind. Truth. It should've been clear, but it wasn't. Hooks and twists made it tricky, like Bernie said.

Was Bernie right?

Was Murphy?

If Hen had to take sides, he'd take Bernie's. And he'd said: *Sometimes truth is what we believe is real.*

So, truth wasn't only what he knew, but what he believed.

Did Hen *know* Tyler did something bad at Miss Sally's that night? No.

Did Hen *believe* Tyler did anything bad at Miss Sally's that night? Absolutely not.

So...

Truth: Tyler didn't do anything bad at Miss Sally's that night.

He wasn't even there. Derek was. Alone. Derek swiped the bracelet from Tyler because he's a jerk. And he left it at Miss Sally's when he did that bad thing.

Truth.

Now Hen had to make everyone believe what he believed, which wouldn't be easy. What could he do?

He thought so hard his brain ached.

By the time he got to school, he had an idea.

A holiday party in his classroom. Teacher instructed them to make marshmallow ornaments for the tree. Hen's plan didn't involve marshmallows.

"Do we have anymore pipe cleaners?" he asked. "And beads?"

Teacher praised him for his originality and set him up with a green pipe cleaner—same color as before—and leftover beads from their project earlier that year.

His favorite colors were still there. He could do the same pattern.

Red, dark blue, yellow, and green.

Red bead. The old barn by the lake.

Dark blue. Tyler's favorite jeans.

Yellow. Golden, fall leaves.

Green. The spindly branches of Miss Sally's willow tree.

And repeat. Red, dark blue, yellow, and green.

Thread enough to make a bracelet.

Barn, jeans, leaves, willow tree.

Hen smiled as he worked. This would fix things. Make everything better.

"Think of someone special you'd like to give these to," his teacher had said. She echoed the same today. "Giving gifts is a way to tell someone you care about them."

Barn, jeans, leaves, willow tree.

Just as he had before, Hen wrapped the wire in a circle wide enough for Tyler's wrist, folding over the extra pipe cleaner.

Christmas 1991

Forget *Silent Night*. No tear-jerker, downer carols allowed. Marcella was all about *Rockin' Around the Christmas Tree*.

She had one Christmas wish and Justice Bowman made it true. He'd granted special permission for a rare twenty-four-hour pass for Tyler to spend the holiday at home.

Bernie put up a Charlie Brown tree, which Hen saved with stringed popcorn and candy canes. Aside from no downer carols, another rule applied: No talk of Tyler's pending trial. Not a word. No mention of Derek, Leon, or Tripp. Especially Tripp. Marcella was set on pretending Tyler was on a break from college or the Marines or somewhere. And she sent Bernie to pick up Tyler from county jail so she could hold onto that fantasy.

At Hen's insistence, *A Chipmunk's Christmas* crooned through the house when Tyler came in. It was like a movie star had arrived. Hen squealed and hopped around like a bunny. Tyler allowed Marcella a long hug—an unexpected gift. His skin held an acidic, medicinal smell, as if he'd just stepped off an airplane. He wore the same ratty

Baja hoodie, and Marcella fought an urge to tear it off him and boil it clean. It did fill him out a little, though. She bit back tears, seeing how thin he'd become.

Bernie came in quietly behind Tyler carrying a bouquet of white flowers—daisies, carnations, and stephanotis. Marcella regarded them askance.

"These are from Tyler," Bernie said.

She eyed her son. "You got me flowers?"

He nodded to Bernie. "I had a little help."

"It was his idea." Bernie set the flowers on the mantle. "I helped fund it, is all."

Marcella's smile was bursting. This holiday was already the best ever.

When they sat for dinner at the kitchen table, filling all four chairs, it felt like a real family. Bernie, sitting across from her, belonged. It made sense, what Sally had hoped for them. She watched them eat, too happy for food. Tyler helped himself to seconds, then thirds of Marcella's spiced roast chicken, homemade mashed potatoes, and wilted spinach. Hen talked about his holiday party at school.

"We made crafts. Most of my class made marshmallow ornaments but I made something else. And then we ate popcorn and watched *Rudolph!*"

"My favorite." Tyler grinned at his little brother. All that ugliness from Thanksgiving at the station done and gone, thank goodness.

Chocolate cream pie—Tyler's favorite—for dessert. As she loaded the dishwasher, the three men in her life scarfed down the pie in its entirety.

If she could freeze time right here on Christmas Eve, she would.

HEN AWOKE BEFORE THE SUN. Had Santa come?

But quiet filled the house. And Hen was cozy under his comforter. The windows had white icing in the corners. The room was snuggly, with a soft rumble of Tyler's snoring across the room. Maybe in a few...

When he next opened his eyes, it was bright and sunny and the window icing had melted. Hen bounded off his bed. Christmas! And it wasn't too early to get up.

"Tyler!"

Tyler looked like a little boy as he slept. Hen smacked a kiss on his forehead, which wrinkled in protest. Hen giggled. Tyler rolled over with a sleepy mumble. His hair was all tangly in the back. Hen twirled it with his finger.

How could Tyler be in so much trouble? Maybe if they pretended hard enough, he wouldn't be. And since he was home, it would be easy to do. That was it. Hen would pretend Tyler right out of trouble.

Hen wanted to wait for Tyler to wake up, but his feet were getting cold. He pulled on his favorite fleece socks. The coffee maker gurgled downstairs. Mom was up! Christmas could start!

He slid down the stairs, closing his eyes tight as he passed by the tree where presents waited for him.

Mom made coffee in her bathrobe. Bernie was there too, already fully dressed at the table.

"Good morning, sweetie!" Marcella sang, gliding over for a hug. "I hope you didn't peek under the tree."

Hen shook his head, grinning. He couldn't help it. It was Christmas!

"I'm making you some hot cocoa. Why don't you have your cereal before Tyler gets up?"

"I'm not hungry."

"Have a little. When we're excited, we don't feel hungry when we really are. Come and sit with Bernie."

Mom was right. As soon as he tasted his Cinnamon Toast Crunch, his belly asked for more. He ate the whole bowl, and then dove his spoon into his hot cocoa. It even had whipped cream on top. Mom and Bernie smiled at him over steaming mugs.

"Think you were on the naughty or nice list this year?" Bernie said.

Hen tightened his eyebrows. He never did find Louis. What if he were in one of those leaf piles that got scooped up and mixed into compost? Oh, gosh. That wasn't nice. And then, he'd seen what had happened at Miss Sally's. That wasn't nice at all. And that yucky thing at Thanksgiving with Tyler wasn't nice, either. He hoped to make up for it today. His lips trembled as worry crept into his heart.

Bernie backtracked. "No, I didn't mean. No, Hen. You're nice. Always a nice boy."

"Oh, Hen," Mom said. "Bernie was just playing. Of course, Santa knows you're a good boy."

Still, Hen's hot cocoa wasn't that tasty anymore. Even with the whipped cream.

Mom cleaned up after breakfast while Bernie started a fire in the fireplace. Hen had enough of polite waiting. He played Christmas with the Chipmunks on the stereo. That would wake up Tyler, for sure.

It worked. Tyler staggered groggily downstairs. Wolfed down a cheese omelet with his eyes closed, almost.

Hen shut off the Chipmunks. "Can we open presents now?"

Mom made Tyler sit in the middle of the couch so that everyone could sit around him.

"Is this where Dad slept?" Tyler fiddled with his hoodie straps.

"Yes, Tripp slept on the couch."

Mr. Tripp-and-Fall.

Bernie handed out the presents. First, from Santa to Hen: a Lego set. "I don't play with Legos."

"Well, sweetie." Mom ruffled his hair. "Maybe that's because you don't have any. This is your first set. All little boys like to play with Legos. Didn't you, Tyler?"

Tyler shrugged, glum all of a sudden. "Don't really remember."

Second, from Bernie to Marcella: gold earrings.

"Oh my goodness, Bernie. You shouldn't have." She put them on. "They're like tiny little leaves." They caught the light within her loose hair, shimmering. Bernie smiled bigger than ever.

"Mom, you're a princess," Hen said.

Third, from Marcella to Tyler: a new Baja hoodie. "I thought you could use another one. The colors in this one will bring out your eyes."

Hen wrinkled his nose. "It's not stinky either."

They all laughed. Even Tyler.

Hen couldn't wait anymore. Tyler's gift was hidden at the back of the tree. Tyler seemed confused when Hen handed him what looked like crumpled tissue paper.

"Open it." Hen hopped on his toes.

"I didn't know you had a gift for Tyler." Pride rang in Mom's voice.

It seemed to make Tyler sad, though. He put it aside—maybe for later?—and turned to Hen. "I'm sorry about Thanksgiving."

"It's okay."

"I have something for you too. It's nothing special, really."

"Okay."

"Wait here." Tyler left the crumpled tissue on the couch and went upstairs to get Hen's present. He held it behind his back. "Close your eyes, hold out your hands."

Hen did.

It felt like a piece of paper. He felt around with his fingers, keeping his eyes closed. Definitely a piece of paper.

"Okay. Open!"

On the paper was a pencil drawing—a cartoony drawing.

"A hedgehog!" Hen pressed the paper to his heart. "A hedgehog, a hedgehog!"

"Do you like it?"

"I love it."

"I made it just for you."

"You're quite the artist, Tyler," Bernie said.

Hen found the crumpled tissue in the crease of the couch, handed it back to Tyler. "Now, you. Now, you. I made mine just for you."

The room warmed as the fire crackled. The tree lights blinked to a slow rhythm. The white flowers on the mantle filled the room with pretty smells. Hen was too excited to keep still. Tyler unwrapped the tissue paper, and—

"What the hell?" He flinched from the thing. Like it was a spider. "What the hell is that?"

Hen stumbled in shock, nearly falling into Mom's lap.

"Tyler? What is it?" Mom craned to see, holding Hen up by the shoulders.

"Is this some sort of sick joke?" His voice was acid. He glared at Hen in a way he'd never seen. Fear spread through Hen's limbs like wildfire. Mom tensed by his side. Tyler threw the thing across the room. *Smack* into the wall near the fireplace.

"Tyler!" Mom called.

Hen's sob was too big for tears. Too big for sound. He opened his mouth in a big, silent wail, heat spreading all over.

"Shh, it's okay," Mom said, then to Tyler, "What's this about? What made you so upset?"

Tyler didn't answer Mom. He stomped upstairs and slammed his bedroom door so hard the whole house shook.

Mom turned to Bernie. "What was in the tissue paper?"

Bernie held up the beaded bracelet, the one Hen made at his classroom's holiday party. An exact copy of the one found in Miss Sally's on that terrible night. Hen wanted to make it better, put things right. Tyler misunderstood. He didn't know what Hen was trying to do.

Hen sucked back his tears and took the bracelet from Bernie.

Mom scrambled off the floor. "Where did you get that? Give it to me."

No. Tyler didn't understand.

Hen ran upstairs after Tyler before Mom or Bernie could stop him. He needed to explain it. Tyler was confused. Maybe he thought this would get him into more trouble. That wasn't it at all.

Tyler lay on his bed, staring out the window.

Hen sat, waited for Tyler to look at him. But he didn't budge. Didn't even blink. He looked like a statue. Or asleep with his eyes open.

"Want your headphones?"

"No."

"This bracelet—"

Tyler jerked to life. He grabbed the beads and jolted upright. "Where the hell did you find this?"

Hen shrunk away.

"Hen, tell me. Where did you get this?"

"No, Tyler, this isn't the bracelet you wore that night."

Tyler shook his head and bared his teeth like an animal.

Hen tried to explain. "Let me tell you—"

"I don't want to talk about the damn beads." Tyler's voice, icy and cruel, stunned Hen.

He mustered courage. "Wait. You don't get it."

"No, *you* don't get it." Tyler pulled at his hair, hard. Tears slid from his eyes.

Hen rushed to explain. "I made you a new one. Since Officer Clapp took the old one."

That made Tyler stop. "What? How did Officer Clapp get the old one?"

"It was...Bernie brought it to me. And Officer Clapp—"

"Bernie?" He gripped Hen's arms. "What did he say when he brought it to you?"

What did he say? Did Hen remember? "He just said, 'Look what we found. It was at Ma's.' Something like that." Hen hoped he gave a good answer.

Tyler pressed on his eyelids, the beads wedged between his fingers. "Okay. Okay. Okay. And Mom? Anyone else? Anyone know... about the beads, Hen?"

Hen didn't know what Tyler meant. "Know about the beads?"

"Damnit, Hen!"

Hen reared back.

"Sorry, buddy. Sorry. I didn't mean to scare you. Okay. So, Bernie and Clapp found it at his Ma's."

"At Miss Sally's."

"Right. At Miss Sally's." Tyler took a deep breath.

"And Officer Clapp took it back. He has it now. This is a new one, see—"

"Okay, wait up. I'm going to ask you a very important question, Hen. And you need to tell me the truth, okay? No matter what, you have to tell me the truth. Got it?"

There it was again: truth.

"Okay."

Another big breath. "That bracelet that Clapp has now. What did you tell him about it?"

"Nothing. I didn't say anything."

"Why did he want it?"

Hen shrugged.

"Does he know you gave it to me?"

Hen frowned. "I think so?"

"Does he know I was wearing it that night?"

Hen blinked at his brother. He remembered Mom's words. *Promise me you'll tell Officer Clapp you never found the bracelet. It never touched Tyler's wrist.*

Why would it matter if he wore those beads? Derek stole them and brought them to Miss Sally's and did that bad thing. Tyler didn't do anything wrong.

Hen wanted to believe it to be true. But suddenly he wasn't so sure.

Tyler talked with his hands. The beads kept clicking. "Hen, give it to me straight here. You gotta tell me right now. Did Clapp know or did you tell him? And if you did, okay-well-fine, but you gotta lemme know. Okay, tell me."

"Tell you what?"

"Does Clapp know that I wore those beads that night?"

Tyler's eyes were frantic. Hen felt uneasy, at the tipping point of a scale. Whatever his answer, one side would outweigh the other. And change everything.

Tyler tried again, his voice gentler. "Hen, does anyone besides you know I wore those beads that night in Miss Sally's house?"

There it was.

Tyler was in Miss Sally's house that night.

Truth.

Hen looked out to the backyard. To the weeping willow that sat between their and Miss Sally's yards. His mother's favorite tree. Now, at Christmas, it looked skeletal, spiky. Not lush and green and soft like it did in summer. No wonder it had such a sad name.

"Hen, answer me. Does anyone else know I wore those beads at Miss Sally's that night?"

Hen was sick with sadness. Too sick for tears. "No."

THE SUN WAS ALREADY on its way down. Hen fought the heaviness in his heart and the truth in his mind. Tyler was there—in Miss Sally's house—that awful night. He said so himself. It wasn't just Derek. Derek hadn't stolen the bracelet. Tyler was there, wearing it.

Hen didn't want to believe it. Bernie had said that sometimes truth was what you believed to be real. Did it work the other way? Could he choose what to believe? Could he choose his truth?

All Christmas day, he noodled it over. He tore into his Legos while Mom cooked up a feast. He wanted to build a big red barn but there weren't enough red pieces. Maybe black would work? He alternated black and red bricks, making a pattern. It helped, the pattern. Snapping bricks together somehow made him feel better.

And then, Tyler was next to him, sorting through the bricks too. "You need black ones?"

Hen didn't answer. He raked through the pile, listening to the plastic click.

"Here's one." Tyler held it up.

Hen took it without looking at him.

Tyler stopped sorting. "I wanted to say sorry."

Hen stared at him.

"Sorry," Tyler said. "Okay?"

"For what?"

A dopey laugh. "For, I dunno. I kinda freaked out on you."

"Is that all?"

Tyler pulled at his hair. "Yeah. I mean, Geez. Seeing that thing was, like, crazy. I forgot all about it, actually. And there you go and shove it in my face. It's like it all comes back."

Hen stared at his Legos. "What all comes back?"

"You know, what happened that night. All that mess."

What happened that night?

Hen wanted to ask. He snapped more bricks together. Did he really want to know?

"So that's why I freaked out on you."

Hen studied his structure. It didn't look anything like a barn yet.

Tyler shucked Hen's shoulder. "Hey, I said I was sorry."

Hen pressed a black brick to a red one. Then a red brick on top of that. He kept going. Black, red, black, red, black, red. His structure was getting taller. It still didn't look like a barn, though. It looked like a bleeding stone wall.

"Did you hear me?" Tyler sounded annoyed now.

"I heard you."

"And? You're supposed to say 'It's okay.'"

"No."

Tyler chuckled. "No? What do you mean, 'no?'"

Hen dropped his Legos and got up. If he stood very straight, he was taller than Tyler. He made his voice really loud. "No, it's not okay."

Tyler sighed. And kind of rolled his eyes. "Hen, come on. I got upset. Can you really blame me? I mean, the sight of those beads makes me think about—"

Hen made fists at his sides. "No!" Everything bubbled up. Steam came out of his ears. His eyes burned red. His chest filled with hot air.

"Hen, you can't expect—"

"I HATE YOU!" Hen screamed.

Tyler's bright blue, Mr. Falling-over-something-eyes stared at Hen in shock. His boxy jaw slackened.

"I hate you!" Hen stomped on his Lego structure, his bleeding stone wall, breaking it apart. The hard edges won against his sock's fleece. Pain shot through his foot. Hot tears sprang from his eyes, but he didn't cry out. He kicked the plastic pieces and they scattered across the wood floor.

Mom called to him in a worried voice, but Hen had turned off his ears. He threw on his coat and boots and ran to the only safe place. Out to the backyard.

Hen followed his boot tracks through the snow under the back porch, to where his play tent was stored. He crawled inside. He shivered—not from the cold—but from fury. He scanned the tent for critters. A small black spider crawled up the tent piping. On reflex, he caught it between his fingers.

His fingers were too mad. They pressed together, squeezing the spider, defeating it, killing it dead. Its slippery insides smushed out and ran down his thumb. He wiped the mess on the tent floor. Tears came, hard and fast.

What did he just do? He just killed an innocent creature. Why? He was a horrible person. Just like his brother.

He curled up, eyes pressed on kneecaps. "I hate you. I hate you. I hate you."

Rocking back and forth, the tears finally stopped. It was dark now. Through the tent window, he could see a billion stars. Past the spiky willow was Miss Sally's house. Her big bay window, dark quiet.

Tyler had taught him not to be afraid. *When it's dark it's dark for everyone.*

What about Tyler? What did he do in the dark? An image of the Monster shadow, its jagged edges. The Scooby Doo villain. Its long shadow—

Hen gasped.

Tall people made long shadows. Derek Hogg was thick and squat.

That jagged shadow was Tyler's, not Derek's.

Hen stared into the dark quiet of Miss Sally's window until his eyeballs got cold. The truth washed over him like a hailstorm. Why did it have to hurt so much?

Tyler was the Monster.

Truth.

Last Spring
April 1991

Ty's mouth hung open, awestruck by the spark. That stuff went up his nose and electrified everything, made his senses burst with feeling. Incredible. Like a super-taster, everything was enhanced.

When Derek emerged from the pink flowery bed sheet, it seemed like an optical illusion. Ty couldn't help laughing.

"We're outta here." Derek walked right to the door. He didn't say hi to Bear. He didn't seem to realize what just went down.

Ty got up, all that muddled stuff from before zapped out of his brain. He shuffled to the door, following Derek. It felt rude to leave without saying anything to Bear. Thank him or whatnot. But a thank you seemed too formal.

"I guess we're leaving."

Bear nodded, and tilted his head back, content in his own internal paradise.

Ty dragged his feet to the truck, sniffling. Sounded like he was crying, which was both funny and depressing at the same time.

As soon as Derek slammed the driver's door, he railed into Ty. "Seriously, dude? My pop will absolutely kill you."

I guess he did realize what went down.

Derek must've found Ty out as soon as he came out from behind the flowery curtain. Ty should've known. Derek's nose was trained like a police dog's.

"Do you think I'm going to feed you that shit? You think you're starting a habit here? Think again, my friend." He peeled out of the gravel driveway and sped down the backstreets toward 87. "You're not getting anything from me. That was a one-time, stupid experiment, got it?"

"Yah, yah. Okay. Got it."

Derek cursed under his breath. Fury stank on him. He drove aggressively. At every curve, Ty got thrown into the passenger door.

Ty watched him coolly. He leaned on the headrest. Despite the car's speed, everything seemed in slow motion. A calm washed over him. And something else—an unfamiliar feeling of self-possession.

Freedom.

The trees they passed were trees. The moon had no face. Nothing happened in his mind as bugs splattered the windshield. No screeching. No voices. For the first time in a long time, he didn't feel like he had to drown something out with loud music. Silence was okay. He had control. Not just over his body, but his mind. Something about that white stuff zapped his brain, shocked him out of it. Like, for the first time in his life, he had clarity. No question what was real.

What bliss.

He thought about his recent episodes objectively, like a doctor. Kind of. As Derek sped along the highway, he felt safe enough to wonder: Why was he so tightly wound? Why did that wheel in his mind spin out of his control and show him things that weren't there?

For the first time, he felt he could slow down that wheel in his mind. Take control.

Then, as he sat in the passenger seat, something shifted. Lifted him. That's how it felt, anyway. Beyond that initial peaceful feeling. Better. Higher than Derek. Higher than God. Ha! Wow, this was good. As if he just had the best orgasm in his life and another was coming. His entire body tingled with it. He fought the urge to moan aloud. Euphoria. That was the word.

Euphoria.

Derek's chain smoking churned like a paper mill. He was still pissed. Ty could tell by the way he smoked. He didn't offer Ty a cigarette, which was fine. Ty didn't need it. Didn't need anything.

About halfway home, Derek punched the radio on, louder than usual. No Guns N' Roses. Some Top 40 crap.

Ty didn't mind. Not at all. Nothing bothered him. He pet the circle of moon through the glass as it tracked them. If he jumped out of the car window and tried to fly, he could reach it. He fanned his fingers, making a silhouette of a bird—slick black against the glowing white moon face.

Time slid by comfortably. It just might have been the happiest Ty ever felt.

When they turned off Route 9 onto Marina Road, the moon disappeared behind a wide swath of trees. When Derek drove onto a dirt road, the truck tires made tiny popping sounds on the gravel.

"Where are we going?" Ty craned to find the moon beyond the trees.

"Not home." Derek tossed his cigarette out. He smacked his armrest and the air turned sharp. "Damnit, Ty. Why'd you do it? I can't trust you for anything."

"I dunno." Ty suppressed the urge to laugh. The uneven back road jostled him. "Where are we going?"

Tall pines surrounded the truck, making the night darker.

"Stoppin' at the lake."

"Schroon Lake? Why? We're almost home."

"Shut up."

Whatever.

Trees opened up and a fat disk of a moon illuminated the lake before Derek's headlights did. The moon was huge. Ty could jump right into it. He didn't even need to fly.

Derek clicked off the headlights, shut down the engine. "Get out." Derek fumbled through the glove box, knocking his fist into Ty's knees. A flashlight appeared in his hand. "I said, 'Get out!'"

"Okay, okay." Ty stumbled onto the sandy gravel, mesmerized by the moon. Someday he'd build himself a big round bed just like it. A waterbed. And it would glow softly like a nightlight and put him into a safe slumber every night.

Derek's flashlight showed a trail. "Come on. Walk."

They were at a remote part of the lake. Undeveloped, with no hint of civilization in sight. If Ty listened closely, he could hear the lake. It sounded like a dog lapping water. "What're we doing?"

"Just do it."

Ty walked in front, following his shadow from Derek's flashlight. The trees grew thicker, the path narrower. Ty kept tripping, his Chucks finding every tree root. It gave him the giggles.

"Shut up."

Ty tried to stop laughing and walk. They walked forever. Soon, his legs ached.

They came to a big, flat rock that sloped to the water. The rock must've messed with the tree roots that flanked it, because the tops all swept inward, making a kind of shelter. Like a fort. Something flew erratically across the moon, and Ty was struck with wonder. Slick black. A raven. But a drunk one. Wait. Not a bird, a bat! It swooped down, licked bugs off the water's surface, and disappeared back into the woods. Hen would have loved it.

"Cool." Ty nestled beneath the brush.

"Cool. Yeah. You will be." Derek's head looked huge silhouetted by the moon. "Get undressed."

Ty laughed. "Yeah, right."

"Dead serious, dude. Strip and get in."

"Get in...the lake? Dude, it's *April*. Lake's barely thawed. Haven't you heard of hypothermia?"

"We're in a bay, dickhead. Temps are warmer here. Don't you know your geography?"

"I don't know where the heck we are. Trampled through the woods to get here. Is this even Schroon Lake?" Ty giggled without meaning to.

"Ty, don't piss me off any more than y'already have. If ya don't get in the lake to shake off that crap in your system, you don't have a ride home."

"Geezum, Derek. It's not like I meant to do it. I mean, I didn't want to do it. But what the hell took you so long? I was sitting there for hours while you're laughing it up with whatever-dude in the kitchen."

"It wasn't hours."

"Felt like hours."

"It was fifteen minutes. Max."

"Whatever. So, this bearded-dude had the lines on the table. Gave me this hollow pen. Kept telling me 'Go! Go!' What the frig was I supposed to do?"

"Say 'no,' Ty. Say freaking 'no.' Didn't your mom teach you anything?"

Ty's gut hitched. A surge of affection for his mother sobered him. Marcella hadn't ever talked with Ty about drugs. She probably didn't even know they existed—in this town or anywhere. He wouldn't want her to, either. She was innocent that way.

"Shut up. Leave my mom out of this."

Derek clicked off the flashlight. Moonlight filtered through the inky pines, dappling light against the rock. Lake water clapped rhythmically, taunting Ty. It even sounded cold.

Derek stared him down, arms crossed. Ty felt his dark eyebrows pointing at him. Pushing him.

"Whatever," Ty mumbled, and flung off his drug rug. It didn't make much sense, but it didn't matter. Ty needed a ride home. Now he stood naked and shivering.

Get it over with.

His feet hit first. Cold shot up his legs faster than lightning. His stomach lurched into his esophagus. His lungs clenched, and he sucked air as if breathing through a straw.

He slapped the water, frantically pulling toward shore. Scraping his fingernails against the rock moss, he found a ledge to grip. He scrambled out, scraping both knees. His body shook uncontrollably. His teeth chattered.

Derek threw him his wadded up clothes, which he hugged to his stomach as it heaved. He puked into the water. Tiny white specks of it caught the moonlight and floated away, looking like chunks of bread he used to throw to ducks when he was little.

He shoved on his T-shirt, which soaked the water like a sponge. Drenched and cold. He slid it off and put his drug rug over his bare chest. He forced his legs into his jeans, commando. He wadded up the rest and threw it as far as he could into the lake. It made a disappointingly puny splash.

He shoved his feet into his Chucks and heard the click of Derek's lighter.

"You good?" Derek grinned, Ty could tell from his tone.

"Screw you."

Back to the car in silence. The only light came from the moon and the tip of Derek's cigarette. Aside from snapping twigs, Ty heard the suction-cup inhale and sighing exhale of Derek smoking.

"Gimme one of those." Ty shivered so violently, Derek had to light it for him. It warmed him a little. He lagged behind, yearning to be alone.

It was still there, that inner tingle. Softer, coming down. Euphoria. He laughed to himself.

Ty might have known it was wrong, if Marcella had ever taught him. He might have understood he had too much to lose, if his father had been around.

And what about Derek? Raised by a fat drug-dealing father, Derek was all of a sudden dripping with morals? Thought he was the bomb after scoring with Roxanne Russo? Mr. High and Mighty over there, driving his piece of crap truck.

Bullshit. He was still high. He was higher than Derek. Always had been. Always would be. He held on to that clarity, and saw Derek for who he truly was. Like an aftershock.

Derek was nothing. A big, fat nothing. Just like his father. Roxanne would see it too.

Ty smiled to himself, as warmth from the truck traveled from his toes to his scalp. He closed his eyes the rest of the way home.

Summer 1991

"WORK FAST," Derek told him as they walked through the doors at Leon's. "I'm meetin' Rox in an hour at the manor."

Ty frowned. Derek could at least use her full name. "What the hell am I gonna do?"

Derek led him to the slop sink near the back room. "Well, first you're gonna mop the floors. Then you're gonna shine the booths. Got it?" His tone was meant for first graders.

"I mean, after, dickhead. While you're at the manor with..." He couldn't say her name.

Derek went to the kitchen, his shoulders jiggling from laughter. "I'm droppin' your ass home first."

Ty's stomach twisted with jealousy. "I thought you guys weren't dating."

"We're not," Derek called from the kitchen.

Ty twirled the mop, slapping the rags against the linoleum, watching beads of water skirt away. Octopus arms.

Heat built behind his eyes, and his vision blurred. Ty shoved the mop between the barstools, angry now. The only sound was Derek's staccato chopping on the butcher block.

Dup-dup-dup-dup-dup-dup

Why couldn't they play music while they worked? Leon didn't like the noise, that's why. Big ol' Leon must have sensitive ears. He emerged from the back room in a black T-shirt and scrub pants. Ty gaped at his belly overhang, exposed without an apron.

"Gotta run out for a minute. Be back to lock up."

"Yo," Derek answered without pausing his knife. Ty froze in place as Leon boomed past. An elephant, huge and lumbering, moving through the diner. Out the door. Car door slammed. Engine revved. Headlights swept across the back wall. A moment later, the engine softened to a distant hum.

Ty forced a stuttering breath.

Dup-dup-dup-dup-dup-dup

Sweat broke out on his temples. He propped the mop against the counter and rubbed his thighs. His legs itched to move. Derek's chopping paused, probably getting another onion or pepper, and Ty waited, his insides humming.

Dup-dup-dup-dup-dup-dup

Ty had to move quickly, even if it felt like he was swimming through the hazy diner. His fingertips tingled as he set the bucket in the slop sink. The back room door was ajar. His stomach got jittery.

He gently pushed through and held his breath, taking a quick inventory of the room. In the dim light of the desk lamp, Ty made out an armoire, a closet, and three filing cabinets.

His breath came back in spurts as sweat broke out on his upper lip. He cupped a fist—a boxer's grip. Ready to fight.

Pop, pop, pop.

Crap. He hadn't meant to crack his knuckles.

Derek's knife was still at it. Thank goodness.

Ty went to the closet first. Through the shadows, he could see the safe. Forget that. He needed something little. A taste.

Inside the armoire, he found linens: aprons, towels, etc.

Near the desk, the lamp emanated a thick heat. Lava started pooling in his shoulders. It crept down his chest.

Stay focused.

Ty's pulse quickened as he worked the drawers. Left top, locked. Right top, a leather-bound notebook. He pulled open the wide middle drawer, making too much noise. Lots of stuff in here, a regular junk drawer.

"Come on," he chanted.

Lava rolled down his arms and into his feet.

Vertigo threatened.

Please, stay focused.

Ty dug in with both hands, shutting his eyes to focus his other senses. Touching. Smelling. Listening.

Something had to be in there.

Boom!

Office door slammed open. Ty hadn't heard the hard stop against the butcher block, nor Derek's clomping footsteps to the back room. Just the door's big boom.

The diner's fluorescent light flooded the back room. Derek's silhouette, his cap like an arrow, shot across the desk.

"Whatcha doin' in here, Ty?" Derek's voice was a warning.

Ty had gotten good at quick lies. "Thought I'd get the key to lock up. Help out your dad."

Derek chewed on a toothpick, like his father always did. "Pop's comin' back. Didn't you hear him say that? There's no key in there anyway."

"Oh." Ty's hands were still deep in the drawer.

Derek snapped. "Ty! Get the hell out of this room. Pop sees you in here, you're done."

"Oh, sorry."

"Come on. We gotta get goin' anyway. Gonna be late."

Ty closed the drawer with fists. He swallowed sourness in his mouth. "Wouldn't want to make Princess Roxanne wait, would we?"

"Hurry up, dickhead."

Derek waited in the doorway as Ty trudged past, hands shoved in his pockets. Derek cursed under his breath as he shut the door behind them.

"Don't go in there again. Back room is off limits. I tole you that."

"Aw'right."

It was already better. Ty blinked away some cobwebs and took up the mop again. He made his own music as he worked now, humming his favorite—Guns N' Roses *Sweet Child O' Mine*. He finished the floor, and then wiped down the booths. From the kitchen, the stretch and zip of plastic wrap replaced the *dup* of Derek's knife.

By the time Leon returned, the whole place smelled of Lysol. The booths' red pleather glistened and the tabletops sparkled.

"Good work, Ty," said Leon.

"Thanks." *Don't talk to me now. I'm at the breakdown.* As the refrain built in his mind, Axl Rose's voice roared in his ears. He had to concentrate on walking calmly to Derek's truck.

Derek threw his apron in the back. He finger-combed his overgrown hair as he slid into the driver's seat.

Ty felt cool all over, that lava having melted away. His hands deep in his pockets, his fingers traced that little packet of white stuff he swiped from the middle drawer. It was all he could do to keep from singing that final refrain, belting out to the stars, matching Axl's gritty falsetto.

Fall *1991*

"SHE THINKS she can control us, D. But she can't," Pop told Derek. They sat in a booth at the diner after closing, twin beers on the table between them. Twin cigarettes in the ashtray. It was late, and Pop's eyes were bloodshot. Derek had thought they'd go right home, but Pop was all hyped up. He went from his cigarette to his Bud without pause, smoke seeping around the bottleneck like dueling snakes.

Derek knew they paid rent to the witch. Big rent. He knew Pop didn't like it. Tonight, though, something else bothered him.

"She's gonna find out, D. This guy has been comin' in the last few weeks for lunch. From outta town, he said. Heard about my famous chili, he said. Bullshit. Had this pad he kept writin' on. Didn't touch his chili or cornbread. Just eyed the place. Watched me like a freakin' hawk. When I went back to the dumpster with a load, he was there—sittin' in a Buick with tinted windows. It was the investigator. I know it."

"Investigator?"

"Hubbard hired him. She's got her hooks in us good, D." Pop slugged his beer. "Good thing is. It's just her right now. Hasn't blown the whistle on us. Hasn't even told her lawyer. We don't have to worry about Clapp as long as we keep him supplied."

Derek drained his beer. His craving for another distracted him.

Pop held up his empty. "Get yourself another. Me too."

When Derek returned with the Buds, Pop took it but didn't drink. "Hubbard gave me the hairy eyeball the other day, told me she had the report. Kind of was a bitch about it. Said she was 'disappointed in the findings' or somethin'."

"What, did she come in here?"

Pop burp-chuckled. "Yap, can you believe? Ordered coffee. Didn't touch it. Scowled at her mug, kinda."

Derek's blood boiled. "Like she's gonna catch something from us? What a wench."

Pop tilted his bottle, slurped the foam. His cheeks billowed with a silent belch. He grabbed Derek's elbow across the table. "Listen up, D. We gotta take control here. We need to get ahold of that report."

Derek glanced at Pop's fat fingers on his arm. He couldn't remember the last time Pop touched him.

"You think you can do it?" Pop squeezed his elbow.

Derek took his arm back. "Me? Do what? Get it from her?"

"Yeah. Go to her house. Sweet talk her or whatever. Bribe her if you have to."

Derek kind of laughed. "How am I supposed to do that? She won't let me in. She thinks I'm the devil."

"You're a smart kid. You can figure it out. Go over there with the little guy."

"Hen?"

"Yeah, let the kid work it for ya."

No freaking way. Derek did not need Hen for anything. "That's not going to happen."

Pop eyed him sideways. "What's your problem with that kid, anyway?"

Derek shrugged. "He doesn't like me either."

"What about Tyler?"

"What about him?"

Pop scratched his scruff, mumbling about the Trout family and being a neighbor and trust and...

Derek stared at his beer, mulling it through. Ty had a weakness. And it had nothing to do with his mental problems. It had to do with that white stuff he'd been pilfering from the back room.

"You think Tyler could help you get in there?" Pop's voice came through the grid of his thoughts.

Fizz from his next sip tickled Derek's nose. A JV-version of what the white stuff must have done to Ty's nose. Ty was becoming desperate for the stuff. He would do anything for it.

"Yeah, I think I could get him to do that."

October 1991
"Cabbage Night"

Stuck behind a school bus, it took Derek a moment to recognize Ty as he put Hen on, giving a thumbs up to his half-brother through the window.

Derek tapped his horn.

Ty swaggered to the passenger side, leaning in like Marcella had done on Hen's birthday.

"Chicken duty?" Derek nodded at the bus as it chugged from the curb.

Ty laughed. "I get it. 'Chicken doody.' Good one."

"Didn't even mean that one. Whatcha got today?"

"Nuthin'. Same old."

"Get in."

Ty slid in and turned on the radio. Commercials. As they pulled out, Derek switched it off. He drove slowly to school, in sync with the gears of his mind. He'd planned it out, mostly. Pop would be proud. He hated to admit, though, that he needed Ty.

"Listen, I need your help with somethin' tonight."

"Oh, yah?"

Derek lit a cigarette. "Besides, you still owe me."

Ty chewed on his drug rug strap, shifted in his seat like he had a load in his pants. "For what?"

Derek blew smoke in his friend's face. "For being such a loser. Back in April."

IN HEN'S FIRST-GRADE CLASS, the instructions were simple: Thread plastic beads onto a pipe cleaner. Choose colors that make a pattern.

Murphy chose black, purple, and orange. And more black. He twisted his eyebrows. "Mine's evil. Bad-guy evil."

Murphy claimed to like bad guys, but joked about them too much. He didn't fit the part, anyway. With a face full of freckles and missing front teeth, Murphy seemed as wholesome as a cornfield.

"What kind are you making?"

Hen shrugged and chose his favorite colors. Red, dark blue, yellow, and green. He tried to push away thoughts of Derek Hogg. How he'd waited there in his truck as the bus pulled away. Where had Tyler gone with his best friend? He had a sinking feeling it wasn't school. "Headed for trouble," he'd heard Miss Sally say more than once. He squeezed a red bead, wondering where trouble might be.

Pushing the red bead onto the fluffy wire, Hen wondered at how it stuck. Almost magnetic.

Red, dark blue, yellow, green.

The pattern. A familiar one.

Red bead. Like the old barn by the lake. Not for farm animals. This one was empty. He and Tyler snuck inside once. It was damp, with mouse poop everywhere. Smelled like mildew and rotting wood. And Hen learned that even if something looks pretty on the outside, it might have a rotten core.

He reached for the next bead.

Dark blue. Tyler's favorite jeans. Tall to fit his long legs. Worn at the knees. Frayed at the ankles. The pockets always bulging. He wore them today as he walked Hen to the bus stop, and as he slid into Derek Hogg's truck.

Yellow. Golden yellow, like fall leaves. Raked into a pile, golden leaves were a hedgehog's sanctuary. A sanctuary was a safe place. Miss Sally taught him that.

Green. Spindly branches of Miss Sally's willow tree in the summertime, hanging to the grass like a big green Snuffleupagus. Tyler showed him how to hide inside.

And repeat. Red, dark blue, yellow, and green. Thread enough to make a bracelet.

"Think of someone special you'd like to give these to," Teacher said, leaning over Hen as he pushed on another red bead.

Hen could give it to Miss Sally. Or Mom.

"Giving gifts is a way to tell someone you care about them." Teacher seemed to read Hen's thoughts.

"Tyler," Hen whispered.

"Your brother?" Murphy made a face.

Hen nodded. His insides warmed as he wrapped the wire wide enough for Tyler's wrist, folding over extra pipe cleaner just in case.

AFTER SCHOOL, the house was empty and silent. Ty felt cold all over. Hen was still at Miss Sally's. His mom hadn't yet collected him after her shift. Ty could go over there now and see about getting that report or whatever Derek wanted. Or he could stick to the plan and wait for Derek to get him later that night. Might as well wait. Confrontation was never something Ty sought out. Besides, this was Derek's thing.

You're such a coward.

The voice from the closet sounded the same as always. Biting and ugly—an older man's, gruff from years of smoking. Ty stood in the foyer, his jacket still on, staring at the closet door. And, because no one was home to hear, he argued back.

"No, I'm not. This is not my deal. I don't even care about the stupid report."

Stupid, freaking coward.

Ty trembled from his fingertips to his eyelids. "Me? Why isn't Derek the coward? He's scared to go by himself. He needs me. He *needs* me."

He banged on the closet door.

Laughter followed from inside. An eerie, hollow laughter that gave Ty goose bumps.

He covered his ears and stomped into the kitchen. He opened the fridge on reflex and, like a switch, the laughing stopped. He stared at the yogurt cups, egg carton, and sparse produce and realized how famished he was. Yogurt wouldn't cut it. In the freezer, he found some microwave burritos.

As it rotated through its two-minute warming, the microwave light shone on Ty's face and chest. A sign or something. Or a test, maybe. He didn't move a muscle. Stayed as still as stone. He held his breath for as long as he could. They were scanning him. Looking for weapons. Or toxins. Who knows what? Heat swirled in his chest and traveled out to his shoulders, elbows, wrists, fingertips. As if he were in the oven too.

Ding!

Light clicked off. Ty blinked at the thing. Cursed under his breath.

A quick glance at the closet to reassure himself. He spoke aloud. "It's not real. It's. Not. Real."

Smells of taco seasoning made his stomach growl. He was too eager. The first bite burned the entirety of his mouth.

He hated waiting. He stared at the thing, wishing for freeze power. Damn, he was starving. Two-burrito-hungry. He fetched another from the freezer and zapped it, being careful to stay clear of the wide beam of light this time.

AFTER SCHOOL, Miss Sally played music that had the twang of

acoustic guitar. Hen built a Lincoln Log tower as Miss Sally tapped her foot on the ottoman. He smiled at her polka-dot socks. She looked so small in her big wool sweater and plaid chair. With closed eyes, she told him, "It's country music, if you're wondering."

Unlike Tyler's music, Hen understood the words in the song. Funny how music made him feel things. Tyler's music made him uneasy. Miss Sally's music made his chest feel full. Maybe a little sad.

It was dark by the time Mom came. Miss Sally still reclined in her chair. Mom hugged Hen, but her eyes met Sally's. "It's getting to be too much, isn't it? Maybe I can find daycare."

Hen's ears perked. *Daycare?*

Miss Sally to the rescue. "Nonsense. He likes it here. And I like the company. So, there you have it."

Hen packed his backpack.

Miss Sally sighed. "Bernie came by. Said he was supposed to fix a window frame at your place?"

"Oh, that was today? Shoot." Mom rubbed her forehead. "The door. I forgot to have Tyler leave it open."

"Gave him an excuse to visit his ol' ma. But speakin' of Tyler." Sally did the grownup whisper thing. "That boy...and the company he keeps."

Mom whispered too. "Sally, I know. It's hard. Without a father, you can imagine. He's seventeen and thinks he knows everything. Didn't we all at that age?"

"Did we? I don't recall."

Mom looked out to the willow tree in the backyard. "The truth is, I don't know what to do. I can't forbid him from hanging out with his best friend, can I?"

Sally smoothed her cheek, her paper-thin skin wrinkling under her hand, saying nothing.

Mom went on. "I mean, Derek's been coming to our house since they were Hen's age. Before that even. He's practically family. The poor kid has no mother. And with that sorry excuse for a father. What am I supposed to do, send him out into the street?"

"Derek Hogg is trouble. Tyler will find trouble with him, mark my words." Sally scratched the fabric of her chair. The room filled with the sound.

Hen had that same icky feeling from this morning when Tyler got in Derek's truck. It had been Tyler-and-Derek since before Hen was born. Best friends. Inseparable. Derek had always teased Hen, but lately the tone was mean. He cursed all the time. Never in a funny way like Tyler did. He smoked cigarettes. Got Tyler smoking, too. Still, he hoped Miss Sally was wrong.

Mom lowered her voice. "Please Sally. You know there's nothing more important to me than my boys. I want nothing more than to keep them safe. What can I do? Coat them in bubble wrap? Tyler's nearly an adult. I have to trust him. He will know—" Her voice hitched like she might cry. "You're right. I'm out of my league."

Hen stared into his backpack, his face heating up. Grownups could do anything. Why did Mom sound so hopeless? Tyler was one of the good guys. Hen couldn't wait to give him the beaded bracelet he made.

Wait—the bracelet!

A panicky feeling came over him. "Where are my pipe-cleaner beads?"

Mom blinked at him. "Your what?"

Miss Sally heaved herself from her chair. "They made a craft at school. Henry made a clever pattern. Let me see if I can find it."

"Oh, please don't get up. We really should go. Tyler should be—"

"Mom. My beads!"

"We can find it later. It's not going anywhere. It will be safe with Miss Sally."

"But—"

"Henry Atticus Trout."

Oh, the full name thing. He frowned and shoved his sneakers on.

But what was in his shoe? The beaded bracelet!

"Mom, look!" He held his beads high, but Mom didn't see. Her face was cinched as she listened to Miss Sally's low whispers. He shoved the bracelet in his pocket. He'd show her later, maybe.

She answered without looking. "Okay, coming. Let's go the back way." Her eyes matched her voice and reminded him of Miss Sally's music—worry hidden in a pretty song.

As he and Mom made their way across the lawn to their house next door, Hen heard the news click on from Miss Sally's living room. The light flashed through the bay window onto the willow tree in the backyard.

Hen's little brown house had only a light on in the kitchen, making the bright orange paint glow. Inside, it smelled like a Mexican restaurant and microwave burrito wrappers littered the table. Hen wrinkled his nose. Miss Sally's house was always clean and smelled like a stick of Juicyfruit. Then it clicked. Burrito wrappers meant—

"Tyler's home!"

Hen ran upstairs to find Tyler on his bed, still wearing his sneakers. Muffled rock music called from Tyler's clamshell headphones as if far away.

Hen knocked on one of the domes, and Tyler's eyes shot open. Red, like he was angry or needed sleep. They softened, seeing Hen. He slid off his headphones.

"Hey, little dude." His voice was scratchy.

Hen pulled the beaded bracelet from his pocket and gave it to his brother.

"What's this? Did you make this in school?"

"Yup. We did patterns. You wear it on your wrist."

"Patterns, huh? That's one stellar pattern."

"Do you like it? It's for you."

"Love it." Tyler put it on his wrist, using all the extra pipe cleaner to make it fit. "Thanks, little dude. What else did you do today?" Tyler chummed Hen's chin.

"I'm learning how to play chess. Miss Sally's teaching me. I'm pretty good at it."

"Oh yeah? Maybe you could teach your thick-headed brother how to play."

"Don't say that. You're not thick-headed."

Tyler rumpled his brother's hair, and Hen felt all that ickyness fade away about what Sally had said. Tyler wasn't headed for trouble. He was home.

Mom called from downstairs. "Hen! Dinner!"

Hen tried to mirror Tyler's uh-oh face and dashed out.

AFTER HEN WENT DOWNSTAIRS, Ty put his headphones back on. Drowning everything else out, Ty let Nirvana's *Smells Like Teen Spirit* take him. The song seeped into the room like a foul odor while Hen did that super nice thing, giving Ty a present. Hen was so...good. How could Hen be his brother? Half brother, but still. Shutting his eyes, shutting it all out, Ty was in the song, part of the lyrics screeching from Cobain's lips. Nothing could get him as long as music played. He botched the lyrics but sang anyway.

Am aloto, am alpino, a mesquite-oh, my limp-it-oh—hey

He peeked through his lashes. He checked his watch, but it was Hen's beads. Red, blue, yellow, green. Simple, pure. Ty chuckled. That kid. So different from him. Even as a boy, Ty was never like Hen. He'd always been scared of everything.

When he was Hen's age, he'd had his first episode. He'd been doing a puzzle in front of the TV. Bugs Bunny was on. Ty liked its bright colors and rounded shapes. Bugs's orange carrot matched their kitchen. "That's all folks!"

Commercial. A guy selling cars. He held a big sign and pointed to the camera, claiming he had "unbeatable" prices.

For Ty, it wasn't just a TV commercial. The car guy could see Ty. Actually see him. He didn't rant about car prices, he yelled at Ty. Scolding him.

"You! You! You!"

The car guy's finger jabbed his shoulder, hot and sharp. Ty had sat, paralyzed, wishing Marcella would save him. She was his mom. Didn't she know what was happening to him? He wanted to scream, but his mouth stuck shut. His insides had frozen. Petrified with fear.

Everything had stopped but his heart, which thrummed painfully in his chest.

Marcella appeared in the doorway, drying her hands with a dishtowel. "What's wrong, honey?"

His lips creaked open. But, nothing. Not even a breath. The commercial went on, the finger jabbing, the yelling, "You! You! You!"

Mom's voice was sugary sweet. "It's nothing, Tyler. A car commercial, that's all." Ages passed before she turned off the TV. He trembled in Marcella's arms. Her soft voice near his ear, cooing. Her hair tickled his face. He raked his nails down his cheek, his gaze pinned on the blank TV screen. Why did Ty still feel the car guy's finger? Still hear his voice loud and clear?

"You! You! You!"

That was the first. Far from the last.

Hen didn't have any of that. So completely different. Like, older already. Secure. Hopeful. Trying to make things better. For Ty. Knowing stuff he couldn't possibly know yet, but sensing it.

Did he know that Ty was different? Ty had always worked to protect him from it. When and if he could determine dream from reality. No doubt it would scare him. Sweet, sensitive Hen.

Yet so naïve. Heartbreakingly so.

These beads. As if they could make everything okay. It pissed him off, kind of. That scary thing inside him was too big. Or, a big swarm, maybe. Lots of little things buzzing, surging, changing all the time. Coming from everywhere. These beads could do nothing against the demons in his mind.

If only they were magic. Maybe if they could make everything disappear. That's all he wanted, to stop being haunted. To quiet the voices.

At least right now it was Kurt Cobain.

Am aloto, am alpino, a mesquite-oh, my limp-it-oh—hey

He ran his finger over the beads. Bump, bump over the plastic humps. Again. Again... The pad of his finger went numb. He squeezed one hard, trying to crack it. Yellow between blue and green.

He once read an article about meditation beads. Each bead was a breath. Each bead, an echo of a mantra. Freedom. Peace. Nothing-ness. A silent prayer. Countdown to stillness. Maybe he could give that a try.

Red, breathe. Blue, breathe. Yellow—

Am aloto, am alpino, a mesquite-oh, my limp-it-oh—hey

Forget meditation. He air boxed in front of the mirror, Rocky Balboa-style, Hen's beads flashing. Red, blue, yellow, green. He imagined Roxanne Russo watching. She wouldn't be able to resist. He'd hold back, of course. She'd have to beg for it.

After the song ended, his heart was pumping good. When he threw down the headphones, silence filled his ears. Time to go. He put on fresh jeans and his go-to drug rug.

As soon as he pulled it over his head, he heard the growling. Really loud. An animal growled right outside the window. Ty checked, leaning over his bed. Nothing there but the willow tree, its waiflike leaves mostly fallen, leaving a dripping, caramel skeleton.

I've got you now.

The voice was right in his ear, as if through his headphones. He wasn't wearing them, though. Blood roared in his brain. His mouth filled with saliva like he might puke. He rifled through his drawer to find a roach. The beads looked funny and strange on his wrist as he smoked it. Like the two didn't go together.

He inhaled down to the end, burning his lips, his lungs stinging.

He squirted some cologne and headed downstairs.

In a flash, Marcella killed his buzz. "Where do you think you're going?"

Dumb question. "Out."

"With?"

Another dumb question. "Derek."

"No, sir."

That was funny. Always funny when Marcella tried to be stern. He looked over at Hen and winked. Hen didn't smile this time. What was his deal? He frowned at his mac-n-cheese.

Marcella grabbed Ty's chin. "What's this? Your eyes are completely bloodshot." She half-whispered, "Tyler, are you high?"

Dumb question number three. His mother might be the queen of dumb questions. Ty couldn't help it. He laughed right in her face. The buzz that made him do it, really. Her puppy eyes looked so insecure and pathetic. Irritation tugged and he felt the good vibes slipping away.

"Chill, Mom. It's cool."

Her voice wavered. "It's certainly not cool, Tyler. And you're not going anywhere. You're staying home."

Meep-meep.

Ty pivoted away from her.

"No, no, no." Marcella followed him.

Geesh, she was annoying tonight.

"Please, Tyler. Don't go out tonight. Stay home. We'll do something fun. I'll pop some popcorn."

Popcorn? Was she for real?

Ty laughed even harder when she tried to grasp his sleeve. As if she could physically hold him back.

"Please, Tyler."

He was out the door without another word.

"Yo, yo, yo!" Ty thumped into the passenger seat. "Got another joint? My mom killed my high."

Derek's lips curled around his cigarette. "I don't wan-cha all daffed out tonight, Ty. You're helping me get that thing later, remember?"

"Dude, I won't be."

"Whatever, let's eat first."

MOM STAYED in the dark quiet watching Derek's truck pull away—her tall, dancer figure shadowed by the porch light. Hen heard her sniffling.

Hen wanted her to come back. Finish her dinner. Scrape the dirty dishes. But she headed straight upstairs to Hen and Tyler's room. Why would she go up there? The kitchen felt too quiet without her.

And too dark. Hen turned on every light he could reach. Better. The orange paint was cheery. Kind of. He pulled out his *101 Facts about Nocturnal Animals* book, flipped the dog-eared pages to the hedgehog section.

Knock-knock-knock.

Hen jumped. Someone was at the door?

Hen expected Mom to skip down and answer the door.

Nothing.

It got really quiet. Maybe he'd been hearing things?

The hedgehog picture was so cute. Hen's giggle echoed in the empty kitchen.

"When first handling your pet hedgehog, wear gloves. If hedgehogs are scared or nervous, they roll into a ball and their sharp spines could stick you. After your hedgehog gets comfortable with you, you won't have to wear gloves anymore."

Hen beamed at the adorable ball of spikes. Those black beady eyes seemed to say, "I love you too."

Knock-knock-knock.

It wasn't his imagination. He looked to the stairs. Still, no Mom.

"Ma-hm! Someone's here!"

Mom's rush of footsteps was a soft drumroll. She gently opened the door.

"Hi, Bernie. Sorry about this afternoon. I keep forgetting. It's absurd. I don't know why you put up with it."

"That's all right." Bernie Hubbard's face was a huge smile.

"You have enough property to manage without worrying about mine."

"I don't mind helping out. Really, it's no problem."

An awkward pause followed. Cool air swept through the open door. Bernie kept smiling even as he shivered. Mom studied her fingers, and then straightened alert.

"You weren't thinking of fixing it now, were you? Oh, geez. Where are my manners? Please, come in."

Bernie shuffled inside, rubbing the back of his neck. "I was just at Ma's. She mentioned, well..." He looked at Hen, his smile fading.

Mom crossed her arms. "What was that? What did she tell you?"

Hen missed what Bernie said next. He whispered it into Marcella's loose, dark hair. Hen's stomach went bubbly, like it did when he saw high-schoolers kissing on the bus.

Mom reared back as if she'd been struck. Her words were quick. "Well, you can rest assured I have the situation under control. You and your mother needn't worry." Then, softer, "Thanks for your concern."

"No offense, Marcella. And I don't mean to pry. But do you have an idea where the boys are right now?"

Hen had turned on too many lights. It was too bright.

"Movies. I think."

Hen perked up. "Movies? Can I go?"

Mom gave him a pained look. "Oh, Hen."

Was she going to cry?

Bernie went to stroke her hair, but patted her back instead. His arm seemed charged with electricity.

Mom murmured into his shoulder. "I didn't know what I was looking for, but I didn't find anything in his room."

So that's what she was doing in their room. What was she trying to find? Secret treasure? Maybe Hen could find it. He snuck across the living room to the stairs, a slight thrill quickening his pulse. The creaky bottom step gave him away, though. Always did.

Mom seemed to have forgotten he was there. "Oh, Hen. It's bedtime."

And then it was like Bernie wasn't there. She hugged Hen's shoulders. "First, a bath. Then, some warm jammies."

Hen couldn't help but whine. Baths were for babies. He trudged upstairs, a great sulk tugging his face.

TY AND DEREK took the booth closest to the kitchen at Leon's. Derek liked to keep an eye on things, he said. As if he owned the place already. Ty cradled the napkin holder and made faces in the chrome.

"What's it like with Roxanne Russo?"

"What's it like with Geraldine Greenbladt?"

"Screw you."

Derek exhaled through a crooked smile, put out his smoke.

"Seriously. What's she like? Yanno, in bed."

"Come on. It was a one night deal."

"It's been more than one time, D."

Derek blushed. "Forget it, Ty. We're not an item."

"Lights on or off?"

"On."

"That figures." Ty's stomach was a pit. He wanted to protect her honor, but truth be told, he would've left the lights on too.

After they ordered, Derek changed the subject. "Okay, about tonight. Let's go over this. It's you against Sally Hubbard. Should be a no-brainer."

Ty nodded rhythmically, hardly listening. He caught bits—report, paperwork, investigation—but he kept eyeing the back room. Was Leon there? Was it locked?

The car dealer, Gary Walsh, unwittingly set him up. He roared in like a wrecking ball, and Leon joined him in a booth, comparing notes on last night's Giants game. Leon was good and distracted. Perfect.

Their Reubens came, and Ty's senses filled with the tang of warm corned beef and sauerkraut. Derek dug in like he hadn't eaten all day. So he was distracted too. Double perfect.

"Gotta hit the can," Ty said.

The back room door wasn't fully closed, and Ty saw the desk lamp on. He could feel its warmth from the hallway. His fingertips went numb. How much longer could he poach these little packets?

He needed his own source, even though he worked here. He had to sneak behind his best friend's back, like a thief, to get drugs that Derek and his pop freaking sold. He'd eventually have to buy from some dude who bought from Derek. With a huge markup. What a joke. Not tonight, though.

Luck was with him. He found a white packet in the first drawer he opened. Weird. Obvious-weird. Like someone left it there for him. Ty wasted no time. He hurried out just before Leon came down the hall. Close call.

He slid into the booth where Derek chewed a fry cigar-style, eyeing him strangely.

"What?" Ty hoped he wasn't going red. His hands shook when he picked up his sandwich.

"You aw'right?"

Ty squirmed under Derek's sideways stare.

"I'm good." After a few bites—it was worth the wait—Ty realized he really did have to pee, which was inconvenient as hell. He'd have to wait or Derek would know all.

Derek started in again about the plan. Ty half-listened, not caring about whatever they had to get from Miss Sally. Or why Derek was so freaked out about it. He finished his Reuben and wiped Thousand Island from his fingers. Damn, those were tasty.

Derek went on. "I mean, 'parently she's got more money than God. Wouldn't know by the way she lives."

That snapped Ty to attention. "What? Miss Sally's got money?"

"Yah. Loads."

Ty giggled. Derek narrowed his eyes. "You say your ma killed your buzz, but it looks like you're still flyin'."

Ty swallowed his laugh. "You're kidding about Miss Sally, right? About her being loaded?"

"Serious as a heart attack."

"No freakin' way."

"Way."

They both laughed now.

"So, you ready? You're gonna do this for me, right?"

Ty's turn to smile, his thoughts consumed by dollar signs. "Let's go."

TY FELT weird when Derek parked in front of Miss Sally's house, even though they were all neighbors. Even weirder how different his street looked from this vantage point. They were, what, twenty paces from his own house but the whole dang street looked foreign. The car door creaked open.

"Aren't you coming?" Ty asked when Derek didn't open the driver's side.

Derek rolled his eyes. "What the hell, Ty? Have you heard anything I said? No. You're going in now, alone. Just get her to hand over the investigation report. Got it?"

"Yah, yah. Right. Okay. So you're staying here? In the truck?"

Derek banged on the steering wheel. "Are you thick? Weren't you listening at the diner? That woman hates me. You're a different story."

"I dunno about that—"

Big, grunting sigh. "Well, she likes your family. Your mom. Hen. You're part of that family. Do you know what you're gonna say?"

"Yah, yah. I got it. Okay. See ya."

With each step up her porch, Ty aged backwards. Step, moody teenager. Step, cranky middle-grader. Step, scared, insecure boy. At her front door, Ty felt no older than Hen—a Boy Scout selling over-priced popcorn.

She answered right away, as if she'd been watching from her window.

"Hi there, Tyler. Are you alone?" She eyed the truck.

"Yah, yah."

"Oh?"

It was an obvious lie. Derek should've parked at his own house. Ty could've walked over. Some plan. Why did he have to sit in his truck in front of her house?

Heat crawl up Ty's face. He wanted to scrap the whole mission. Miss Sally's house smelled like a giant vat of potpourri.

"Can I get you anything? I have Ginger Ale."

"Um, water? If you have some."

"I happen to have some water. Comes right from the faucet. Have a seat."

While she fetched his water, Ty noticed Hen's school picture—

wallet size—in a little pewter frame on the sideboard. He liked that picture of Hen, even if he wasn't smiling. Kind of candid. Like they didn't tell him before they snapped it. And his hair was messy. His cowlick curling up like a ram's horn. Ty felt a pang of sadness. He tipped the frame down so he couldn't see his little brother's face.

The water glass Miss Sally gave him trembled in his hands and the water rippled. He downed the whole thing without taking a breath.

"My, my. You were thirsty. Is there anything else I could get you? A lollipop, maybe?"

"Lollipop?"

"Isn't that a side effect? Doesn't it make you want to suck on something?"

"What?" For some reason, his thoughts went to Roxanne Russo.

"A side effect of—what's it called? Ecstasy, I think. Aren't kids doing ecstasy these days?"

Ty felt a little sick. "No, ma'am. I've never done ecstasy."

"Oh, I see."

Miss Sally perched daintily on the arm of her plaid chair. On the mantle, the tick-tock of her old fashioned clock grew louder in the quiet room. Ty wondered if it chimed every fifteen minutes. If it was one of those kinds of clocks. After what seemed like hours, nothing happened. He was prepared to hear them, the voices, but they were quiet. Maybe waiting. Maybe the clock ticking was some sort of test.

To his astonishment, the ticking relaxed him. Or maybe it was the colors in the room, or the way Miss Sally decorated her house. The odor of potpourri in the air. He could see why Hen liked it there so much. It was calm. Quiet. Sleepy. Safe. He'd never been inside her house long enough to notice.

A lamp sat on the end table near Miss Sally's plaid chair. A ceramic lamp. Ty had seen a similar lamp on a show recently. The same exact one. It had a hiding spot. A secret compartment for money or drugs or whatever. Very cool. Sneaky. Who'd look in a stupid lamp? Hey, maybe that's where she stashed her cash? He breathed in deeply through his nose, and could almost smell it.

Aha. That was the test. They were quiet so he could focus on the lamp. The hiding spot. They had sent him on a mission. For the lamp. And what was inside it. Through Derek. He was, like, their spokesperson this time. Why else would Derek have Ty come in here all by himself for some stupid piece of paper? The lamp was at arm's length. How easy it would be to reach out and—

As good as dead. A different voice. Not the older man with the smoking voice. This one sounded like a radio announcer. Ty glanced at the dark screen of the sleeping TV.

"Did you hear that?" he asked Miss Sally, his voice faltering.

"Hear what?"

Ty forced a swallow. Told himself it wasn't real. "Nothing."

He concentrated on breathing. And the voice didn't come back. The room filled with the ticking again.

"To what do I owe this surprise visit, then?" Miss Sally's voice was not unkind.

Ty stole a look at Derek's truck. Rubbed his jeans. He couldn't leave without trying. He forced the words, eyeing the lamp now. "Miss Sally, I actually need something from you. It's really important."

"What is it, Tyler?" Miss Sally was either amused or concerned. Ty couldn't tell which.

"Yah, so. You did an investigation on Leon's Diner?"

Miss Sally held his gaze.

"I need the report."

Now she laughed. "Silly boy. Did Derek put you up to this? Is that why he's waiting in the truck?"

"No, really. I just need it. Come on."

"*Come on?* That's your persuasive argument? That's your big line?"

Ty's mouth fell open. A desperate thirst hit him all over again.

"Tyler, you listen to me." She leaned on splayed knees, looking more like a basketball coach than a little old lady. "That boy is no good. You've got to get in with a nice group of friends. You become who you hang with, you know. Their aura rubs off on you. Choose wisely, Tyler. Surround yourself with quality people in this world, you hear me?"

He didn't understand at all. "Yes, ma'am."

They sat in silence for some time. When Miss Sally left to refill his water glass, Ty was stuck. Couldn't move. Couldn't go to check out the secret compartment in the lamp.

He stared at the TV, willing it to speak again. As usual, when they saw him looking, they were quiet. If Ty had access to his emotions, he would let himself cry. Right there in Miss Sally's living room near the picture of Hen in the little pewter frame. It was all so hopeless and sad.

Nothing. He had nothing. He was empty.

His suffering smoldered inside. Everything swirled. On the outside, he kept up the normal act. He mixed in with the potpourri. Like taking on its vibe.

Damn, he was thirsty.

"Here. Drink, and then you're on your way."

Water never tasted so good. It seemed she saved a little bit of his life right then. He didn't have a chance to thank her.

She pointed to the bay window. "You tell that hooligan waiting in that truck to forget about it. He's not getting that report."

Ty didn't care about the stupid report anyway. Still, he waited until they pulled away before telling Derek. Miss Sally watched from the front door, Ty could feel it.

Derek sighed, but didn't seem surprised. "On to plan B."

"What's plan B again?"

"Late night break in. Find it ourselves. She's left us no choice."

Ty nodded, and his head went numb. He reached inside his pocket and wrapped his hand around the little packet of white stuff.

January 1992

Running errands after school was no fun. Why did Mom always drag Hen around in the car on their free afternoons? He'd be in the backseat for hours. It would be dark by the time they got home. All he wanted was to play outside. He wanted to forget Christmas and everything about it, his Lego barn and all. Hen hadn't seen Tyler since Christmas day. He hadn't spoken to him since telling him *I hate you* over a week ago.

After Tyler left, they had a huge snowstorm, like the sky was mad at him too. But Hen loved the snow. He built a huge igloo. And it still stood, frozen solid in its dome-like shape. His winter play tent. He liked to escape there, especially on sunny days. The sunshine shone through the icy igloo walls and it felt like he was inside a giant crystal. There, he imagined none of the bad stuff happened. He pretended that he'd never gone to Miss Sally's after school. He pretended he didn't have a brother.

Out the window, they passed snowcapped trees. They looked like they were wrapped in cotton. Hen wished he were one of them. Just for the day.

"Hen, sweetie. I was hoping we could stop in and see Tyler."

Hen's stomach swooped, hearing his brother's name. He kept watching the trees.

"Hen? What do you think?"

Hen didn't answer.

"He's still your brother, you know. Don't you want to see him?"

No. Hen was still pretending.

"Hen, it's okay that you two had a fight. It's okay to be mad with Tyler. That happens between brothers. But you still love him, right?"

Still love him.

Hen imagined love was like Play Dough. He could keep it warm in his hand and mush it around, change its shape. It would get under his fingernails and into the grooves of his thumbprint. Once, Hen ate some. It tasted okay. Sometimes, tiny specs fell onto the kitchen floor and dried into hard pebbles. Mom would sweep them up and throw them away.

Was love like that? Could it change like that?

Heat gathered under Hen's knit hat. The snowcapped trees now seemed too tall. Maybe he didn't want to be a tree after all.

Mom parked by the bank. She turned to Hen. "Do you want to talk about why you're upset with Tyler?"

Hen shook his head.

Mom sighed. "You know, forgiveness is an important part of being a family. In some ways, it doesn't matter why you're upset with Tyler. What's important is that you find it in your heart to forgive him, because you love him no matter what."

Hen tried to forget about the dried Play Dough pebbles.

Next to the bank was a gray house and attached office. He knew that house. Gears spun in his mind.

Mom pressed. "You love Tyler no matter what, right? Just like I love you no matter what."

"Okay." The gray house. He had to knock on the door.

Worry fell from her brow. "All right. I have to make a quick deposit. It'll only take a minute. Will you come in with me?"

"Can I wait here?"

Mom gave a tired smile. "Sure, sweetie."

After she went through the glass doors, Hen ran through the snow mounds to the old gray house that held the sign: Hon. Carl Bowman

He could hear Murphy's voice now: *A judge is the mack-daddy of it all.*

To his surprise, the judge himself answered the door. He had soft starbursts around his light brown eyes, like Bernie did. He smelled like pinecones and warm apple cider. Hen grinned widely. He wore normal clothes, a sweater and slacks. Hen would love to see him in his judge robe someday.

"Oh, Henry Trout! You must be here to pick up your mom's pie plate. Come on in." He never seemed in a hurry.

Pie plate? Hen shrugged.

He sat on the small beige couch. In less than a minute, Mom's ceramic pie plate was in his hands. He rotated it like a steering wheel.

The judge gave an awkward grin. "That'll be all, I think? Is your mom out in the car? Don't want to keep her waiting now."

As if on cue, the door flew open and Mom appeared, her cheeks wind-kissed and her eyes tearing from the cold.

"Oh my, Henry Atticus Trout. You gave me such a scare! Why did you leave the car?" And to the judge. "I'm so sorry, Carl."

"That's perfectly all right. I figured he came by for your pie plate. It was quite delicious, by the way. Like always."

"Oh, good. And thank you. For everything." She studied her shoes. "Letting Tyler come home for Christmas, I mean."

"Well. I'm glad it all worked out," the judge said softly. He must've known Tyler needed forgiveness too.

Marcella ground her heel into the rug. "Carl, I…if there's anything you can think of. To help Tyler, I mean. Anything I can do?"

Judge Bowman's starbursts disappeared. He gave Marcella a sad look.

Mom's smile looked more like a frown. She adjusted her purse strap. "Well, we better get going. I'm sure Mr. Bowman is busy. Come on, Hen."

"Wait, I have to show the judge something." Hen turned to Judge Bowman, who always listened as if what Hen said was important.

"Oh, Hen. Mr. Bowman doesn't have time—"

Hen held up his treasure: a beaded pipe-cleaner bracelet. The one Hen had made for Tyler for Christmas. The one Tyler had thrown across the room.

"What's this?" The judge's wide grin was back.

Marcella gave a nervous laugh. "Mr. Bowman doesn't have time to look at your crafts from school, sweetie. He's got lots of grownup work to do."

She reached for the beads. Hen wanted the judge to take it. "Tyler didn't want it."

His grin faded. "I don't understand."

"I wanted to give it to Tyler. But he didn't want it. He never put it on." Truth. He'd worn those first beads that awful night. But these? Tyler had thrown this very bracelet across the room when Hen tried to give it to him at Christmas. *These* beads never touched Tyler's wrist.

"Okay? I'm not sure why you wanted to show me this."

"He wasn't wearing it. He never wore it. Not that night or ever." Truth.

The judge sat on the beige couch. "I see."

Mom started to speak, but the judge stopped her with his hand.

"This is about the charge against your brother. You want to help prove his innocence." The judge smiled, and his starbursts came back.

Hen wished he'd taken off his knit hat. Was the judge asking him a question? He was trying to find forgiveness. The judge could find it too.

"I'm sorry, Carl," Mom whispered.

"That's quite all right." He tapped his knees and towered over Hen. It was like he'd grown taller since Hen first came in. "Tell you what, Mr. Henry. If you'd like to submit this as a piece of evidence, it belongs in the hands of Tyler's attorney. Do you know Mr. Gerrity?"

"But you're the judge." Hen almost said, *you're the mack-daddy of it all*, but got shy.

"I know it's confusing." The judge rubbed his chin, noodling it out. "You know what? Why don't I hold onto it then? Would that make you feel better?"

Hen held tightly to the bracelet. "What are you going to do with it?"

He didn't mean to make a joke, but the judge's laughter boomed. He put up a wait-a-minute finger and stepped into the other room.

While he was out of earshot, Mom hunched down. "Hen, listen. I know this is all very strange. I know you want to help your brother. But—"

"I'm not confused."

"That bracelet—"

"I'm telling the truth."

Marcella's words came fast. "There's no reason to bring the bracelet out in the open like that. If no one has asked about it, you don't need to bring it to the judge's attention. I'm not sure what you're trying to do."

Hen paused. Just a few minutes ago, in the car, she'd told him: *You have to find it in your heart to forgive him.* He imagined going into his heart and searching its chambers. A big, red maze. Forgiveness was a happy, yellow triangle of cheese like you see in cartoons. If it were there, he'd find it. He was good at mazes.

"I'm finding the cheese," he said.

"The what?" Mom's forehead wrinkled.

"Forgiveness."

Mom's face smoothed into a small smile.

Judge Bowman came back, holding up a plastic sandwich baggie. "Here we are. We'll put it in here for safekeeping. I'll call Mr. Gerrity and make sure he gets it before the trial. Then it will be official."

"Official?" Hen shot off the couch, clapping his hands together. He dropped the beaded bracelet into the plastic baggie.

"How's that, then? It's now an official piece of evidence." Judge Bowman's tone was more *Sesame Street* than *Law & Order*, though. He pressed the seal closed, and pressed his lips in a *Sesame Street* smile.

Hen nodded, but a tinge of uncertainty kept him from smiling back.

GERRITY WOULDN'T SIT DOWN. It made Ty antsy, too.

The room was too small to pace. Gerrity took two steps left, two steps right. Like he was the one going through withdrawals, with this fidgety lawyer dance. He also had this habit of cracking his neck. Ty noticed it on their first meeting. His neck spun nearly all the way around like an owl. Wary, Ty wondered if this was all a ruse. If they sent him to deliver messages in code. He listened carefully for clues.

"It's time to start talking. It's time you stop protecting your best friend," Gerrity said, slathering on invisible aftershave.

A laugh escaped. Ty glanced furtively at the UFO gadget in the corner.

Gerrity did his owl-neck thing. "Not funny, Tyler. You are being charged as an adult with a very serious crime. The DA and Clapp, they assume it's a done deal. They have their evidence against you, however flimsy it may be, and, in their minds, that's it. You could be locked up for the next twenty or thirty years if we don't plea bargain our way out of this. You need to start telling me the truth. Now. None of this cool-guy silent treatment. Don't you know I'm the only chance you've got?"

"I tole you—"

"You told me that you were high that night. You don't remember anything beyond smoking a joint in Derek's truck. Tyler, you and I both know that's a bunch of crap." Gerrity leaned across the table, his neck tendons flexing. His voice got low. "Listen, I'm your lawyer. It's my job to turn this around for you. Just because I'll know the truth doesn't mean the rest of the world will, do you get me?"

Ty shifted in his chair. His mind was murky. His memory of that night mixed with the girl huddled by the roadside, who wasn't actually real, turns out. What else that night wasn't real? He couldn't think of Miss Sally without all kinds of noise getting in the way. And now the UFO camera tested his last ounce of sanity. The gadget seemed to be asleep, oddly. The red light winked out. Just an empty box now.

Gerrity rifled through his briefcase. He tossed something down on the table—a Ziploc bag full of color.

"What...?" Before he got the question out, Ty recognized the beaded bracelet. A surge of panic got his heart racing. He clammed up. Averted his eyes.

"You know what this is?"

Ty barely nodded.

Gerrity used an odd voice. "I get this call from Judge Bowman, the town justice, the other day. Apparently, your little brother delivered this to his home office hoping to save you." Gerrity's laugh was almost sad. "What's the deal with this beaded thing, Tyler? Can I really use this kid-trinket as a piece of evidence?"

Ty glared. Why the hell would he ask Ty? He was the freaking lawyer.

"What's the story with the beads, Tyler?"

Memories of Christmas morning made Ty burn with shame, while a surge of love for his baby brother filled his chest. He glanced up at the UFO camera. Still sleeping. Maybe it was okay to talk. "It's a bracelet. Hen made it for me."

"Apparently, Henry told Bowman you never wore it."

Ty stared at the thing in the Ziploc. Such a silly thing. Hen had been so proud. Regret stung. Ty loved Hen more than he could handle sometimes.

"No, I didn't." *I threw it across the room. And Hen told me he hated me. I ruined Christmas for everyone.* Ty couldn't speak the words. But he could still hear Hen's anguished voice: *I hate you!*

Hen had never said anything like that before, ever. A sick feeling rose in Ty's throat, remembering.

Gerrity took a long breath and mumbled something like "worth a shot." Ty soured and tucked into himself as Gerrity rifled through his briefcase again.

An envelope appeared on the table next to the Ziploc.

"You know what this is? It's an eviction notice. Addressed to Mr. Hogg, from Mrs. Hubbard. She was trying to evict him. Imagine that? Leon's Diner has been a landmark in this town for thirty-five years. She was taking it down. And she could've, too, if she had good enough reason. She was his landlord, you know."

The letter faced Ty, but he couldn't focus on the words. He couldn't read. It seemed like another language.

Gerrity kept talking anyway. "If this eviction threat is connected to the incident that night, this letter could be submitted as a piece of evidence. Evidence that would incriminate the Hoggs and potentially help get you a decent plea bargain."

His lawyer's fast talking made Ty's head fuzzy. "What do you mean?"

Big sigh. "Did the Hoggs know this was coming? Did Derek know Leon was about to get evicted? Maybe he had a plan. Sent you two over there?"

A plan. Derek's plan.

Gerrity's voice seemed to echo. "If we can establish a motive for them, the evidence against you is weaker. Do you see what I'm saying? It would give reason to believe the Hoggs wanted Miss Sally out of the picture, so to speak."

Out of the picture.

Ty held his breath, studied his hands. He traced the callous from raking the backyard before Clapp picked him up. Marcella had wanted him to clear the leaves. The last chore he'd been assigned, and he couldn't even finish it. He'd gone off to get locked up in county jail with only half the yard raked. Tears built, which surprised him, shocked his senses alert.

Gerrity stared him down. "Tyler, did this letter have anything to do with you paying a visit to Mrs. Hubbard's that night? Did Leon send you over there?"

Ty picked at his hangnails, pulling off little rice-shaped pieces.

These hands. Slender, boy hands. They never played an instrument or wrote a decent term paper. They couldn't even get the freaking yard raked.

"Yah. Leon sent us over there."

Gerrity grinned, his eyes slitting like a cat's. "That's my boy. Tell me everything. Tell me the whole truth."

The tears somehow stayed inside, swarming with memories of what happened that night, now somehow clear as crystal.

"It was Cabbage Night."

"What's Cabbage Night?"

"You know, the night before Halloween."

"Ah, the prankster night."

Ty snickered. "Worse than April Fool's."

February 1992

Derek felt weird knocking on the Trout's door, his home away from home. Would he be welcome if Ty wasn't there? He silently cursed his nicotine craving and shifted in his basketball shoes, which were, he realized, unsuitable for the current cold, snowy weather. It seemed fitting, though. The clouds told his story. Gray, gloomy, rolling into a storm.

Marcella answered, still wearing her diner uniform, her long stockinged legs punctuated by the fluffiest slippers he'd ever seen.

"Derek?" She searched past him warily before letting him in.

With the door shut, Derek felt a wave of warmth. His cheeks and fingertips tingled with it. Chunks of snow fell off his basketball shoes and melted onto Marcella's area rug. As she slid his flimsy jacket off his shoulders, he began to weep.

She didn't ask any questions, giving Derek another reason to love her. Her fluffy white slippers swished as she led him to the couch. It seemed like just yesterday he and Ty had babysat Hen and watched

Rugrats. The tears came steadily now, remembering. It was not a proud day.

As if Marcella could see into his memory, she called to the kitchen, "Hen, why don't you work on your coloring in your room? We can have dinner in a little bit."

Through the tempered glass of his tears, Derek saw Hen at the kitchen entryway, watching them with eyes bigger than his head. His small figure unmoving. Prominent, though. Wielding power that Derek had never possessed here.

Derek wanted to hide. He sniffed hard and sunk into the couch. Let it swallow him up.

"Go ahead, Hen." Marcella's voice was firm now.

It took ages for Hen to go. His tiny feet moved soundlessly across the room—too close to where they sat—and started up the stairs. Just a few steps before turning back to stare at Derek.

Marcella couldn't see Hen looking at him. Studying him. Derek felt a chill blanket his now-dry eyes. Every muscle in his body tensed. Anger dampened his sadness. How could he hate a little boy so much? He was just a boy. It made him angrier, knowing he couldn't help but hate the kid. What kind of thug was he?

Only when he heard Hen's bedroom door slam shut did he relax somewhat.

Marcella waited, her arm slung across the back of the couch. Not a hug, exactly. But close. He smelled her flowery lotion. He sunk deeper into the cushions, hoping to find her embrace. She took back her arm, hugging herself.

He spoke through a throng of frogs in his throat. "They came for Pop. Clapp's gone, too. Can't help us anymore. He musta got spooked. Got a transfer to Plattsburgh or someplace."

Her mouth opened but she didn't speak.

Derek wiped away fresh tears. "I'll be next. They're comin' for me. Probably at my house now."

"Are you sure?" Marcella glanced out the window. Her eyes had filled, and Derek saw love there.

"None of this shoulda happened," he heard himself say. "I dunno why it got so fu—I mean, messed up."

She touched his knee, and warmth traveled through the rest of his body. If he closed his eyes, he could've slept. Right there on the couch.

"I'm scared," he whispered.

"I know," she said, her voice pure song. The next thing he knew, his face was nestled in her bosom. He thought about all the crude things Pop had said about Marcella's breasts over the years. Maybe it should've been arousing—like it was with Roxanne Russo—but it wasn't like that at all. It was soft and safe. He rested his head there, letting tears slip out. *Mom*, he said silently, his lips grazing the coarse fabric of her uniform.

She eased him upright. "Derek, look at me."

Her eyes were wide with hope and love and goodness. He poured himself into them.

"Derek, I have to ask you something."

"Anything."

"What about Tyler? What does this mean for Tyler?"

What? What about *Tyler*?

It was like being hit. It took a moment for Derek to register it. He slowly came back to himself. Realization struck in waves—a set of marbles knocking down his vertebrae. He was wrong. Her tears weren't for him at all. They were for Ty. Or Hen. Or Sally Hubbard. Or, heck, maybe even Bernie now. Never for him. His love was a one-way street. She didn't love him. He wasn't another son to her. He was the kid next door, Ty's best friend, and Hen's worst enemy. And he was headed for prison. She didn't care. It didn't matter to her life. He was an extra in that movie. Inconsequential.

He shouldn't have come here. Straightening, the wet soles of his basketball shoes squished against Marcella's oak floor. He shot off the couch, hurried into his jacket.

"Sorry, Mrs. Trout. I should go."

"Wait." She reached for him. An embrace? No. She meant to stop him from leaving. "Please, tell me what happened. With your dad. With you. And what it means."

"I dunno. I'm not a lawyer."

"I know. I know. But if Leon is arrested and they arrest you too, that must mean something for Tyler's case, right? There's hope yet." She caught herself then, and her eyes softened as if she'd just now started to see him.

Her voice kept creeping up in pitch, like a tone-deaf piano. "Oh, Derek. I know this must be hard for you. I know you must be scared. Please, I'm trying to...I mean, maybe you could help each other. I don't know. I'm not a lawyer either." She started crying—a desperate, shaky cry that distorted her lovely face.

"Please," she choked out, wiping her nose. Tears streamed, streaking mascara to her chin.

That familiar, heavy tangle settled in his chest. How pathetic she looked, hunched over in her uniform and ridiculous slippers. How he hated her for not loving him.

He threw his arms up. "What do you want me to do?"

She glared at him, tears stopped in her eyes. "Tell the truth!" she yelled back, a pearl of spit shooting from her mouth.

He felt the power shift. In a moment, he was fortified. He felt himself fill with it, heating his limbs, lifting him up. If Hen were still in the room, it would've done nothing against what built inside him. His basketball shoes squeaked as he stepped toward her, his face mere inches from hers.

"The truth will crucify him."

Marcella recoiled as if he'd delivered a blow. She stared, her mouth agape.

The rest played out like a movie scene, but Derek held his power.

Blue lights rotated outside, blinking into Marcella's bay window in a telltale rhythm. Marcella babbled on about Ty. How he'd never do such a thing. *Blah, blah, blah.* It was noise. None of it mattered. He felt himself pulling away from Marcella, the closest thing he'd had to a mother. Something clicked. He knew who she really was—a broken woman who lived in denial. She loved the wrong people, suffering valiantly, hurting those who loved her most.

He was done. He understood his place in the world. And Marcella Trout had nothing to do with it.

He zipped his jacket and opened the front door to the blue lights. When he turned back, Hen was balled up on the bottom step, hugging the wooden spindle.

"Sorry about your floor."

The blast of cold felt good. Shocked his senses. Blue light washed over him as he filled Marcella's doorway. Stepping out, his basketball shoes crunched in the hard snow. Hands to the sky, he met the officer's gaze across the driveway. Clapp's replacement was taller, thinner than his associate. Looked younger, too. Just out of the academy. That would be his luck, getting arrested by a freaking kid.

One step. Two. It would be a hundred to the cruiser.

Something tugged on his jeans.

"Is it true? Did Tyler do it?" Hen's voice. He'd run outside in his footy pajamas.

Marcella called, "Hen! Come back inside, sweetie!"

Derek kept his hands where the officer could see them. "Go back inside, Chicken."

"I need to know for sure. What's the truth?"

One look at Hen's eyes and it was clear he already knew.

"Hen, come back here this minute!" Marcella's voice was worn down.

Derek swallowed. A sick feeling coated his stomach. "Truth doesn't matter, Chicken."

Hen ran in front of him, between Derek and the cop car. A tiny silhouette against the blue lights, he stretched out his arms. His little voice rang out. "Yes, it does! It matters. It's the only thing that matters!"

Derek: "Go home, Chicken."

Officer: "Get in the car, son."

Marcella: "Hen, come back inside!"

Hen advanced. Derek saw his face clearly now. Tears swam in his huge eyes. His voice was a whisper. "Tyler did it, didn't he? He hurt Miss Sally. He didn't mean to, but it was him. Wasn't it?"

Derek stepped around the boy. That tangle in his chest soaked in pity. As he made his way steadfast to the cruiser, Hen kept whining behind him, "Was it him? Was it him?"

He sounded so desperate and pitiful. Any other day, it would've annoyed Derek. Today, it depressed him.

Keep walking. One foot in front of the other. Almost to the cruiser.

Hen's voice faded, muffled with tears. "Was it Tyler? Did he do it?"

Derek didn't look back. Zoned in on the blues. Hen wouldn't hear, but he said it anyway. "I'm sorry, Hen. For everything."

Trial of Tyler Trout

The courtroom reminded Marcella of what she'd seen on *The People's Court*, with wooden church-like pews and burgundy curtains giving a false sense of warmth in the too-bright room.

Though Gerrity mapped out the process weeks ago, it seemed unfair that the prosecution presented their case first. What happened to innocent until proven guilty? The way the prosecutor, Peter Docker—or *Dock*, as Gerrity called him—disparaged her son, it all seemed a lost cause. Marcella could hardly stand to listen to it, and consciously tuned out the heinous accusations that couldn't possibly be true.

And that was just his opening statement.

When he called his first witness, Officer Robert Clapp, Marcella thought she might vomit. Was this the kind of twisted game law enforcers played in the name of justice? Couldn't they see this whole thing was rigged?

She refused to acknowledge the smarmy officer on the stand, and instead took an acute interest in her fingernails. She pretended to be elsewhere, biding her time at a bus stop or airport terminal. Anything but give credence to this loser in a uniform.

Until two words piqued her interest: *beaded bracelet*. She listened eagerly, then, fear encompassed her every nerve.

"It was found in Sally Hubbard's home the day after the incident," Clapp said. "Bernie Hubbard was there with me and explained how she babysat the boy next door. We figured it belonged to him."

"And from what I understand, you took it away at that time? Away from the crime scene?"

Clapp's well-rehearsed line held no apology. "Typically nothing leaves a crime scene, but considering this was such a kid-specific object, it was automatically classified as non-evidence. Obviously, this was an incorrect classification. But as they say, hindsight is 20-20."

Marcella's head hurt trying to make sense of what Clapp just said. Did that mean the bracelet was important or not?

Dock didn't ask that question. "What did you do with the bracelet?"

"Actually, Bernie gave it back to the boy."

"Anything unusual about that interaction?"

Gerrity: "Objection. Hearsay. Officer Clapp wasn't present for that interaction."

Dock: "On the contrary. My witness accompanied Bernie Hubbard next door to the home of the boy in question and absolutely *was* present for the interaction."

Judge: "Overruled."

Clapp puffed his chest. "Yes, so, when Bernie gave the bracelet back to the boy, he didn't take it back right away. It was like the boy was scared to take it, or he knew something."

Gerrity: "Objection. Witness had no way of knowing emotions or thoughts of this boy."

Judge: "Sustained."

Dock: "Officer, is the boy in question related to anyone in this courtroom?"

"Yes, sir. His mother is sitting in the gallery."

A thousand pairs of eyes stared at her. Heat crawled up her back.

Clapp gestured to Tyler. "And his brother is the defendant."

Dock made a face to the jury. "Did you say his *brother* is the *defendant?*"

Marcella rolled her eyes at his superfluous inflection.

"Yes, sir."

Dock's voice boomed through the courtroom. "Your honor. I'd like to submit this piece of evidence as People's exhibit A."

He waved a plastic bag in front of the jury before handing it to the judge. Marcella easily saw it held Hen's beaded bracelet craft. Tears started, seeing it in this context—an extension of her baby boy. She fought an urge to run up and collect it for him. It didn't belong here. Still, Hen's little voice rang in her mind and sent a chill through her. *The beaded bracelet. He was wearing it that night.*

"Objection!" Gerrity leapt out of his chair, waving his own plastic baggie in the air. Marcella nearly tipped out of her seat trying to make it out. She blinked a few times, as it seemed to be déjà vu. What the—?

Gerrity spoke fast. "Your honor, I also have a beaded bracelet I was planning to submit as evidence. I think you'll find it is identical to the one Mr. Docker is trying to submit."

The courtroom buzzed with commotion until the judge pounded his gavel and requested a sidebar.

Aside the bench, the two lawyers remained stoic as the judge examined the contents of the two plastic baggies. Marcella gripped the seat back in front of her, wishing for the ability to read lips. But maybe it didn't matter. Dock's neck reddened and his expression soured, while Gerrity's grin was absolute. As the dueling attorneys made their way back to their respective tables, the judge made an announcement.

"Because two identical beaded bracelets are presented and since the original bracelet at the crime scene has been compromised, there's no way to know which, if any, were actually at the crime scene. Therefore, both items are excluded from evidence."

Excluded from evidence. For once, the legalese was perfectly clear. Marcella nearly collapsed with relief.

By the time Mr. Docker had finished presenting his case and rested, Marcella felt wrung out. The judge called a recess.

Gerrity led her to a sitting room to rest. "You need to get your energy back. Next is our turn and I need you. You're going on the stand, remember?"

How could she forget?

It was Gerrity's idea to throw her on the stand. A risk, he'd said, since it would give Dock the chance to cross-examine. She'd seen his tactics play out. Dock-head Dick-head was the master of turning things around. Her nerves were already frayed. She wasn't sure she'd survive a cross-examination.

"I'll be fine," she lied. "I just need to lie down for a few minutes."

She reclined on such a scratchy couch, she was sure she wouldn't sleep. But then...

When Marcella came to, the first thing she saw was Bernie's face, a heap of worry on his features.

"It's okay," he kept saying, his voice soft.

"Bernie?"

"There she is." Bernie's smile was back. His warm palm covered her hairline and it dawned on her he'd been stroking her hair. That was a first. And, a balm. She closed her eyes, comforted by the weight of his hand. She could stay like this for hours. Maybe get some more sleep.

"Where am I?" she whispered.

"Gerrity sent me back here to get you. But here I find sleeping beauty. I wouldn't dare wake you."

It all rushed back. All those awful things the prosecutor said about her son. She tried to sit up. "Oh, no. I have to—"

"No, no. Stay right where you are. They can wait." He eased her head back onto the pillow. He handed her a glass of water. "Here, drink."

The water was lukewarm—the way Hen liked to drink it. *Oh, my*

Hen. Another jolt of panic. If Bernie was here with her in Elizabethtown, that meant—

"Wait. Where's Hen?"

"At Murphy's. It's all arranged with Murphy's parents. They're feeding him dinner, too."

Gratitude filled her. Hen was safe.

Couldn't say the same about Tyler. Shame crept into her heart. How much could that boy take?

"How is Tyler? Do you know?"

Bernie moved to the end of the couch, near her feet. "I haven't seen him. Haven't heard anything. They're going to put him on the stand tomorrow, though. That, I do know."

A headache spiked. She massaged her temples, trying to clear her mind. No use trying to come up with a plan. No use trying to solve for this. Tyler's situation had taken on a life of its own. Completely out of her control.

A sigh escaped. Hopelessness was pervasive. The room seemed too quiet all of a sudden.

"I failed my telecourse," she blurted.

Bernie's eyebrows lifted. "What's that? Telecourse?"

"I signed up for a marketing course. Did you know that? But then when all this happened, I dropped it like a hot potato." Marcella laughed lightly and palmed her forehead. "I thought I could work toward a degree in business. How foolish of me."

Bernie straightened. "Now, don't you start with all that. I won't have it. I don't know anything about any telecourse. But I know you. And you are a good person. One of the best."

"Oh, Bernie, you don't have to say that."

"I'm not just sayin' it to say it. I mean it. And I want you to be nice to yourself now. You hear me? You be kind to Marcella."

"Be kind to myself?" She leaned back on the pillows. "I can try."

"Please do."

She blinked Bernie into focus. He sat with her stockinged feet in his hands. As he gazed out a window, natural light fell over his face and shadowed his profile. Handsome, in his way. Plain, yet smart.

Thoughtful. This was a man of integrity. The way he wore his heart on his sleeve. The selfless way he helped her with everything.

You be kind to Marcella.

He turned toward her. Like she was caught in a windstorm, it struck her so acutely. He loved her.

He *loved* her.

Something released in Marcella's chest. A surge of adrenaline warmed her from inside out. She could breathe freely for the first time all day. She felt like singing. Or running. Or flying.

Or laughing.

"What's so funny?" Bernie half-grinned.

Why did she laugh? Marcella silently scolded herself. But while a part of her world was falling apart with Tyler trapped in that courtroom, she felt another part of her world open up. How could she have never seen it before?

Bernie was here. Had been here all along.

She sat up. "Bernie."

"No, lie down. Take it easy, you—"

"No, Bernie. Come here." She reached for him.

"What is it?" He tensed as she pulled him close. Confusion wrinkled his brow, but yearning shone in his eyes.

She looped her arms around his neck. Like she'd done it a million times before. "Kiss me."

He took in a sharp breath but didn't move. His skin smelled like metal and oil and earth. He was warm. She breathed him in and closed her eyes. She pressed her lips to his. Like she'd done it a million times before. Now it was her turn to stay still. Waiting.

Until he kissed her back.

MARCELLA HELD on to that sweet calm with Bernie as long as she could. Until Gerrity, impatient now, came to collect her. Was she really going on the stand? At once she felt utterly incompetent. What good would she do? But Gerrity was hard-pressed for character witnesses. Someone who could vouch for Tyler's "quality of character." Too bad Hen didn't count.

Although they'd rehearsed at Gerrity's office, nothing prepared her for the real deal. All that careful prep floated away.

As she walked the aisle, feeling incongruently bride-like, she felt at any moment someone would call her bluff and send her away. Surely, they wouldn't let her go up there and make a fool of herself and her son, both. But alas, she made it to the stand somehow.

In the leather-cushioned hot seat, she swore her oath with a hand on the Holy Bible to tell the truth, nothing but the truth, so help her God.

So help me, God. If I only knew the truth.

It was like she was on another planet. Was this really what mothers were expected to do? Was this on the list of responsibilities?

Tyler sat unmoving at the defendant's table. She studied him from her perch. Now that she could see his face, she tried to recall better times. Tried to capture that tenderness she'd once felt for him. When he was a baby, perhaps? Did she really want to resurrect those memories? What a whirlwind. Hurled into motherhood at twenty-two, she survived what she thought was the brunt of it years ago. The bone-tired exhaustion when he was a newborn, the heart-stopping fear when he gashed his forehead stepping in front of a swing set, and later, the blatant rejection when puberty hit.

Nothing prepared her for this.

What the hell was this? Sitting in an oversized casket, as men in suits circled like hungry sharks, peppering her with questions about her son who was accused of murder. Her son. Murder. The idea made her insides curdle. It felt like some sort of sick joke.

At least Gerrity was on her side. After the formalities were done, like stating her name and relationship to the defendant, Gerrity set the stage for the jury to imagine a "broken household." Which ticked her off a little. But Gerrity insisted it was part of the strategy.

Gerrity's questions were softballs, which she answered mindlessly, unable to tear her eyes from Tyler. He should have been terrified. Yet...was he?

Tyler leaned his elbows on the table, slouching like he was at a boring lecture at school and not on trial for a criminal offense inside a courtroom. He didn't seem to get it. He appeared to be waiting this out, his mind on the next thing. And what might that be? What the heck went on inside his head?

He wore that strange expression she'd seen too often in recent months. His eyes darted to the security cameras near the ceiling, with a knowing expression. Like he saw something that wasn't there. It was maddening. Didn't he know she was trying to help him, to save him? The least he could do was look at her.

The second wave of questions set up the fact of the drug operation in the back room of Leon's Diner. Those were harder to answer. White lies sound different inside a courtroom. Thankfully, Gerrity saved the tough questions for Tripp when it was his time to go on the stand.

No time to prepare for cross-examination. The transition between the two lawyers was swift. Dock stood as Gerrity sat, a well-practiced routine. Marcella fought an urge to flee. She braced herself as if Dock planned to physically strike her. He paced before her and the judge, his face drawn and serious.

Wow, she was beat.

Had to hand it to Gerrity, though, he was thorough. He fidgeted in the seat next to Tyler, who still hadn't met her eyes. She decided to pretend he wasn't in the room at all, considering the vein of questioning.

Dock's voice was as cocky as before. "So, we've established that Tyler's father is estranged. And Tyler's half-brother is about ten years younger. Correct?"

"Right."

"That's quite a wide gap. How do the half-brothers get along?"

"Oh, we don't say half-brothers. Just brothers. Tyler's a good big brother."

The memory of this past Christmas gurgled up like acid reflux. When Tyler threw Hen's gift away and Hen screamed *I hate you!* She pushed it back down.

How about a happier moment? She forced a smile. "Last summer, Tyler took Hen to the lake to hang a bat box Hen made at school. It was a production, to say the least. Hen's always had a concern for wild animals. Tyler respects that. He took the bat box thing seriously. Hen idolizes him."

"Could you tell us about Tyler's childhood?"

As if it were a closed chapter. Wasn't he still a child? "I don't know. I guess he was, you know, a regular boy. Lots of energy. Maybe a little hyper after dessert."

"Tantrums?"

"He threw the occasional temper tantrum. What child doesn't?"

"I'm not sure. We're talking about your son, who seemed to have quite a lot of physical altercations at a very young—"

Gerrity: "Objection."

Judge: "Sustained."

Dock: "Did Tyler fight with his peers?"

A loose hem thread found Marcella's fingers. "Some. The normal playground spats."

"Tyler's former principal said he often found himself in trouble at school."

Marcella willed her trembling lips into a smile. "Boys play games."

"Games of picking fights?"

The thread broke between her fingers. "I don't know what else to say. He was never a malicious child."

Dock looked at a paper on his desk. "Didn't he vandalize school property in the sixth grade? A broken window?"

Was Dock trying to corner her? A stupid laugh fluttered out. "Vandalism? Oh, no. That was an accident. He was a boy. You know, rough and tumble. He and Derek liked to catch frogs and tackle each other in the backyard. They stayed in the woods for hours. Came home covered in mud. Once they did karate in my kitchen and dented my oven door. I wouldn't call that vandalism."

"You use the expression 'rough and tumble.' Isn't that the same as saying he's violent?"

Gerrity: "Objection."

"I withdraw the question." Dock had the nerve to grin at her.

Hot flash. Did she give the wrong impression after five minutes on the stand?

Her words scrambled out. "Boys do that sort of thing. Wrestle around and pretend to be ninjas. Gosh, they imagine pinecones as guns and play cops and robbers. This is boy stuff. It doesn't mean they're violent."

"Did you ever witness rough play between Tyler and his younger brother, Henry?"

"Oh, absolutely not. Tyler would never hurt Henry."

The Christmas fight involved hurt feelings, not sticks and stones, Marcella told herself.

"Would you say it was difficult raising Tyler with an absentee father?"

As if Tripp were marked absent from school. So easy to categorize. Bitterness filled her. "Yes. But I managed."

"It must've been hard for Tyler as well."

It wasn't a question. Gerrity had told her not to speak unless a question was asked. But her defenses flared. "I think we did just fine. I work very hard to give my boys what they need. To keep them safe..." That last word stung.

"But a boy needs his father." Dock looked pained.

What a haughty acting job. She glanced at the jury. Couldn't they see through this?

No way. Tripp would not be made a martyr. Not on her dime. She didn't hide her irritation. "Not that father. Honestly."

"He grew up without a father. That's bound to affect a young boy. Perhaps change him."

Every muscle tensed. "I'm a good mother. I love my boys more than anything in the world. I'm not perfect. I've tried—I, I try to do—no, I do the best I can. The best I know how. I'm a good mother."

Why was it hard to say? Doubt pressed down on her. Part of her knew she was nothing but a hack, band-aiding her children's needs only when they became too obvious to ignore. Ripped shoes, overgrown fingernails, *Mom, I'm hungry,* holes in the socks, late permission slips. She'd never been ahead of the game. Many days, that's what it felt like. A game with no instructions. A game she was destined to lose. No one taught her what to do. Was she supposed to magically figure it out? She should've learned how to be a better mom. Where was the telecourse for that? She loved them so much it ached. But long ago, she realized love was not enough.

Bernie's voice cut through her ugly thoughts: *Be kind to Marcella.* It seemed impossible right now.

Dock waited a few beats. Marcella's words—*I'm a good mother*—hung in the air like a body odor. "May I remind you, Mrs. Trout, that you are not on trial here?"

"Yes, I know that." She swallowed hard, sealed her lips.

Ages passed before Dock spoke again. Marcella burned in her chair. He deposited a manila folder at the judge's bench. "I submit this as evidence—records from the school nurse at Tyler's school. These records indicate he suffered from severe anxiety."

"What teenager isn't stressed about school?" Marcella blurted.

"More than one report indicated he claimed to see or hear things that weren't there. Interacted with them."

Marcella's tongue swelled dry. She sought out Tyler. *Look at me.* It was no use. He was elsewhere. What was going on in his mind?

"Mrs. Trout, have you seen evidence of such behavior at home?"

Darkness pierced Marcella's heart. Her hands shook too much to take her water glass. How to answer such a question? "Not really. I mean, sometimes a commercial on TV would scare him. But, that's nothing."

"Oh? Like a trailer for a horror film? That kind of commercial?"

"Um, no. It was a car commercial. That was a long time ago." Her voice trailed off. Why did she bring this up? It had nothing to do with—

"A car commercial." Dock over-enunciated.

Marcella flushed. That was only the first hint that her son was different. His fear of that stupid car commercial was real, though.

Over the years, a handful of other odd things would set him off.

The phase when the telephone ringing made him cry. At school, he didn't make many friends. He had a hard time understanding coincidences, saying there was a higher power at work that made him and Artie Foy buy the same exact windbreaker. Then, on long drives, he'd insist the radio stay on scan and tally something on his fingers. Like he was patching together snippets of radio programs into something that made sense. Those were quirks. Right? Surely every child had them. Besides, this kind of behavior stopped after Hen was born. Didn't it?

She hit rewind in her memory bank. Since Hen was born, she kept coming up blank when it came to Tyler. Hen filled most the space there. Seven years ago, Tyler was eleven—nearly old enough to take care of himself. Hen had needed her more.

The difference between the two brothers was obvious from the start. One look into their eyes told her everything. Hen's were vibrant and eager, while Ty's had dulled and...gone empty. Growing pains. Hormones. Teenager stuff. He just needed some space.

"Mrs. Trout?"

"Yes? Sorry." Had he asked another question?

"Have you ever seen evidence of Tyler's visions? Paranoia?"

Gerrity: "Objection."

Judge: "Sustained."

"Strike that last word from the record." Dock's sneer was hateful.

Visions? Paranoia? What was he now—a witch doctor?

Anger flamed up her chest. "Tyler is a normal teenage boy. Lately he keeps to himself. That's what kids do these days. When he was little, he may have been—I don't know—nervous. Scared sometimes. Night terrors and the like. This is all completely normal. But visions? Paranoia? You're describing a different kid."

"Who might that be?"

"Excuse me?"

"The different kid."

Marcella bristled. "I don't know. I'm not an expert on children."

"No, you're not."

Her jaw dropped. Did he just? No, he didn't! That was a direct insult. She clamped her mouth shut, simmering.

A long, excruciating pause. Dock glanced at his legal pad. When he approached Marcella's casket again, his expression hardened. Marcella's ears clogged. Defense mechanism.

"When did you become aware Tyler was abusing drugs?"

What? Her mouth fell open again. Tyler? Abusing drugs?

Gerrity: "Objection."

Judge: "Sustained."

Dock: "If you would allow, Judge, this question will not be objectionable once I call my psychiatric witness."

"Then you'll have to wait until after that evidence has been submitted. Please strike that last question from the record."

But it didn't matter. She'd already heard it. Silence fell down around her. Abusing drugs. No way. Impossible to get her mind around. Tyler... taking drugs? Like pot? Booze? What kind of drugs could he mean?

Her mind raced. Could it be true? Was that why he'd been such a jerky kid lately? It hit her with a sick sort of relief. But abusing drugs? That didn't compute. It was too disturbing, the logistics too foreign. Drugs? Tyler? Which? How? When?

Too many questions spun. She was at a loss for words.

At his table, Tyler's cheeks pinked up like they used to when he'd play in the snow too long. She dug a fingernail into the pad of her thumb.

"Let me ask you a different question. When did you become aware that your former husband abused drugs?" Before she had a chance to answer, Dock placed a stack of paper on the judge's bench. "I submit this as evidence—a record from Ark Renewal in Springdale, Arkansas. Tripp Trout was treated for drug addiction in 1986. And again at the same facility in 1990."

Well, there it was. The blame fell on Tripp, then. Marcella took her first full breath all day. Ha! No one would question his role in this crisis. He should probably have been on trial himself.

Dock went on. "It's clear from this report that Tripp's drug habits were not new. He'd been abusing for several years. So, I'll ask it differently. During your marriage, when did you become aware that your husband was abusing drugs?"

And back to her. What a sucky volley. They wanted to pin this on her? "It's not my fault he took drugs. I had nothing to do—"

"That's not the question, Mrs. Trout."

She recoiled. His tone was like venom. She shook it off and tried to think. Again, she hit rewind in her memory bank. An image of Tripp came to: a red, unseeing glaze to his eyes, a possessed-like laugh that gave her a full-body chill. Had he been high? Well, sure. It seemed obvious now.

But how the hell was she supposed to know? She was no doctor. She knew nothing about getting high. She'd never tried anything. Not even cigarettes. It was no secret that Tripp did whatever he wanted, whenever he wanted. Trying to control that sonuvabitch was like trying to tame a hyena.

"I didn't know anything."

"You didn't know Tripp Trout was abusing drugs during your marriage?"

"That's right."

"Were you aware that he worked with Leon in selling drugs when he lived in Severance?"

She traced her throat with her fingertips, glanced toward the jury. Would that make her an accomplice or something? "No. I was never aware that Tripp sold drugs. Not at all."

"You knew the drug operation was going on. But you didn't know Tripp had any part in it?"

"Right." The word weighed a thousand pounds.

Dock didn't believe her. Who knew what the stone-faced jurors thought?

Heat erupted from every pore. Marcella prayed her face didn't show it.

Dock changed tack. "What was your relationship with Derek Hogg?"

She blinked away thoughts of Tripp. A tear settled in the corner of her eye. "He was Tyler's best friend. Since they were little."

"Yes, I'm aware of that. I'm asking about *your* relationship with him."

She blotted the tear with her thumb. "He was at our house a lot. Shared our pantry. That boy had an appetite. He was kind of folded into our family, I guess you could say."

"So, you were like a mother to him?"

"I wouldn't say that—"

"That's how he described you."

"He did?" Marcella's throat went dry. Derek thought of her like a mother?

An image of Derek clomping in his big sneakers, his backwards baseball hat framing that wide face that still held a hint of baby fat. That face she'd wiped chocolate and dirt from industriously, like a daycare provider. And then it seemed to happen overnight. He grew into a massive man who towered over her, so much like his father.

And yet.

The way he turned on his manners whenever she was around, almost bashfully. He'd defended her at the diner on Tripp's first night here. And then, at the time of his arrest—a time she'd been praying for—he'd come to her. Nuzzled against her, sobbing into her uniform, needing a mom. Needing to be loved. Needing her.

She had to ask Dock to repeat his last question.

"To your knowledge, did either Tyler or Derek have any conflict with Sally Hubbard?"

She cleared her throat. Grief for Sally was still fresh. "They were loud sometimes. She didn't like that."

"She didn't like the noise?"

"She...thought they were headed for trouble."

"How do you mean? What kind of trouble?"

How could he ask such a question, knowing what he knows? "She was worried about Tyler. She thought Derek was a bad influence."

"Drugs?"

"I don't think she knew anything about that, assuming it's true." She hoped Sally hadn't kept it from her. "But she didn't exactly say."

"What was your opinion of Derek in that regard? Did you agree with Mrs. Hubbard?"

"Did I agree?"

"Did you think Derek was a bad influence?"

Marcella wiped lint from her skirt. Derek thought of her like a mother. She couldn't shake the idea.

Derek's trial would be later. And Leon's. She would be called for a witness for those, too. She would testify about the back room, the illegal drug operation Leon had going there—white lie after white lie. Bernie would be called to testify about the documents found in Sally's house. The rent, the eviction notice, the investigation report. Leon's guilty verdict and harsh sentencing would bring a sigh of sweet revenge for Marcella.

But Derek. That situation just messed with her head. Derek would most likely be found guilty of possession of an illegal controlled substance with the intent to distribute, money laundering, and drug trafficking—fancy lawyer words for the things he'd done to ruin the lives of others.

Not murder, though. Not even involuntary manslaughter. According to Gerrity, Derek would probably be sentenced to eight to ten years in state prison and fined ten to fifteen thousand dollars. Months from today, Marcella would read about his fate in the *Schroon Daily*. She could already feel a rotten mix of fear and grief and betrayal and anger—a tangle of emotions that clogged her throat. Derek Hogg—a real and true criminal. Put away like human garbage.

She'd opened her home to him. She'd trusted him with her eldest son. Tyler had spent more of his young life with Derek than anyone else. Why hadn't she seen Derek for the toxic person he was? How many times had Sally told her? What had she been waiting for? A siren? Police to intervene? Right there in her living room, on the very couch where Derek had cried on her shoulder. It was like the blue lights still flashed, snow clotted off his shoes, his hot tobacco-laced breath hissing: *The truth will crucify him.* How close had she been to danger?

All of this was Derek's fault. That was clear as day.

Dock sounded impatient now. "You still haven't answered the question. Do you believe Derek Hogg was a bad influence?"

"Yes. He was. I think that's been established." In her peripheral, Tyler squirmed in his chair.

"How so?"

"If it weren't for Derek, Tyler obviously would never have experimented with drugs to begin with."

"Mrs. Trout, you do realize that Derek's drug screening came back clean. He's sworn under oath he's never taken a single drug in his life beyond marijuana, tobacco, and alcohol. Several people have corroborated his testimony."

Marcella's voice shook. "What do you mean? This is all his fault. He sold drugs. He gave them to Tyler."

Dock stared hard at Marcella, drawing out his words for emphasis. "Theft is among Tyler's charges. Derek didn't provide them to Tyler."

"But—"

"Tyler stole them."

"Objection!" Gerrity's voice jarred Marcella. She shot him daggers. About time.

WORDS. Ty hated them.

His mother's words on the stand had made his chest ache. Gerrity constantly used words he didn't understand. The worst was the judge.

It was a new day. But it felt the same as yesterday. Gerrity and Ty sat together at a wooden table, waiting for the judge to arrive.

Gerrity's words always came fastest. "I have some news to tell you. I've been trying to get your father here to put him on the stand. I was having a hard time getting a straight answer from anyone, but it seems that—"

He stopped himself, like he just thought of something. His gentle tone was almost nurturing. "Tyler, were you aware that your father suffered from psychosis?"

"Psychosis?"

"Yes. More specifically, paranoid schizophrenia."

Schizophrenia. What a word. It kept pinging around, his ears echo chambers. Schizophrenia. Gerrity pronounced it with a long E. Schizophrenia. Made it sound worse.

Ty chewed on his lip. "That means crazy, right? Like, serial killers and rapists kind of crazy. Homeless bums. Not my dad. He was a musician. He had tons of friends. He charmed the pants off everybody he met."

"It manifests differently person to person. But the commonalities are fear, paranoia, sometimes hallucinations. I have some information on it." Gerrity put a stack of papers on the table. "Is that a surprise to you? He was very sick. For years."

Ty couldn't respond. A strange, itchy fuzziness possessed him. What Gerrity described wasn't Dad.

It was *him*.

"This diagnosis will help you."

Fear crept in. Why? *Because I'm crazy too?* His thoughts were too fragile to be spoken. "How?"

"We have our own psychiatric expert witness. Based on your medical history and your father's, the case for genetic predisposition will be clear, the mental instability as well. I think that will be enough. It has to be. And, if it comes to that, we can plead insanity defense. I've already notified the DA. Expert evaluations are underway. Of course, this would imply an admission of guilt..."

His words fell like rubber erasers in this courtroom that held so much tacit garbage. The words bounced off the table and fell to the floor.

"You think I'm crazy."

Gerrity almost rolled his eyes. "Tyler, schizophrenia is a serious mental illness. It will help us get a good deal for you. You may not have to sit inside a cell at all."

"You think I'm crazy."

"I think you have a genetic predisposition for mental illness, specifically schizophrenia. I'm going to bring in my psychiatric—"

"I want to see him."

"Who? The shrink? You will. That's part of the process."

"No, my dad. I want to see my dad."

Gerrity blew out a big breath. His tone was strange. "I'm sorry to say that that's just not possible."

"Why not? He came here before. He can come again."

"I'm afraid he can't."

"Why not?"

"Tyler, I hate to be the one to tell you this..." His words kept cutting out, like they had a bad connection. Static on the radio. Filling Ty's ears. Words were elusive to him. Ty only caught a few. Enough to understand the gist.

Your father. Drug overdose.

Your father. Won't be able to testify.

Your father. I'm sorry.

"He's not coming?" He was supposed to save the day. That's what fathers do.

"Tyler, I'm sorry. But your father's drug overdose was fatal."

"What?" Air rushed near his ears like he was on an amusement park ride.

"Your father didn't survive. I'm so sorry."

"He's dead?" Ty's vision blurred.

Gerrity talked and talked. More words. Ty's ears were full.

His mouth filled with saliva. His stomach erupted into his throat. "My father's dead."

They had finally come. All those weeks in that little room with the UFO camera watching. They'd seen enough. Now it was time. Judgment day. The aliens had descended.

Worse yet, Gerrity kept at it. He hardened his gaze on Ty. Flipped the switch to business. "Let this be a lesson to you. Those drugs that make you feel good? They are especially dangerous for you because you may have this condition. It is a dire situation. You do not want to become a statistic. We're going to work to get you help. Therapy. Rehab. I don't want you to worry."

"My father's dead." He decided he hated Gerrity. His fist pounded the table with a muted thump. His face twisted in pain.

Gerrity hardly noticed. "So now, when I call you to the stand, make it about emotions. Cry like a baby. Convince the jury you were a goner from the start. That as soon as you emerged from the birth canal seventeen years ago, you were destined for addiction."

The pudgy, red-faced judge entered the courtroom. Everyone was supposed to stand.

Ty couldn't stand. He wanted to shove his fist through the table. Throw his chair against a wall. Angry tears pricked. The room stretched into a narrow hallway, its walls closing in. He was being sucked down into the tunnel. An airless vacuum. He coughed, holding his throat. Tears slid from his eyes—the eyes he got from his father—and tumbled down his feverish face.

Though Marcella would've preferred to have Bernie beside her on the day Tyler took the stand, knowing he was caring for Hen comforted her. Besides, she'd been sitting for over an hour and nothing had happened yet.

She craned her entire body toward Gerrity's table. She studied the back of Tyler's downturned head. It kinked to the side, shy-like. Near his collar, she saw fine blond hair on his neck.

He needed a haircut.

The fury. They didn't have the decency to give him a haircut before the trial? There he sat, alone. Up at that stupid table with his hair overgrown. With all the evidence pointed against him. And now, his deadbeat father had broken his heart once again and wouldn't be there to testify in his favor. And she couldn't even go to him.

Gerrity folded his hands apologetically before the judge's stand. His soft-spoken words rippled through the courtroom like lake-effect snow.

"Oh, I see," the judge said.

Wait. What did he say? Although she'd heard it plainly enough. She still couldn't believe it. It was the last thing she expected to hear out of Gerrity's mouth.

Found in motel bathroom. Autopsy results pending.

Tripp was dead?

Apparent drug overdose. Possible suicide. Investigation underway.

Oh, my god. Tripp was dead.

Her breath got chunky. The room spun.

Gerrity glanced back at Marcella, genuine apology in his eyes.

Why look at me? Tyler sat there all alone. Her oldest son had just learned his father dropped dead. And she was stuck in a pew, wrapped in polyester, silenced by courtroom etiquette.

She gripped the bench in front of her until her fingers went numb. She searched the courtroom for a sign—any sign—that would tell her son's fate. What would happen now that Tripp, the bastard, was dead? This had to lead to a recess, right? They couldn't keep up this charade of justice. The defendant's father freaking died!

Tears welled up. Her heart pounded so hard it hurt.

A few members of the jury shook their heads pitiably. Most remained expressionless. Bastards. All of them. What were they thinking? Have they looked at her son? Did they even see him? Did they know what a crappy hand he was dealt as spawn of such a loser as Tripp Trout? It wasn't fair. None of this was fair.

Gerrity kept talking.

His client was grieving. He'd always wanted more from his estranged father.

His voice droned on as the courtroom swirled around her. Wood and burgundy leather and velvet curtains and that flag and the other flag and the robe and the men in suits. Everything blurred together.

Gerrity kept talking.

The circumstances under which his client's father passed reinforce the argument for rehabilitation.

Meaning what? This legalese way of speaking was maddening. Impossible. Everything went into the haze. Dizzying. Marcella pulled herself up. Screw courtroom etiquette. She would go to her son. He needed his mother right now.

"Tyler," she called.

He straightened but did not turn in her direction.

"Tyler!" Louder this time. "Ty!"

She sidestepped out of the pew, her voice cracking. "Tyler, I'm here."

In the aisle now. "I'm here, Tyler."

Then, he did turn. His eyes were wet and raw, but menacing. Tripp's icy glare. A warning: *Don't come any closer.* What? He didn't want her to make trouble? He didn't want her causing a scene?

No, he couldn't be mad at her. He needed her. Maybe he didn't understand what was happening. He was confused and angry and—

She didn't care about the trial or courtroom antics or even the law. Her son's father had died. She needed to go to him.

She wobbled toward Gerrity's table, ignoring the guards who flanked her. "Tyler, I'm here." Her voice broke.

Guards caught her by the elbows.

"He just lost his father. Let me go to him. Let me go to my son!" Her cries cracked through the courtroom. "Let me go. Please. I have to go to him. Please."

Tyler turned away, showing his unshaven neck. The unruly hair on the back of his head.

No...

She fell into the guards' arms. Right there in the aisle of the courtroom. Then...

Blackout.

Ty blinked, and it was the next day. Back at it. Same, same in the courtroom. But everything felt different because he was alive and breathing and his father was dead. Last night's terrors were unspeakable and he hadn't even slept. Ty's insides felt like someone had used a tenderizer on them. His brain, too. So many times he had to check to see if he was still breathing. He was amazed to find he was. He couldn't imagine anything worked inside. But his heart still beat and his lungs brought oxygen into his body. Why, though? Why bother? His father was dead. He should be, too.

Marcella wasn't, though. She was quite alive. She made that clear yesterday with her little breakdown in the courtroom.

"Tyler! I'm here," she'd called.

He'd turned back to glare at her. And she was his mother, but not his mother. She was also Ellen Ripley. Sigourney Weaver. Same, same. They were all a part of *Alien*. He'd watched the movie many times. Ellen Ripley defeated the alien, but not until it terrorized her and the rest of the ship.

The courtroom-ship shifted on its course, and Ty's stomach lurched. Everyone had a part. Everyone played against him. They'd gotten to everyone. Even the judge had transformed into an alien, scaly, slick-black. Like an enormous insect. The man who turned into a bug. *The Metamorphosis*. Where was that book?

The giant bug, no, the alien was there. Big kahuna alien was in charge. He had a long, dagger-shaped head that clicked open when he spoke—in code—fangs flashing. Screeching, gaping jaw—saliva stretching. Claws floating, swimming, waiting for the right moment to pounce.

The movie played out.

Ty's mother—Sigourney Weaver, Ellen Ripley—fought her way to the aisle, wailing inconsolably, until kahuna alien's guards came after her. Her cries had echoed in the courtroom even after they took her away.

A heaviness had fallen over him. Lava filled his chest and his whole body.

And today. Same, same. His body was breathing and alive as he sat in the courtroom. But it didn't matter. Nothing mattered. Because he knew it wasn't an overdose. His father hadn't done anything wrong except be related to him, to Ty. Even way out in Arkansas, they found him. The aliens got Dad. Punished him. Silenced him.

Ty gritted his teeth, wary of them all now. Everything was connected. This would play out as they saw fit.

"Tyler Trout."

Ty stepped woodenly to the stand. It was like a stage. In the audience, his mother's face was all screwed up with worry. Besides his own lawyer and Dock, there were some random people. And then, the jury. They looked far from amused. Bored as hell, actually. Policeman guy came over with a Bible. Told him to put his hand on it. Raise the other.

"Do you swear to tell the truth, the whole truth, and nothing but the truth, so help you God?"

"Yes." He knew his line.

Policeman guy went back to his corner and Gerrity stood in front of him.

He'd asked Ty to cry like a baby, show what a sorry sack he was. He should've been able to. He should've been crying for Dad. Sad about that. But the tears wouldn't come. He tried. Even pulled at the hair on his arm. But the tears were so far buried. Impossible to reach.

He answered all Gerrity's questions—questions designed to portray Ty as a hopeless mental case. Whatever. It didn't matter. No one could do anything about it now. The aliens had taken over.

On Gerrity's cue, he started talking about how the aliens had always been there, controlling him. They fought to get a message through—from the UFO cameras—but there was too much congestion. His head was thick with tedium. For once in his life, he yearned for the distraction. They were strangely quiet, though. But they were there.

He talked and talked. It got quiet in the courtroom.

Gerrity, wide-eyed and slack-jawed, seemed to swell on the spot. Maybe he was unhappy with Ty's performance. Who knew? Ty was no actor. What did Gerrity expect? Ty spoke the truth. Starting with the commercial, then the scan code on the radio, then the voices in the closet he attacked with a poker, and then the screeching animals at night that kept him awake at all hours.

It all sounded stupid when he said it aloud. He felt himself turning bright red and wished he could take it all back. Keep his secrets to himself.

When Gerrity turned to the subject of his father, though, Ty had a strange out-of-body response. Like, floating. Maybe going to heaven for a visit. Up, up, and up. Everything else erased. Light, airy, like clouds. He was vapor. Nothing. Until someone in the jury sneezed and he came crashing down into the leather-studded chair so abruptly, he felt like he might puke.

This was torture. He would kill for a fix right now. Not literally. His stomach turned with the thought, though. The cruel irony tormented him.

Then it was Dock's turn.

His questions started. About Derek. His truck. Miss Sally. His father. They were like a slow burn. Waves of them. Incessant. One after another and another. They seemed so dumb. Obvious. Ty hated that he had to answer them all. It was excruciatingly monotonous. His head pounded. Ages passed before he asked about Cabbage Night. Ty felt something close to relief.

But something was wrong. Dock's lips were moving, but Ty's ears went numb. His hearing was on the fritz.

On reflex, he studied the corners of the room. There were four UFO cameras in here. Four! One in each corner. Oh, no. They were supposed to be done. It was over. This was it. Tyler's palms got sweaty.

He heard Gerrity's voice in his mind.

That's my boy. Tell me everything. Tell me the whole truth.

Gerrity's catlike eyes and oversized Joker grin circled before him. Laughter echoed. Everything else drowned out.

That's my boy. Tell me everything. Tell me the whole truth.

Was this their message? Part of their plan?

Fighting through the noise in his brain, Ty started talking. Fast. "I didn't borrow Derek's truck. That's never happened. Not that night or ever. He wouldn't let me drive it. We went together to Miss Sally's. We had a plan."

"What—"

Ty wouldn't let him in. "We were just going in for some stupid piece of paper. I was high. Kind of out of my head."

"What drugs did you—"

"The good stuff. Cocaine." He glanced at Marcella, whose eyes were shocked open. Like the living dead. That word must've hit her like a ton of bricks. It almost looked like *she* might puke. That endless worry in her watery eyes.

Everything else clicked off. UFO cameras blinked out. Laughter shut down. Congestion cleared. Silence fell down around him.

It was just the two of them in the room—him and his mom. He spoke directly to her, looking her right in the eye.

"Do you know what it's like when your mother doesn't know you?"

Her face went blank, stunned.

His lip twitched as he held back tears. "I was there that night, Mom. I went into Miss Sally's house. I didn't give a shit about the paper Derek wanted. The report or whatever. I wanted money. She had it hidden in there. She was asleep. Right there in her chair in front of the TV. The light made her look creepy. It weirded me out." He paused. Swallowed. Took some water to clear that crud on his tongue. And kept talking. "Then she woke up and it was just me and her in the room. Just us."

Marcella wrapped her arms around herself. Her lips trembled.

"Yes, Mom."

She kept shaking her head.

He pulled at his hair. "Don't do that. Don't—why can't you see me? I was there. It was me."

"No," Marcella whispered.

"Yes. I was there. It was me."

Dock's voice: "Hold on, son. Start from the beginning. This was—"

"Cabbage Night."

"The night before Halloween."

"Right. The night of pranks."

...ROXANNE RUSSO WASN'T at the bonfire that night. They'd stayed in the truck, he and Derek, smoking weed and watching the flames. No one paid attention to how dangerously high the flames were. Neon orange, mud yellow, electric purple. Hot spikes teased the tall pines, licking the trees' shadows.

He yearned for Roxanne. Imagined her glazed-cranberry nails scratching his back, tracing her name over his flannel shirt. Her name, then his. A big heart around both.

"Ready to roll?" Derek smacked his chest, waking him with a start. Ty hadn't realized he'd fallen asleep. Weed sometimes did that, made him sleepy.

He rolled his tongue against his teeth. "Got any water? Thirsty."

Derek offered him a half-drunk, warm Coke leftover in his cup holder. Ty slurped it down.

Nirvana's *Lithium* had come on and they were halfway to Miss Sally's when Ty remembered the little white treat in his pocket. "Dude, I need a bathroom."

"I'll pull over. Grab a tree."

Ty bit the inside of his cheek. Fingered the packet. "Tree won't work." He made a fart noise with his mouth.

"Geezum. Aw'right."

Derek pulled into Stewart's on Route 9.

A public restroom wasn't Ty's favorite place to do it, but he wasn't picky tonight. And he was prepared. He pulled out the white packet, his tightly rolled bill at the ready. That shit was up his nose faster than Leon could fry an egg. He stayed on in the bathroom, making sure he didn't bleed. He sang Pearl Jam's *Jeremy*, swaying in front of the mirror. His reflection looked pretty good. Maybe he was too good for Roxanne Russo after all. Anyway, this was better.

So much better.

"You good?" Derek asked as Ty slumped back into the truck.

It was late when they got to Miss Sally's. Ty had no idea what time. The moon was high in the black-as-pitch sky. The car door made a screeching sound when it swung open. Too loud for this quiet night.

Lights flickered from Miss Sally's front window. Lights from the TV.

"Shit. Is she awake?" Derek said. "It's almost midnight."

"She falls asleep in front of the TV a lot." Ty surprised himself, knowing this.

The front door wasn't locked. Weird. Like she deserved to get robbed. Derek had been ready with a T-shirt-wrapped fist, but no need. They walked right in. Didn't bother to take off their shoes. Miss Sally slept right through it, open-mouthed, in her plaid chair.

The house was strangely quiet. The TV muted. And the old-fashioned clock on the mantle didn't make a sound. Its arms were frozen, as if time had stopped.

The only light came from the TV and it danced over her in an erratic pattern, changing the shadows of her sleeping face.

Creepy. She kind of looked dead. A shudder went through him.

While Derek hurried to one of the back rooms, Ty went to the ceramic lamp on the end table.

Derek's voice rang in his mind: *I mean, 'parently she got more money than God. Wouldn't know by the way she lives.*

Derek might be here for some report. Ty was here for money. Money would solve everything. No more sneaking around, stealing from the diner. He'd have his own stash. Maybe get to that house down in Rensselaer himself somehow. Buy it straight up.

There was money in the lamp. Hidden there. He'd seen it on that TV show.

Inspecting the bottom of the lamp, though, he couldn't find the hidden opening. Ty laughed at himself. Of course, he couldn't find it. It was *hidden*.

Miss Sally stirred, and Ty jumped inside his skin. Then his skin wouldn't quiet. Like his blood grew spikes, and poked him from inside out. With the lamp in one hand, he slapped his legs with the other, trying to stop it. That only made it worse.

"Where's the money?" he said aloud, angry at the spikes in his blood getting in the way of everything. That euphoria from Stewart's bathroom faded into an irritable, murky fog.

"Where's the money?" He yanked the plug and pulled the cord from the lamp's base.

Miss Sally, suddenly on her feet, blinked him into focus.

"Tyler? What are you doing here?"

Then something shifted. Her voice screeched like a bat. "You shouldn't be in here. Get out of my house!"

The light from the TV made her look ghostly. Her polka-dot socks looked so funny and odd, he might have laughed a little. That's when Derek came back.

He was still empty handed. Whatever they came in for—what was it again?—Derek hadn't found it.

"The hell you doin'?"

"Derek Hogg? What is going on?" Miss Sally looked from one to the other, shaking her head like she kept saying *no*. "How did you get in here? What were you doing back there? Both of you, out!"

Derek held up his hands. "Sorry, ma'am. It was Tyler's idea."

Miss Sally turned on him. "Tyler, put that lamp down and get out of my house this instant. Before I call the police!"

Aha! So there *was* money in the lamp. Why else would she insist he put it down?

He had to get inside it. Maybe smash it against the wall?

Miss Sally came at him, her veiny arms extended. Did she mean to hit him?

Bold move.

Ty lifted the lamp over his head. Instead of grabbing the lamp, Miss Sally smacked his face. Her bony fingers knocked into his nose. Hard. Inside, a million explosions. A million tiny veins popping.

"Shit!" Blood dripped. He wiped with his free hand, and it came back red, red, red.

Countless tiny things popped inside his head. Like little shocks. It filled his ears and messed with his vision. A cruel headache surged. He squinted against it.

Miss Sally studied her own hand, stained with Ty's blood. She yelped in shock. "Oh, my. I didn't mean to... What happened?"

Derek was at her front door now. "Ty, come on. We're out."

The light from the TV was like a strobe light at a dance club.

Then things started to change.

Everything closed in. She morphed before his eyes.

Shape-shifter. The metamorphosis.

She became an insect. A slimy, iridescent creature—glowing against the light of the television. Her head expanded like a balloon. Her skin paled and became translucent. Her hair vaporized, like steam from a teakettle. Her eyes changed shape and glowed from within. Her voice had changed, too. She spoke a different language. Computerized gibberish—*oo-lah, blong-oi, see-mrah*. Her hands grew claws as she scratched at him.

They were here. From the UFO. They'd channeled her. They'd been waiting for him here. All this time. He wouldn't let them get him.

He heard the voice clear as day, but couldn't detect its source: *As good as dead.*

A strange, fluttery rage built up in Ty. He felt his body inflate, filling all the space around him. The room flushed neon like he was inside one of Hen's glow sticks.

As good as dead.

Frantic, he searched for the voice in the erratic lights of the TV. They jabbed his chest, like in that car commercial.

You. You. You.

Miss Sally yelled, demanding something, her voice super harsh.

You. You. You.

He thrashed, swinging the lamp. It struck something, broke apart. Then everything went dark. When he blinked into focus, Miss Sally lay in front of the TV. A gory wound on her head seeping blood. It pooled on the carpet all around her.

Ty's ears clogged. Derek's voice reached him through the fog.

"Ty! What the hell did you just do? What'd you do? Oh, no. No, no, no, no, no. We're so screwed. Totally screwed!" Derek jumped all spazzy around the living room, like a monkey at the zoo. Knocking into all the insect-ghostlike-creatures that lined the walls.

They surrounded him now. They'd come in from their UFO and were here watching, making sure it happened the way they'd planned.

"Let's get the hell outta here!" Derek opened the door with the T-shirt fist. Ty ran too, away from the insect-ghostlike-creatures lurking in the corners. The neon flamed up behind him, like a rocket. A giant bonfire. And the creatures vaporized like Miss Sally's hair, zooming to their ship that hovered in the upper atmosphere. A Star Trek spacecraft.

Ty froze, his eyes on the sky.

Derek yelled and waved him over. But his voice was on mute.

Ty couldn't breathe. Couldn't move. Derek had to physically pull him back into the truck, where Ty tucked into himself on the passenger seat. Their ship ticked loudly, the sound shaking the ground, the truck. Ty plugged his ears and squeezed his eyes closed, waiting for it to stop. It whirred and croaked and threatened to crush them, squash the truck like the shell of a beetle. And then it went black. Silent.

The courtroom held an eerie silence, and Ty wasn't sure of anything. He felt spent. Exhausted. But, after all that talking, he didn't feel the relief he expected.

Dock's voice: "Tyler Trout, is that a confession?"

Gerrity: "Objection. I'd like to request a recess, your honor."

Recess. Like in elementary school. Swings and slides and monkey bars. An hour of freedom that seemed endless.

Gerrity's request was denied. He looked strung out. "I'd like to call a mistrial."

Dock's voice again, louder this time: "Tyler Trout, is that a confession?"

Gerrity shouted, "Objection!"

The judge glared at Ty's lawyer. "Overruled." Then, he said a bunch of other things Ty didn't understand, pounded his gavel, and nodded to the policeman standing in the corner.

Things shifted in the courtroom. Police guy came to his side and grasped his arm. "You're coming with me."

Ty felt the clogging spinning top in his chest. Racing like an electric drill.

"Mom? What's going on?"

She wasn't looking at him anymore. She wept into her hands, hiding from him and everyone.

The lights on the UFO cameras flickered. Spun, too.

His arms were forced behind his back. Handcuffs clicked around his wrists.

Wait. Help. Something had gotten off track. This wasn't supposed to happen. This isn't what Gerrity said would happen. Something was wrong.

Frantic, Ty looked up at the judge's bench. That pudgy, red-faced dude with glasses wasn't there anymore. It was the kahuna alien.

Spinning top buzzed like electricity in his chest. Was it too late? Shit. Shit. Shit.

His words were fast. "They were watching the whole time. They called me names. It was an order. I had no choice. They weren't going to let me go. They have a plan. And I'm part of it."

Ty trembled. Everything vibrated. The whole freaking room. The walls were closing in.

"They're here right now. Watching me. Watching everything."

Police guy tried to lead him away, out of the courtroom. But Ty stayed put. He couldn't tear his eyes from UFO cameras.

Red eye went solid. The buzzing became a slow hum. Was that it? Did he do it? Were they satisfied?

The judge was talking to him now. To Ty's surprise, it was the pudgy, red-faced guy looking over his glasses at him.

"...do you understand?"

More words. One stuck. It was for Ty alone.

Confession.

The weight of the word was oppressive. Another word would come later, after deliberations, from the jury foreman:

Guilty.

That would be for Ty alone too. He could hear it already. It screamed from the walls. Fear erupted, started at his feet and grew. Filled the whole room like smog. Consumed him.

They were immune, at a safe distance in their UFOs.

They were done. And they had won.

EPILOGUE

September 1992

Lots of things changed in second grade. Some good, some not so good. Some just weird.

Good: Hen could go to the bus stop all by himself. After all, he was eight now.

Not so good: Second grade was a lot of work, with a lot of homework.

Just weird: Tyler was gone. He didn't babysit him after school. Tyler couldn't make him a snack or teach him to ride a bike. Hen had the whole bedroom to himself. Which was sometimes scary and all the time lonely.

Off the bus today, Hen's street was quiet and breezy. He breathed in the autumn air. The damp leaves that plastered the pavement smelled like salt and sulphur, like morning sleep.

Miss Sally's house had sold during the summer. The new owners —newlyweds from Massena—hadn't yet moved in. Her house was empty. Had been empty for months and months. It seemed peaceful, though, now. Not so sad.

Miss Sally would always be with him. How she insisted on table manners even with after-school snacks. Her snickerdoodle cookies. The pile of coffee table books. Playing long, quiet games of chess. Her plaid chair. The Juicyfruit house. All her love, all the memories of her, he kept inside, close to his heart.

He weaved in and out of the leaf piles all the way home. Leaves were changing fast. Soon all would be off the trees. Last week, when he and Mom drove down 87, the mountains had turned from green

green to speckled green. Reds and oranges and yellows mixed in. Driving through the winding Adirondack valley was like driving along a big, coppery quilt.

Now it was leaf pile time.

Hen half expected to see Bernie in the backyard, rake in hand, making his own piles. But he wasn't. He sat with Mom in the living room. She was home already?

They were waiting for him.

"Hi, sweetie." Marcella smiled in a way he hadn't seen for months. Since before the trial, before Tyler got in trouble. Hen stayed by the door.

Bernie's smile was big too. "Hen, come on in and sit down. We have something we want to tell you."

"What?"

Mom still smiled. "Take off your things, silly. And come sit down."

Hen dropped his backpack and shucked off his sneakers. They had something to tell him. He had to get his words out, fast. "There are leaf piles again. I know what I need to do. It will be way easier to catch one if we make a nest. Like, a little den. We can use mud and dried leaves. Like, a mini cave. We can put a strawberry inside."

Mom kind of laughed. "What are you talking about?"

"To catch a hedgehog. Right, Hen?" Bernie said.

Hen nodded, and pulled off his jacket. "I want to name him Louis. I'll get my markers. I'll draw it and show you what I mean."

"Wait, Hen. Please. Come and sit. We want to tell you something important."

Hen's stomach dropped. Important might mean bad. It had before. The last time Mom told him something important, she explained where Tyler had gone.

He'd been sentenced to rehab.

Rehab. He'd heard the word a lot lately. Grownups let it roll off their tongues like a song lyric. When the mail delivered a letter from Tyler, Hen saw a similar word in the return address. Hen had to ask what it meant.

"Rehabilitation," Mom had said. "Like, working to get better."

"Is he sick?"

She had looked sick herself. Hen wished he hadn't asked.

"Yes, Hen. He needs to get better."

"His letter says he's in a special hospital. So, he's not in jail?"

"No. But he can't leave the rehab."

"So it's kind of like jail?"

Big sigh. "We can still visit him."

Was this what they wanted to talk with him about? Visiting Tyler? The idea scared him a little. He made his way to the chair near the sleeping TV. The air in the room thickened. Mom and Bernie sat so close, their knees touched. Their interlaced fingers were like a knit blanket.

"We have some happy news."

Hen waited, feeling some relief. If this wasn't about visiting Tyler, though, what was it about?

"Bernie's going to live here. With us."

Hen waited. Blinked a few times. This was the happy news? It hardly seemed like news.

"Did you hear me, Hen? Bernie's moving in."

They expected him to say something. "When?"

"We wanted to talk to you about that. Wanted to see how you felt about everything."

"Everything?"

"Well, you know. If it was okay with you."

Hen wasn't sure what they meant. Bernie was here all the time. He didn't see how it would be any different.

"Okay," Hen said.

Mom let go of Bernie's hand and leaned forward. "Hen, how does this make you feel?"

Hen shrugged.

"What do you think of it? Are you okay with it?"

"Yeah, I'm okay."

Mom laughed for real. It was nice to hear her laugh. "Really? I was worried."

"About what, Mom?"

Bernie seemed concerned too. "Do you have any questions? I'm not going to take your mother away from you. No one could ever do that. You know that, right?"

"Yeah." Hen gave Mom a small smile.

"You sure?"

Hen fidgeted. "Uh-huh. Can I draw my picture now?"

"Hen, this is very much about you. Bernie and I care for each other, but you are the most important thing."

"To both of us," Bernie added.

Mom glanced at Bernie in a sharing-secret kind of way. "It took me a while to see it, but Sally was right all along."

"Miss Sally?" Hen's throat closed, hearing her name.

"Yes, Miss Sally wanted us together. This was her hope for us. For you."

"For me?"

Bernie scratched his chin. "It's complicated. One day you'll understand."

A few beats passed. Hen scrunched his eyebrows. Miss Sally wanted Bernie to move in? Grownup stuff was more confusing than a game of chess.

"Can I draw my picture now?"

"Sure, sweetie."

He left them there on the couch. He wasn't sure if they went back to holding hands, but if they did, he was okay with it.

THE MUD CAVE turned out better than Hen had hoped. Like a mini earth-igloo. Bernie helped him. After dinner, they found the perfect place for it in the backyard. Along the tree line among small piles of dead leaves.

Bernie was unsure. "There's nothing keeping the critter in. You know, once they get in."

"That's the point. They don't have to stay."

"Doesn't seem like much of a trap."

"It's not really a trap. More like a home. They're supposed to want to stay."

"And then you'll bring them inside and they'll get all prickly trying to find a way back out."

"Maybe I won't bring him in. Maybe I'll let Louis stay right here in the backyard. In his little den."

Bernie smiled, his eyes flashing in the evening light. "Good luck, then." He heaved off the ground and brushed dirt from the seat of his jeans.

"Bernie?"

"Yahp?" Bernie sank onto a hip as if he had all the time in the world.

Hen wanted to ask a question but didn't know how. Bernie sat back on the ground, getting his jeans dirty all over again.

"What's up?" Bernie's voice made Hen feel safe. But he still didn't know how to ask.

Bernie gave their hedgehog trap a little pat. "You got a good den, here, Hen. You did a nice job. Any critter would be lucky to call it home."

"Thanks."

They were quiet awhile. Hen studied the stubble on Bernie's usually clean-shaven chin. Spikes stuck out around the dome of his jaw, like a hedgehog.

"Gonna be dark soon." Bernie looked at the sky.

The sky looked huge.

"Was it hard?" Hen's voice was hoarse, as if he hadn't spoken in hours.

Bernie's eyebrows went up. "Was what hard?"

"Forgiving."

Bernie took a long breath. He looked Hen right in the eye. "You're talking about Tyler, aren't ya?"

Hen nodded.

Another big breath. Bernie's smile was long gone. He looked over to Miss Sally's. "Yes, it is. It was. Thing is about that, though, I love your mother. I have to say I've never loved another human being as much as I love your mother. And your mother? Well, she loves Tyler. She loves you and Tyler more than her own self. And when you love somebody, you love what they love. I love everything she loves."

"Mom loved Miss Sally too."

"Yes, she did."

Miss Sally's house was dark quiet. The big bay window was like a sleeping TV. Hen tried to remember what it was like inside, but it was hard.

Hen whispered, "I miss her. I loved Miss Sally."

"I know you did. I loved her too."

"She was your ma."

"She was. Still is. Always will be."

"Don't you miss her?"

Bernie's voice was soft. "'Course I do. Miss her every day."

"It's not fair." Tears sprang from Hen's eyes, as sudden as a summer storm.

Bernie let Hen cry. "I know, buddy. You got lots of feelings. It's okay."

"You're not mad?"

"Oh, I was. I still have my moments. I ask God 'why' all the time."

Tears fell over the hedgehog den. Hen felt he'd never stop crying. His voice was all wavy from it. "How could you forgive him?"

When Hen looked up, he wished he could take the question back.

A tear had rolled down Bernie's cheek, leaving a wet streak like a shiny scar. Hen blinked at Bernie, amazed at how quietly he cried. He didn't make a sound. His face didn't change. If it weren't for the streak of wetness on his face, Hen wouldn't realize he'd been crying at all.

Hen sniffed his tears and wiped his face, smudging it with soil. He smelled earth and drying mud in the air.

Bernie didn't move to wipe his tear-scar away. It looked like a strand of tinsel in the evening light. His words were slow and careful. "I can't say it was easy. It ain't easy even still. I guess I'm working on forgiving him, because that's what Ma would've done."

"Miss Sally would've forgiven him?"

Bernie gave him a sad smile and got to his feet. "That's what Ma would've done." He left Hen there with all his feelings. He made his way back to the house without bothering to brush off the seat of his jeans.

HEN STARTLED AWAKE. He hadn't meant to fall asleep. His digital clock read 11:42. He got his flashlight from under his bed and headed downstairs. He grabbed his coat and headed outside before he was fully awake. The cold night air stung. It was the darkest night he'd ever seen. No stars in the sky. No moon. It was deep night. Dark quiet all around. But Tyler's voice found him: "Think of this, Hen. When it's dark, it's dark for everyone. You don't even need to hide. It hides you."

Hen paused at the top step. Tears built as a yearning for Tyler took hold. Hen sank down onto the worn wood. The light from his flashlight jockeyed as he shook with sobs.

How could he ever forgive him for what he'd done?

For so long, he denied it. He didn't believe it. Tyler couldn't have possibly done such an awful thing. But then, the bracelet, Judge Bowman, Derek, the visit when Tyler sent him away, the trial. The days and weeks of Mom being gone. The waiting at Murphy's for what seemed like a lifetime. Then, after Mom collected him and brought him home, he learned that they decided Tyler was guilty. He had confessed, which meant he admitted he did that awful thing. Which meant he *did* do that awful thing. Not Derek or anyone else. He did it. Tyler. His Tyler.

Then he got Tyler's letter.

Dear Hen,

I don't blame you for hating me. I kind of hate myself right about now. I've been a rotten brother. Sorry for sending you away when you came to visit at Thanksgiving. Sorry for yelling at you and throwing your bracelet across the room at Christmas. Sorry for not helping with your hedgehog trap.

I did a very bad thing. I was sick when it happened, kinda. They decided to send me to a special kind of hospital for a long time and they are fixing me up. I think about what happened all the time. I feel really really really bad about it. I cry about it at night. I know you are sad because of what I did. I cry about that too. I'm so sorry. Sorry, sorry, sorry. I will keep saying it until you tell me it's ok. That you don't hate me anymore. I hope that time will be soon.

Love, Tyler

Hen could read now, and read it himself. He didn't need Bernie's help. Or anyone else's. He read his brother's words himself. And read them again. And again. And again. And then he folded it up and put it in his sock drawer because he didn't want to read it anymore. He didn't want his brother to say sorry anymore. He didn't want to hear it. He knew the truth. He could never forgive him.

But Bernie could. And did.

Even though he put the letter away, he'd read it so many times, the words found him. They found him all the time. The last thought of the night as he stared at the ceiling of the bedroom they used to share. The first thing each morning, as his lids clung together with sleepies. He'd rub the crust from his lashes, trying to free the words from his mind. It was no use. It replayed in his little mind like a song on repeat.

How many times would Tyler say sorry? Did it matter? Sorry wouldn't bring Miss Sally back. Sorry wouldn't change the fact that he lost Mom to the trial for days and days—so many he lost count. Sorry wouldn't get Tyler out of prison or rehab, or wherever he was, for years. Hen would be fourteen or fifteen before Tyler got out, maybe. A teenager himself. Eating microwave burritos and listening to music on huge headphones. What would Tyler be like then? All grown up. Would he still be his brother?

Would he be able to forgive him then?

He clicked his flashlight on and off, splashing the distant tree line with a burst of white. Hen's face was wet, but no new tears fell. His nose was clogged, and his head felt sleepy. His play tent stood a few feet away. He was bone tired suddenly. Just a little rest. The den was probably empty anyway. It didn't seem to matter anymore.

He slunk into his play tent and lay down. The cold ground

beneath the thin canvas of the tent gave him a chill. Waking him alert. That wouldn't do at all.

With new resolve, he marched out of his tent, did an about face and brandished his flashlight like a sword. The light grew into a big circle as he moved closer to the tree line, panning across like a spotlight against a stage, trying to find the hedgehog den. Little piles of leaves made a berm, like a barrier protecting his house from the darkness of the woods. A warm, safe feeling came over Hen.

His next thought wasn't about Louis, the hedgehog that may or may not be resting in his new den. It was about Tyler. His brother. At seventeen, at twenty-seven, at thirty-seven...he would always be his brother. His next inhale went deep. He felt it in his fingertips and toes. When he breathed out, he let it all go. A big cloud of fog took his breath into the night air.

In the middle of his backyard, he turned off the flashlight. In the total darkness, he took another deep breath. He felt it go right to his heart. When he breathed out, some of the anger went too. He wiped his eyes dry.

When it's dark it's dark for everyone.

It was Tyler who taught him not to be scared of the dark.

He didn't need his flashlight anymore. His eyes had adjusted, like night vision. He tiptoed in the direction of the den, hoping he'd find it. Of course, he did. Eagerness bubbled up, and all that careful breathing went away. He was too excited to breathe. He could feel it. Something special was about to happen.

A few feet from the den, Hen sank down onto his belly and army crawled the rest of the way. Nighttime ninja, sneaky and silent. Hen smelled the raw earth of autumn—damp soil, dead leaves, and moss. The den was like a little hobbit house, its opening a welcoming upside-down U. He dipped down to look inside. He couldn't believe it. He grinned super big, remembering Bernie's unshaven chin.

"Louis?"

NOTE TO READERS

Schizophrenia is a serious mental illness. Although there is no cure, with proper medication and treatment, it can be managed. If you or anyone you know exhibits symptoms, please contact the National Alliance on Mental Illness at 1-800-950-NAMI (6264) or go to mentalhelp.net.

ACKNOWLEDGEMENTS

When my middle son (Adam Henry) still talked like Elmer Fudd, he was obsessed with nocturnal animals. "Only noctuwnal animals, mommy." He especially loved hedgehogs. We lived in Texas at the time, in a neighborhood that was neatly organized like a giant's garden. Good-sized homes blocked in with good-sized fences, stacked against each other like puzzle pieces. One night before bed, my little guy begged to go out in the backyard to find a hedgehog. Seeing all the naive eagerness in his huge hazel eyes, we couldn't say no.

Flashlight in hand, he headed out the back door in his bare feet and favorite green pajamas. As I watched him from my kitchen, I noticed my neighbors' windows just beyond our fence. It being so dark outside, their windows were like movie screens. It struck me how clearly I could see inside their homes and how they must be able to see into mine. And there was my Adam with his flashlight, panning our backyard with an innocent hope to find himself a pet.

And the story idea hit...

Originally titled *Henry Trout Saves a Hedgehog*, then *Paradox Lake*, and finally *Boy on Hold*.

A bit about the setting. I grew up in Lake George, which is about 45 minutes from Paradox Lake. Oddly, I'd never visited Paradox until after the book was contracted. My writer friend, Linda Marshall, hosted me at her lake house there for a lovely lunch and an insightful tour. Recently, I learned my old neighbor, Brian Turner, grew up in Severance and attended Schroon Lake Central School. Having lived there in the nineties, he was happy to answer any random question I had while in the throes of revisions.

Paradox Lake is so named because it both is fed from and feeds into Schroon Lake, depending on water levels of the lakes and Schroon River. Paradox is just one of the many lakes in the Adirondack Region. The Adirondack park's over six million acres hosts thousands of lakes and is the only national park that has over 100 towns, villages, and communities in addition to its protected nature reserves. In 1963 it was designated as a National Historic Landmark. I urge anyone who hasn't visited the Adirondacks to do so.

I owe a huge debt of gratitude to my father, James R. Davies, Esq —or in some circles, "Jimbo." An attorney who spent his career practicing law in upstate New York, his insight into the legal process was key. I did take some small liberties to help my story. Tyler's arraignment occurs in a fictitious home office of the Town Justice (Bowman). This would usually occur in Town Court, however it is not uncommon in small towns for arraignments to occur in a judge's home office. Also, Tyler would've been held prior to his trial in Essex County Jail, which is 40 minutes from Severance. To avoid introducing another set of police officers/guards to the story (no less driving time for Marcella), I put the county jail in Schroon Lake.

Mike Spero, my father-in-law and former narcotics officer, described how young people typically get hooked on heavy drugs, which informed Tyler's "euphoria." My cousin in-law Doreen Burns made a comment at a family wedding about the pervasive link between mental illness and drug abuse—thus the character of Tyler was revised from a baseless criminal to a teen suffering from undiagnosed, terrifying psychosis. The bulk of my research for Tyler, though, was first-hand accounts of people suffering with schizophrenia and similar psychoses, as in *Recovered, not cured, a journey through schizophrenia* by Richard McLean.

I wrote a huge chunk of this book during the 2014 Sandy Feet Writer's Retreat alongside my dear friends Aly Aiello, Michelle Curran, Betsy Devany, and Anika Denise.

I'd like to thank the following writers/editors who gave me feedback: Cassandra Dunn, Christy Morgan, Aly Aiello, William Belcher, and the team at Immortal Works—specifically Beth Buck, Melissa Meibos, Ashley Literski, Staci Olsen, Holli Anderson, and Jason King. It was a thrill when Beth liked my pitch on #pitmad...The rest, as they say, is history.

Thanks to my mom, Janet Davies, and brother, Dr. Jim Davies of

Carleton University, for reading early drafts. Thanks to my mother-in-law Judith Basile for being such a supporter. Thanks to my boys—AJ, Adam, and Chaz—who can't wait to read this book. Always, thank you to Anthony, who makes everything possible. Upon reading the first draft of this book, he told me, "This book will change your life." It already has.

PLAYLIST

Duran Duran, "Shadows on Your Side," *Seven and the Ragged Tiger*, EMI, 1983

Eurythmics, *Sweet Dreams (are Made of This)*, RCA Records, 1983

Guns & Roses, "Sweet Child o' Mine", *Appetite for Destruction*, Geffen Records, 1987

Loggins and Messina, "Danny's Song", *Sittin' In*, Columbia, 1971

Nirvana, *Nevermind*, DGC Records, 1991

Pearl Jam, "Jeremy", *Ten*, Epic Records, 1991

Public Enemy, *It Takes a Nation of Millions to Hold Us Back*, Def Jam, Columbia, 1988

BOY ON HOLD
DISCUSSION QUESTIONS

warning: contains spoilers

1. The story is told through multiple points of view and not in chronological order. How do these author choices affect how readers receive the story?

2. It's been said that parents can't be blamed for their children's bad deeds. At the same time, they can't take credit for their children's good deeds. Do you agree or disagree? Does Marcella deserve any credit or blame?

3. It's clear that Marcella loves her sons. At one point, she claims that she learned long ago that her love wasn't enough. What did she mean? Do you agree or disagree?

4. Who holds more power in town—Sally Hubbard or Leon Hogg?

5. How does Marcella deal with the sexual harassment and abuse she's suffered?

6. Is Derek a villain?

7. What are Officer Clapp's redeeming qualities? How about Leon?

8. Bernie is kind and unassuming. What faults does he have, if any?

9. Tyler silently suffers every day with an undiagnosed, terrifying psychosis. Why doesn't he seek help?

10. Does Marcella do the right thing by inviting Tripp back into her home?

11. How are Tripp and Tyler different?

12. Hen searches for the meaning of truth and eventually believes he's found it. Do you agree with his definition?

13. Hen believes he can save Tyler by making a duplicate bracelet. Does he?

14. The original title of this book was *Henry Trout Saves a Hedgehog*. Who is the hedgehog?

15. If you were Bernie or Hen, would you be able to forgive Tyler?

ABOUT THE AUTHOR

Johannah Davies (JD) Spero's writing career took off when her first release, *Catcher's Keeper*, was a finalist in the Amazon Breakthrough Novel Award in 2013. Since then, she's found similar success with her young adult fantasy *Forte* series, winning recognition from National Indie Excellence Award (2014, 2016), Adirondack Literary Award (2015), and Book Excellence Award (2016). Having lived in various cities from St. Petersburg (Russia) to Boston, she's now settled with her husband and three sons in the Adirondack Mountains, where she was born and raised.

This has been an
Immortal Production